ST. MARTIN'S

MINOTAUR

MYSTERIES

OUT ON A LIMB

Joan Hess

St. Martin's Paperbacks

To Mary Lightheart,

whose act of courage inspired so many of us

Acknowledgments

I would like to thank Kyle Russell and Rob Merry-ship for helping me muddle through the complexities of property development. All errors contained herein are due to my faulty notes, and not to their generously offered information. I would also like to thank John Dixon, a geologist at the University of Arkansas, who went so far as to supply me with a geological map so I could ponder the infamous Fayetteville Fault.

CHAPTER ONE

"So all is forgiven and you'll be moving into the castle with Prince Perfectly Charming?" asked Luanne Bradshaw, my best friend and toughest critic. She took a slice of pizza from the box on the coffee table, studied it as though it were a slide from a lab, and cautiously took a bite. She does not suffer pepperoni gladly.

We were sitting in my living room in the top half of a modest duplex, which has two small bedrooms and a cramped and often cranky bathroom but redeems itself with a view of the campus lawn undulating gently down the slope from Old Main. Undergraduate classes had been dismissed for the day, and only a few students were cutting across the grass or lingering on the marble benches meant to inspire thoughts of Plato and Aristotle. The sky was blue, with a cloud here and there to break the monotony. Luanne and I had closed our respective businesses for the day—hers a vintage clothing store, mine a bookstore down the hill from Farber College. Both of us clip coupons.

"I don't know," I said. "Peter swore he was never interested in his ex-wife, and pulled all that nonsense just to make me jealous. I suppose P. T. Barnum had me in mind when he delivered the line about a sucker born every minute. I think I showed maturity and restraint, however."

"Oh, yes, you had all of us fooled. It never occurred to me when you called at least once a day to rant that you were the tiniest bit perturbed. I just assumed it was an extended bout of PMS." She picked up her beer and took a sip. "So Lovely Leslie, as you called her, has scuttled back to Manhattan and you and Peter are back to whining and dining?"

"He's coming by later."

"And?"

"He's coming by later—that's all." I picked up the clicker and turned on the local news. "Unless, of course, a disgruntled Kappa Theta Eta goes ballistic and takes out the housemother, thus demanding the attention of the CID. It never seems to happen between nine and five."

"There ought to be a law," Luanne murmured.

I was going to point out that there *was* a law when the image on the TV screen caught my attention. "Oh, my gawd! Is that who I think it is?"

"Unless we're under the influence of errant microwaves," she said, as stunned as I. "What on earth is she doing in that tree—or any tree, for that matter?"

Caron, my not-so-mild-mannered daughter, came through the front door in time to hear the question. Chronologically speaking, she's sixteen years old, but she swings back and forth between toddlerhood and jaded savoir faire. The latter was the mode of the moment as she dropped her backpack on the floor. "I was Absolutely Humiliated. After school, everybody went out to see what was going on with this tree business, and Rhonda could barely contain herself when she saw who it was. You really ought to pick your friends more carefully, Mother. I have to live in this town, too."

"Not necessarily. I'm sure I can find you a job in a hospital in Guatemala or Sri Lanka. You'll have to start with bedpans, but after a few years you'll be allowed to clean gangrenous sores."

Caron grabbed a slice of pizza and slouched into a chair. "You are so not funny."

I turned up the volume on the TV. The reporter, her hair shellacked and her pert nose powdered to prevent even a glimmer of shininess, stared earnestly into the camera. "For those of you just joining us," she began, her tone making it clear that those of us who had failed to join her earlier might well be residing in a swamp, "this is the situation thus far. Local environmentalists calling themselves the Farberville Green Party are staging a demonstration to stop developer Anthony Armstrong from cutting down a stand of oak trees in order to begin construction of the second phase of Oakland Heights. The demonstrators arrived during the early hours of the morning and built the platform you see behind me." Her voice grew huskier, as though she were describing some sort of catastrophe in which scores of innocent victims had perished due to the cruel caprices of nature. "Its occupant, retired high school teacher Emily Parchester, has chained herself to the tree and vowed not to come down until the city council takes action. Other members of the Green Party say they will hold a vigil around the clock. And now the clock is ticking. The bulldozers are scheduled to arrive in the morning. Will Miss Parchester be able to defend this beloved tree?"

The camera shifted to a group of a dozen or so people holding posterboard signs that claimed the developer to be an "herbicidal maniac" and other less-savory designations. The reporter approached them but remained prudently out of range should they descend into whackery.

"Would you like to explain your position to the viewers at home?" she asked.

Their designated spokesman, a man in his thirties with a neatly trimmed beard and wire-rimmed glasses, stepped forward. His tweedy jacket, turtleneck shirt, and corduroy trousers did not suggest he was a dedicated ecoterrorist, and I was not surprised when he said, "My name is Finnigan Baybergen, and I'm an assistant professor of botany at Farber College. I am also a concerned citizen who feels that the city council and, more specifically, the planning commission, failed to follow the city landscape ordinance designed to protect the environment from those who would make a profit from the destruction of our precious ecosystem. Drive by the mall and look at the acres of pavement, with only a few sickly saplings to replace trees that were here when Farberville was nothing but a sleepy little market town. Those apartment complexes across the road were built on what used to be peach and apple orchards planted by families that endured hardship to find a better way of life. Must we sacrifice hundred-year-old trees so that developers like Anthony Armstrong can make a few dollars? The members of the city council were elected to preserve and protect the unique ambience of Farberville, not to sell it to the highest bidder."

"Disgraceful!" snorted a stout woman behind him. Beside her, a rotund man with a shock of white hair bobbled his head emphatically, as did the rest of the protesters.

"Bunch of damn tree-huggers!" shouted someone beyond the range of the camera.

"Kiss my oak!" shouted another.

Unwilling to be upstaged by amateurs, the reporter gestured for the camera to follow her as she moved toward the tree. "Let's see if we can get a statement from the demonstrator on the platform. Miss Parchester, are you confident you can remain there indefinitely? Have preparations been màde for your comfort and safety?"

Caron took another slice of pizza. "When we saw who it was, Rhonda began to laugh so convulsively that Louis had to steady her. How fortunate for her that he was conveniently nearby. It would have been such a tragedy if she'd plopped into a puddle. I would have been underwhelmed with grief."

"Miss Parchester is hardly a close friend of yours," said Luanne. "Considering your mother's epic reign of ineptitude and meddling in murder investigations, I should think your classmates would understand."

"You are so not funny," I muttered, meriting a dirty look from Caron. I leaned forward as Miss Parchester peered down from her perch some ten feet above the ground.

She had chosen a cardigan sweater and a dress with a lace collar and cuffs as the appropriate garb for tree-sitting. Her bifocals glinted as sunlight found paths through the foliage. "Oh, yes, I'm quite nicely equipped. My friends have provided me with a sleeping bag and an air mattress. I have a small duffel bag with clothes and personal items, as well as a transistor radio and a flashlight to read by at night. A box contains provisions and several jugs of water. I have a tarp in case it rains. I shall be quite comfy up here in my leafy bower with the birds, butterflies, and squirrels."

The reporter gestured at those who had gathered at the edge of the parking lot. "Do any of you have an opinion that differs from that of the Farberville Green Party? Does Phase Two reflect economic progress or—"

"You got a potty up there?" jeered a thick-necked man in a grimy T-shirt that did little to hide his protuberant belly. His companions, one with the pinched features of a weasel and the other with the flattened nose of a bulldog, guffawed at his witticism.

Miss Parchester's lips tightened briefly. "There are some questions a gentleman doesn't ask and a lady doesn't answer. This is not to imply I'm confident that you are a gentleman, but perhaps you might pretend to be one in order not to embarrass yourself on television."

"Why don't you head on home to your outhouse?" added Finnigan Baybergen. The rest of his supporters inched forward, although they were less than menacing. With the exception of their leader, they appeared to qualify for Medicare and senior discounts at movie theaters. The yardsticks stapled to their signs would not fare well against the tire irons and monkey wrenches that the trio of troglodytes were likely to have in their pickup trucks.

The reporter hastily moved away from the tree, wondering, perhaps, if Miss Parchester had a chamber pot at her disposal. "This is Jessica Princeton, on location for KFAR. Let's go back to the studio for more local news." She smiled brightly until the image faded and her twin, albeit a male, began to drone on about revised costs for renovations to the football stadium.

"Goodness," I said as I turned down the volume, "Miss Parchester does seem to create awkward situations, doesn't she? Were there any police officers there?"

Caron shook her head. "A private security cop was trying to keep people from parking in the spaces in front of the condos, but nobody paid any attention to him."

"How large was the crowd?" asked Luanne.

"Maybe twenty-five, not counting the television crew and the protesters. Most of them probably heard about it on the radio and stopped by on their way home. Do you think Miss Parchester is really going to stay in that tree night after night?"

"She might," I said. "She may appear to be scatterbrained, but she has a great deal of determination to fight whatever miscarriages of justice she perceives. After all, as she is so fond of telling us, her dear papa was on the state supreme court."

"While her dear mama stayed home and made elderberry wine," Luanne said through a mouthful of mozzarella. "I hope the designated martyr doesn't have any alcohol with her. Stubbing one's toe in the living room is momentarily uncomfortable; falling off a high platform is a bit more grievous."

I wasn't pleased at the idea of again becoming embroiled in Miss Parchester's affairs, having once aided and abetted her when she'd been charged with a murder in the teachers' lounge, and on another occasion having retrieved her beloved basset hounds when they'd been stolen by a repulsive dealer. But despite all that, she'd offered me tea, cookies, and her trust—and I doubted Finnigan Baybergen had her best interests in mind when he allowed her to take the stage, so to speak, in this current drama.

"I'll drive," I said to Luanne as I put down my glass. "Caron, you'll have to come along and show us how to find this place."

Caron picked up her backpack. "I have already endured enough mortification for one day, thank you very much. Besides, I have a test tomorrow in algebra. Inez is coming over after dinner so we can study together."

She looked at the remains of the pizza. "*Her* mother fixes things like pot roast and baked halibut."

"You wouldn't know a halibut if it bit you on the—" I stopped and took a breath. "Just give me directions. If Peter shows up, tell him I'll be back shortly."

Luanne fiddled with the radio as we drove up Thurber Street, passing not only our businesses, but also the bars and pool halls that lured in Farber College students on weekends. If I believed a neon Budweiser sign in the window of the Book Depot might do the same, I'd have purchased one years ago. Caron and I skimp by without resorting to thrift shops and soup kitchens, although my gloomy accountant implies the possibility is not remote. I could easily imagine him perched atop a doorway, pointing at the pizza box and rumbling "Nevermore." It was unfortunate that my deceased husband had met his demise without the benefit of a life insurance policy, but he'd found coeds more worthy of his attention than his family's welfare. Then again, he hadn't anticipated a chicken truck careening down an icy mountain road.

"Wasn't there something in the news last year about Oakland Heights?" I asked. "A fire, maybe?"

Luanne found a country music station to her liking and sat back. "A fire caused by a gas leak, I seem to think. Nothing worthy of Jessica's breathless coverage."

I shrugged, then turned my attention to the increasing amount of traffic as we approached the scene of the demonstration. Oakland Heights was on the east side of Farberville, within the city limits but in an area that still had a few farmhouses, pastures, and stretches of woods. Several sprawling apartment complexes had sprung up since I'd last driven that way. I wondered if Anthony Armstrong was responsible.

A car pulled out, allowing us to find a space near the

entrance to the condos. The lot itself was packed with vehicles parked haphazardly, including a van from the TV station. Jessica Princeton was likely to be inside it, making sure her lip gloss would still glisten if she had to emerge to provide live coverage of Farberville's first brawl that did not involve fraternity boys, alcohol, and football. As we walked toward the back of the lot, where we presumed Phase Two was in the works, a very irate young man shouted, "Do something, damn it!"

I stopped, hoping he was not addressing me since I had no idea what he had in mind. Haul Miss Parchester off the platform? Bulldoze the oak tree? Tie a yellow ribbon around it?

"Over there," Luanne whispered.

In front of one of the units were two young men. Neither was smiling. The one with the more ferocious expression had shaggy black hair that flopped over his forehead, thin lips, and the angular jaw of a pugilist begging for a right hook. He wore a gray sweatshirt and jeans, standard campus attire for all but the dedicated preppies who aspired to become partners in their daddies' law firms. The other man, his face round and flushed, wore a blue uniform with a patch on his shoulder, leading me to deduce à la Miss Marple that he was the security officer Caron had mentioned.

The latter began to sputter. "Why doncha give me a break? I already told you I can't do anything. I warned them they was trespassing when they parked here, but nobody listened. Even the folks from the TV station ignored me. You want I should shoot them all?"

"I have a seminar in thirty minutes. How am I supposed to get there—hitchhike?"

"Beats me," the officer said, then walked toward the back of the parking lot, where the crowd had gathered.

"This is insane!" howled the floppy-haired man. "There's no way I can get my car out! What's happened to my rights as a private citizen? What about my seminar?"

I decided to intervene before he went berserk and attacked Miss Parchester and the other Farberville Greens. "Excuse me," I said, "but we can give you a ride to the campus in a few minutes. I just need to speak to someone, and then I can drop you off in front of whichever building you prefer."

"Who are you?" he demanded, huffing and puffing as only a graduate student can.

Luanne, whose Yankee blood comes to a boil every now and then, nudged me aside. "She is someone who has offered you a ride. If you are concerned that this is a ploy to take you to a remote county road, steal your wallet, and leave your battered body beside a scummy pond where your bodily fluids will be sucked by mosquitoes and leeches, then by all means start hitching a ride. I suggest you do so briskly."

He gaped at her, then pushed back his hair. "No, I'd appreciate a ride. It's just been—well, a bad day, and now this. I'll get my backpack and wait here for you." We watched him walk over to his condo and enter it.

Luanne and I resumed walking. A few people were heading in the same direction, but an equal number were coming the opposite way, now more interested in getting home than in staring at an elderly woman on a platform in a tree. The rednecks were milling around at the edge of the pavement, mumbling among themselves and, I hoped, tiring of the situation. The Farberville Green Party postured near the tree, clearly prepared to bash anyone who might dare to approach. The security officer had managed to evaporate for the time being. Where he'd found refuge was hard to determine, but I doubted his presence would do anything to help.

"Miss Parchester?" I called as we arrived at the now-infamous tree. "It's Claire Malloy."

Her pink face, ringed with fluffy white hair, appeared at the edge of the platform. "How delightful of you to drop by, Claire. I'd offer you a cup of tea, but I cannot allow anyone to join me up here. You would, I think, enjoy the view, especially now. I can see the towers of Old Main as they are silhouetted in the rosy hues of the sunset. I wish I'd thought to bring my watercolors and a pad."

"I need to come up there," I said flatly.

Finnigan Baybergen moved in as though I'd brandished a chain saw. "Miss Parchester has chosen to hold a solitary vigil. No one will be allowed to join her."

Luanne poked him so hard he nearly fell backward. "Listen here, buddy, if you don't back off, I'll back you off the bluff. Miss Parchester is not a poster child for your movement. She is more than capable of deciding for herself if she does or does not wish to entertain guests on this thing you've built."

"We had a meeting last night," he said as he rubbed his shoulder.

"I don't care if your meeting was in Yalta."

"Actually, it was at the Unitarian Center."

Luanne advanced again on him. "And you drew straws to determine who would risk his or her life to sit in a tree? What about you, Assistant Professor Baybergen? Afraid of heights?"

I ignored both of them. "Why can't I join you, Miss Parchester?"

"I really don't see why not," she said, looking a bit

confused. "It's not as if you're going to drag me down, is it?"

"No, I promise I won't do that. I'd just like to make sure you're safe up there. Why don't you drop the ladder and allow me to join you for a few minutes?"

A dubious contraption of rope and wooden cross-pieces tumbled off the platform. I reminded myself that Miss Parchester, who was at least thirty years older than I, had used it to scramble up.

I may have been breathing heavily when I reached the platform, but I was reasonably calm. Miss Parchester helped me crawl away from the edge, then hauled up the ladder, squeezed my hand, and said, "This is so very kind of you, Claire. I must admit this is a bit stressful. Finnigan has done everything he can to assure my comfort and safety, but . . ."

"Are you sure this is what you want to do, Miss Parchester? Perhaps Finnigan or one of the other Green Party brigade ought to be here. Why did you agree to do this?"

"How about a nice cup of tea? I have this darling little propane stove. It won't take a minute to heat a kettle of water."

"Why you?" I persisted.

"Because I believe in the cause, my dear. We must pass along a proud heritage to the next generation, and the generations to come. How would you feel if you knew your grandchildren would spend their lives surrounded by asphalt? The Earth is precious, and we must fight to preserve it—trees, fields, birds, rivers free of pollutants that cause diseases, expanses of clover and black-eyed Susans, deer and foxes coexisting with domesticated animals. How can we sit at home and allow this to be destroyed by greedy men who would eradicate the intrinsic essence of nature in order to build tacky condominiums?"

I refused to be distracted by her utopian manifesto. "Miss Parchester, your heart may be righteous, but it's going to be cold tonight. At best, you can delay the bulldozers by a few days. The deer and the antelope are going to have to play somewhere else sooner or later."

"Then it shall be later. Lemon and sugar?"

"You'll be arrested for trespassing."

"So be it. Papa always admired those who availed themselves of civil disobedience when no other options were left. If I am physically removed, I shall be kicking and screaming. Finnigan has assured me that legal assistance will be available." She glanced down at the protesters. "He has also assured me that should this developer choose to have me forcibly removed, national media will be on hand to record the brutality. It's quite likely I shall have a heart attack."

"Miss Parchester—" I gurgled.

"Or perhaps a stroke," she added. "I haven't decided which might be more effective. In either case, the film clip of an old woman being dragged to the ground will be the lead story on every channel. Finnigan has been in touch with the major cable news channels. CNN has promised to send a crew in the next few days, as have its competitors."

I accepted a cup of tea from the Mad Hatter. "So you volunteered because of the potential publicity factor?"

"I've never underestimated you, dear."

She began to stir her tea as if she and I were sitting in her parlor, surrounded by piles of ancient yearbooks and yellowed newspaper clippings trumpeting her papa's accomplishments in the courtroom. Below us, voices were belligerent as opposing parties debated the issue.

Luanne and Finnigan Baybergen were in each other's faces; I couldn't hear the exchange, but I could see it was not amicable. The rednecks were no longer present, although I was not at all confident they were gone for the night.

"Miss Parchester," I said without much hope, "it's dangerous for you to sleep here. The temperature's going to drop to forty, maybe lower. If you should happen to wake up and not realize where you are, you might—"

"I am linked to my tree," she said as she held out her ankle so I could see the cuff attached to a chain that wrapped around the trunk of the tree. "I suppose I might take a misstep and dangle, but I cannot fall all the way to the ground. It may well be uncomfortable, but Finnigan has the key."

The tea turned to acid in my mouth. "If you fall off the platform, only Finnigan can release you? You'll swing by your ankle until he rescues you?"

"Like a pendulum," she agreed with a giggle.

It took me a moment to respond. "And he will be here all night, right?"

"I shouldn't think so. He and the other members of the Green Party will stay until the media and sightseers leave. After that, I shall crawl into my sleeping bag and watch the moonlight through the branches. The whip-poorwills will keep me company until dawn breaks."

"But what if . . ." I said weakly. The platform was ten feet above the ground. The image of her taking a tumble and then swinging helplessly made my stomach churn. I wasn't sure exactly how old she was, but I had no doubt she was too old to take up this newly created gymnastic event. "If you should fall . . ."

"Then I shall be a martyr, and Anthony Armstrong will never find the nerve to destroy this tree and those around it. The public outcry will be too much for him. I would rather have this vibrant stand of oak trees than a cold marble slab in a cemetery. A tasteful plaque would be nice, perhaps at the base of the tree. Bronze, I think."

She might be able to think, but I certainly wasn't. I finished my tea, then said, "Is there any chance I can talk you out of this? What about your dogs? Who'll look after them?"

"Nick and Nora are staying at my niece's house in the country. She doesn't appreciate their sensitive natures but has promised to see to them until I return. She's a fine girl, very solid and reliable. I shall miss them, but Papa always said that civic responsibility was more important than individual needs. Mahatma Gandhi sacrificed his life for the good of humanity; surely I can survive minor deprivation and discomfort to do what I can to protect our legacy."

"Just how long are you prepared to stay here?"

"Well, Mr. Constantine—he's the unfortunately flatulent gentleman behind Finnigan—is a retired lawyer. He's planning to file a suit tomorrow that claims this particular grove is an essential stopover for migratory hawks, which means there would be a violation of EPA regulations concerning protected species if the habitat was destroyed. We may not win the case, but we're hoping for an emergency restraining order. He hopes to get a hearing within a day or two."

"A day or two, Miss Parchester?" I said, trying not to sound exasperated. "Couldn't the Farberville Greens have chosen someone else?"

She gave me a look that must have quelled whispering in the back of her classroom. "What is it you're trying to say, Claire? Am I too old to protest injustice?

Should I sit in a rocking chair on the porch and quietly wait for my eyesight to fade and my memory to diminish?"

I caught her hand. "Of course not, Miss Parchester. It's just that, well, it's going to be a hardship for you. You're in danger from the elements, as well as those unsavory men. I'd feel better if your supporters planned to stay the night."

"Finnigan has classes in the morning, and Mr. Constantine will be at the courthouse. I don't see how the others would fare much better than I. My sleeping bag is filled with down. Miss Whitbred gave me a lovely set of thermal underwear and woolen socks, and the Margolises contributed a thermos so that I can keep my tea hot all night. Eliza Peterson brought along several paperback books, although, I must admit, I question her taste. Some of the covers are quite racy. Louis Ferncliff baked his special almond coconut brownies. Would you like one?"

"You had a tree-sitting shower?"

Miss Parchester smiled sadly. "I'd always dreamed of a bridal shower. This will have to suffice."

I had run out of things to say that might persuade her to come down from the tree. The night would be chilly, but she seemed well equipped. Finnigan Baybergen had not struck me as someone capable of staring down a bulldozer. Miss Parchester, on the other hand, had survived forty years at Farberville High School. Thousands of teenagers, year after year, all with acne and shifty-eyed excuses, all presuming they could outwit her. Despite their youthful bravado, there had never been a level playing field.

"Do you have a cell phone?" I asked.

"Yes, Finnigan insisted I take his, although it's a peculiar little thing and I doubt I can operate it. So many buttons, you know." She brandished a rectangular object that very well might have been an almond coconut brownie, minus the crumbs. "He explained at very great length. I don't suppose you remember when one could merely pick up the receiver and wait for the operator to ask whom you wished to call. When I was a child, I could ask for Mama and the operator would track her down. These days there are so many numbers to be dialed or punched or even entered—whatever that means. I've entered rooms and entered contests, but I've never entered numbers. It's all quite alien, I'm afraid."

I leaned forward and kissed her cheek. "If you're the least bit worried about this . . ."

"Not at all, dear Claire. Anthony Armstrong will never risk the negative publicity that should arise if I, a gentlewoman of a certain age, were to be dragged from this platform. He knows well that the media will capture it all and he will find himself the object of outrage not only locally, but across the country. I shall protect the tree, and it shall protect me from harm's way." She dropped the ladder off the edge of the platform and gave me a twinkly smile. "Thank you for dropping by, Claire. Do come again when you're in the neighborhood."

I had been dismissed. I fumbled and swung until I reached the ground, then watched helplessly as she pulled the ladder back up and disappeared from view. I wondered if I should confront Finnigan Baybergen and try to convince him of the insanity of the scheme. It was, however, devious and well thought out. Construction workers might have been able to drag a squirmy, greasy-haired youth out of the tree, even breaking a few bones in the process, but the very idea of anyone causing harm to Miss Parchester, with her rosy cheeks, porcelain

complexion, and faded blue eyes, would be reviled in
the national spotlight.

"Let's go," I said to Luanne, who was glaring at the
demonstrators as if she were a bull charging into an
arena. The slightest flicker of red and bloodshed would
ensue.

"These people are morons. Oh, yes, good cause and
all, but the very idea of allowing—"

I caught her arm. "It's as much Miss Parchester's
scheme as theirs." I told her about the hoped-for injunction, then added, "This whole situation may be resolved
by tomorrow. There's nothing we can do short of pitch-
ing a tent and toasting marshmallows over a candle."

Luanne shrugged. "I suppose not."

Finnigan Baybergen was hovering nearby, looking as
though he was torn between punching me in the nose or
scratching a bad grade on a midterm paper. I'd spent too
many years in academia to feel threatened by either. I
let go of Luanne and went over to talk to him. His lips
receded, but he held his ground.

"Who are you to interfere?" he demanded.

"A friend of Miss Parchester," I said evenly. "I find
it irresponsible that you and your merry band of
mischief-makers are willing to go home and allow her
to stay here alone tonight. What about those rednecks
who were here earlier? They or others of the same sub-
species could come back, you know. Your goals may be
lofty, but you seem to be willing to put a woman of her
age in danger while you watch yourselves on the late-
night news."

"After you take a hot shower," Luanne said, looming
over my shoulder, "and make yourself a toddy. You're
half her age, for pity's sake. Have you been camping
since you were a Boy Scout?"

Finnigan stiffened. "I happen to have spent three weeks in Alaska last summer. Conditions were quite primitive, and on two occasions we discovered evidence that a bear had been prowling outside the cabin. Nonetheless, that is irrelevant. The Farberville Green Party has its agenda. Miss Parchester was not coerced; she volunteered."

I nudged Luanne away and stared at Finnigan. "So you're going to allow her to sleep on the platform with no one but that inept security guard to make sure she's safe?"

He gave me a supercilious smile. "I don't understand why this is any of your concern. You insult Miss Parchester by implying that she is incapable of deciding to take a stand to protect these trees. You said you were her friend. Do you think she's feebleminded, a lamb to be sacrificed for our evil goals?"

"She's not that," I admitted, glancing at the platform.

"And she's armed," he said softly. "Despite her objections, Joseph Margolis insisted that she take his handgun. She argued vehemently, but we persuaded her to tuck it in the duffel bag. With the ladder pulled up, nobody should be able to disturb her. But if someone does . . ."

If ever I had felt the blood drain from my face, this was the moment. "She's armed?"

I did not add that she was, therefore, dangerous.

CHAPTER TWO

I wasn't sure how much Luanne had heard of my conversation with Finnigan, but I could see no reason to set her off while she was still fuming. As long as the rope ladder was furled, no one could menace Miss Parchester. And, I reminded myself, the cause was defensible but unlikely to stir up unrestrained fury from those who favored development over scruffy oak trees, no matter how old they—or the players—were. Only one person would profit from Phase Two, and he was conspicuously absent. Jessica Princeton had done her best, but squabbles at city hall and political corruption on the county level had now captured her viewers' attention.

"Let's go," I said to Luanne before she could throw a punch at anyone in range, including the Green Party demonstrators, bewildered gawkers, or even a few curious chickadees. "Miss Parchester can take care of herself."

The security cop was still undercover in the literal sense of the word, but I doubted he would be of much use. The platform was high; anyone who attempted to climb the tree might discover that Miss Parchester had not only a chamber pot but also a thermos of scalding tea at her disposal (and, well, a gun, but surely one of minimal caliber). And the issue might be resolved the next morning, either in court or by brunt of a bulldozer. Anthony Armstrong might well be the perpetrator behind the demise of fruitful orchards and babbling brooks, but I could not believe that he would welcome the adverse publicity should physical harm come to Miss Parchester.

The student was pacing near the road. "My seminar starts in less than ten minutes," he announced as if we cared.

"Seventeenth-century French literature?" Luanne asked in a sugary voice. "Will Molière sink into obscurity without your profundity?"

"Wow, like sorry," he said as he followed us toward my car. "This is really nice of you. I didn't mean to sound so rude. My name's Randy Scarpo. My wife, Jillian, and I have lived here for almost two years. I'd planned to go to the library earlier this afternoon, but she was upset because the baby's been running a fever. I had no idea what was going on until I came outside, at which point there was no way for me to get my car out. I have orals at the end of the semester, and the last thing I want to do is piss off a professor on the committee."

"Don't worry about it," I said. "I live next to the campus, and dropping you off won't be inconvenient."

He folded himself into the backseat of my perpetually messy hatchback. "Are you two faculty?"

Luanne appraised him over her shoulder, then said, "I regret to say that we're merely outside agitators who may have been protesting the cause célèbre alongside your parents before they opted to beget you."

"Not my parents. They were in their sanitized dorms,

watching televangelists pray for your mortal souls."

I waited until a van passed, then pulled onto the road. "Is the baby better?"

"It wasn't anything. Jillian gets upset when Connor so much as sneezes. Last month she insisted we take him to the emergency room when he got the hiccups. You can imagine how that went down. Our pediatrician has tried to talk to her, but she won't listen."

"Doesn't she have some sort of support?" asked Luanne. "A group of mothers her age with whom she can share concerns?"

"I wish she did, but she's kind of reclusive. Her only friend at Oakland Heights moved out. No one else has a baby, or even a toddler. Her only sister is a lesbian who does stand-up comedy at college campuses. Jillian hasn't spoken to her in years." He paused, then added, "My parents adore Jillian. They bought us the condo for a wedding present."

I glanced at him in the rearview mirror. "Where shall I drop you off?"

"Koenig Hall, if that's okay. And my seminar's in differential vectors, not French literature."

Moments later I pulled to the curb in front of his destination. "I'd like to ask a favor of you, Randy. The demonstrator on the platform is a friend of mine. When you get home, would you please go out there and see if she's all right?" I found a taco wrapper on the floor of the car and scribbled my name and telephone number on it. "Then give me a call so I won't worry about her."

"It'll be a couple of hours."

I gave him the greasy paper. "I'd appreciate it."

I watched him disappear into the building, then drove Luanne to her apartment above Secondhand Rose.

"Miss Parchester will be fine," she said, patting my

arm. "She outsmarted Peter and all his CID lackeys. They're a lot tougher than an itty-bitty bulldozer and a few gorillas with more tattoos than brain cells."

I decided not to mention the gun. "I just don't like it. If Finnigan Baybergen were up there on the platform, I wouldn't bat an eyelash. In fact, I might pack a picnic lunch, find a shady spot beneath an endangered oak tree, and root for the bulldozer."

Luanne got out of the car. "If you aren't overly occupied with Peter, call me after you hear from Randy."

I promised I would, then drove home and parked in my allotted half of the basement garage. The downstairs tenants seemed to change with the seasons. The current one had no ascertainable gender and was rarely at home. Caron found him or her spooky, but I had no problem as long as music was not played so loudly that my floor vibrated.

Caron met me in the kitchen. "We've got a problem," she whispered. "Peter's in the living room. I can't explain, but you have to get rid of him."

"Is he the problem?"

"Just get rid of him—okay?"

I put down my purse and stared at her. "What's going on, Caron? Have you and Inez done something illegal?"

"Of course not," she said as though the two had never skittered near the brink of felony charges and been yanked back by dint of a metaphorical apron string. Her eyes began to well with tears. "I can't tell you until Peter's gone. Trust me, Mother—This Is Serious."

"All right," I said, giving her a hug. I went into the living room, where Peter was sitting on the couch, his feet propped on the coffee table. He'd managed to find a beer, and the pizza box was empty. He was flipping through one of the magazines I receive monthly and rarely find time to read. The domesticity of the scene was unsettling, but I put it aside to think about later, when Caron wasn't hopping about in the kitchen as though she'd given sanctuary to a serial killer, which was far-fetched but not beyond the realm of possibility. She has an extraordinary track record.

"Hey," I said, "how are you?"

He looked up, his eyes as appealing as warm gingerbread and his teeth as white as whipped cream. "Wondering where you were."

"I gave Luanne a ride home," I said truthfully. "I hope you haven't been waiting too long."

"Go anyplace else?"

I sat down next to him. "Well, let me think. I went to the grocery store this morning, then came back here and made myself a peanut butter on rye for lunch."

"Peanut butter on rye?"

"It's quite intriguing. After that, I spent the morning at the Book Depot, doing the crossword puzzle and trying to prevent my science fiction hippie from shoplifting several paperbacks. He claims he's a Marxist and therefore repudiates the concept of private property unless it involves the sale of galactic battleships and nubile slaves with multiple appendages. At noon, I walked to the bank branch and deposited a very minuscule amount of money, but enough to cover the outstanding checks."

"And then you ate peanut butter on rye?"

"Yes, I did. I then sold a few books, banged on the boiler, and dealt with a sales rep who'd had one beer too many. Luanne came by at five and—"

"Let's talk about Oakland Heights."

"Why would I go there?" I said.

Peter Rosen had not achieved the rank of lieutenant in the police department because of his talent for disarming witnesses with an adorably dimpled smile. He certainly hadn't done so in order to collect a monthly paycheck; his family was wealthy, and the cost of one of his suits would have covered my rent for several months. He was stubbornly unforthcoming whenever I tried to find out why he'd chosen to settle in Farberville, an insignificant city of perhaps thirty thousand with only the college to give it a smidgeon of charm. Smidgeon as in pigeon, as in droppings.

He grinned, knowing it would annoy me. "You might have gone there because your friend Miss Parchester is chained to a tree."

"I was there briefly," I acknowledged. "Luanne and I happened to catch the local news."

"And you were worried about the rednecks returning after everyone else had left?"

I nodded. "Good guess, Sherlock. Is there any way a bona fide police officer can stay there during the night? Preferably one with more than a tin badge and a beeper?"

He started to answer, but Caron came into the room and glowered at me.

"Mother," she said, enunciating each syllable as if it were a crystal on the verge of shattering, "I told you I need to talk to you. It's urgent."

Peter looked at her, but she turned away. After an uncomfortable moment, he stood up. "Maybe I'd better go."

"I suppose so," I said, unable to offer any explanation. I participated in a lingering kiss by the front door, then waited until I heard him go down the stairs and leave through the front door. I locked my door and turned around. "Okay, dear, what's the crisis? Did Inez fail to show up?"

"Inez is here," she said grimly. "She's in my room."

"And that's the problem?"

"She's not alone."

"She's not? Someone else is here? Who is it?"

"Yes, someone else is here, and we don't know who he is, much less his name. You'll have to ask him yourself." She raised her voice. "Peter's gone, Inez. Come on out."

Inez Thornton is Caron's best friend, and proof that opposites not only attract but cling like burrs. She's soft-spoken and marginally anemic, and the throes of adolescence have left her thus far unscathed. Caron is full of sound and fury. Inez merely wheezes.

"What on earth are you talking about?" I demanded.

Inez came down the short hallway carrying a large wicker basket. "This is for you, Ms. Malloy."

In the basket were not Easter eggs or foil-wrapped chocolates. Those I could have dealt with. In the basket was a baby, perhaps a month old. A bit of dark hair, a rosebud mouth, defiant bluish-gray eyes. Tiny pink fists. Cheeks marred with rough red patches. All in all, and with no way to deny it, a baby.

"What the . . . ," I said, stunned.

Caron stared at me as Inez placed the basket on the floor near my feet. "We haven't been trick-or-treating, Mother. The person downstairs found this on the porch, along with a denim bag and a letter with your name on it. He—or she—pounded on the door and insisted that I take delivery. I didn't know what else to do. Then Peter showed up, and I thought I'd better talk to you first."

Inez blinked at me. "It's a boy. Whoever abandoned him left some diapers in the bag. I changed him while Caron heated up a bottle. There are a couple more diapers and cans of formula in the bag."

"A letter?" I said weakly. "Did you open it?"

My daughter gave me a contemptuous smile. "Of course not."

Inez handed me the missive, which was suspiciously moist, as though innocent parties might have tried to steam it open. I accepted it, although I was distracted by the baby, who seemed content to gaze at me.

I finally averted my eyes and opened the envelope. Inside it was a sheet ripped off a legal pad and covered with a scrawled script that was nearly indecipherable. As best I could tell, it read: "You're the only person I can trust to take care of Skyler. Just for a few days. Don't let anyone take him away. I promise I'll come back for him. Please do this for both of us."

"Oh, dear," I said as I put aside the note and looked more carefully at the resident of the wicker basket. Caron and Inez had both managed to lean over my shoulder and read the terse message.

"Skyler?" said Caron.

"It's a complicated story," I said as I went into the kitchen and poured several inches of scotch into a glass. It had been about a month ago, late in the afternoon, with dark clouds in the sky. Caron had disappeared from a local inn, and although I had been frantic to find her, I'd found myself delivering a baby. Claire Malloy, bookseller and hastily recruited midwife. The mother, a teary, malnourished, and abused teenaged girl, had agreed to be transported to a battered women's shelter and then, I'd hoped, to a hospital for postpartum and neonatal care. I hadn't followed through, since she had been a sad yet determinedly anonymous figure.

I had told no one about the episode, not even Luanne.

"Who are his parents?" asked Inez as I came back

into the living room. "I mean, why would they leave this baby with you?"

I glanced at Skyler, who thus far seemed docile but could quite possibly be the personification of the calm before the storm. "His mother's about your age. She was living on the streets. I had . . . an encounter with her, and I guess she found out who I was and where I lived."

Caron crossed her arms. "That doesn't explain why she left this baby on our front porch."

Inez went so far as to purse her lips, albeit briefly. "It really doesn't, Ms. Malloy. This isn't a hospital or a convent. Why would this girl abandon her baby here?"

"She hasn't technically abandoned him," I said as I reread the note. "She wants me to take care of him for a few days, that's all."

"But why you?" demanded Caron.

"I don't know. I guess she doesn't have anyone else."

"This is a baby, not a puppy! I don't care how old she is—she isn't supposed to dump her baby like a sack of potatoes! What if no one was home? What if that person downstairs had gone off to dig up bodies or paint swastikas on overpasses? Inez and I were in my room. We couldn't have heard anything. You came up the back stairs. What would have happened to Skyler if . . ." Her indignation gave way to sobs interspersed with hiccups. "Leaving a baby like that!"

Skyler, no doubt sensing emotional upheaval, began to whimper. I took him out of the basket and cradled him against my chest. "It's okay," I said, speaking to both of them as I savored the redolence of baby powder.

Caron went into the bathroom and reappeared with a handful of tissues. "It Is Not Okay, Mother. What are you going to do?"

"This isn't kidnapping, is it?" asked Inez, glancing

over her shoulder as though anticipating the intrusion of a squadron of social workers armed with assault weapons.

Skyler quieted down. I eased him back into the basket, which was well padded with a slightly grimy quilt.

"It's not kidnapping," I said firmly. "I have the letter to prove that I'm the designated caretaker for no more than a few days."

"So what are you going to do?" demanded Caron. "Shouldn't you call somebody? Leaving a baby on the doorstep is clearly negligent, and probably criminal."

"But you didn't tell Peter," I pointed out.

Inez cleared her throat. "Well, we discussed it, but we figured he'd call some brawny lady to come scoop up little Skyler like a bag left at the bus station and take him off to some dreary, roach-infested house where he'd be left in a metal crib in a cold room. He's just a little baby."

"That he is," I said as I took a swallow of scotch. "His mother knows who I am, but I have no idea who she is. I don't even know her first name, much less her last name or where she lives. Any suggestions?"

Caron seemed to be recovering from what I suspected was more than momentary shock over the present situation. "Well, you are the legal guardian for the time being," she said. "I really don't understand why you won't tell us any more, but I suppose I can live with it for a couple of days. Just don't assume I'll baby-sit."

"Of course not," I said numbly as I tried to remember how I'd handled the situation sixteen years ago. I'd resumed my graduate assistant duties after three months of maternity leave. Carlton never changed a diaper, much less dealt with strained prunes and rubber duckies. I dealt with it all, although I gave up hope of writing a dissertation on an obscure English novelist who would continue to rest in anonymity until some predatory graduate student stumbled across the body. The college had a philosophically enlightened day-care center where the babies and toddlers had been encouraged to express themselves via finger painting and pudding fights. Caron had thrived.

"So what are you going to do?" asked Inez.

"I'm not going to do anything tonight," I said. "Skyler's mother will undoubtedly call me tomorrow and make arrangements to collect him after she resolves her problems."

Caron stared at me. "So you think you can care for this baby?"

"I've been there, done that," I answered. "The stork did not keep you in a nest until you were potty-trained and capable of uttering a complete sentence."

"But, Mother—" she said, then stopped and shrugged.

I wasn't pleased with the scenario, but I most certainly wasn't about to call social services and allow my temporary ward to be whisked away in the night. I hadn't conceived him, much less carried him for nine months and gone through the ordeal of birth, but I had, by damn, been the first person he'd encountered and the one who'd wrapped him in a towel, kissed his forehead, and handed him to his biological mother. I'd severed the umbilical cord, but not my involvement.

"Two cans of formula?" I said. "How many diapers? Any clothes?"

"I'll check." Inez skittered down the hall with more alacrity than necessary.

Caron sat on the far end of the sofa. "I don't see how you can handle this, Mother. Unless you want to call me in sick, I have to go to school. You have a business to run." She looked at Skyler, who was sucking on his fist. "You can't just hand him a bottle and leave him in your office all day. Babies do all sorts of disgusting things, and I'm not talking about burping and spitting up."

"Oh, yes, I know very well. What do you suggest I do?"

"Maybe Luanne can take him."

I reached out to touch her arm, but she shrank away. I sat back and said, "And Luanne can give him to her first customer of the day, who can pass him on to some guy at the car wash, who can—"

"Where's he going to sleep?"

"At the moment, he seems content with his basket. This is only for a day or two, Caron. If we don't hear from his mother and the time comes when you and he need bunk beds, I'll call social services."

"You're joking, I assume."

"I don't think we can persuade Miss Parchester to drop a line and haul him up. What is it you think I should do?"

Inez came back. "Two cans of formula, three diapers, a cotton nightie with drawstrings, and a pair of tiny socks. I went through all the side pockets in the diaper bag in case I could find a clue, but there wasn't so much as a scrap of paper."

Skyler was fast asleep, at least for the time being. He was tiny, no more than nine or ten pounds. I had enough essentials to last until morning, when I could, if necessary, buy a box of disposable diapers and a few more cans of formula. His mother would return with apologies and excuses, and swoop him away. All I was doing was baby-sitting. No big deal.

Caron glared at me. "This is ridiculous, Mother."

"That's a harsh word," I said. "This young girl must

have been desperate in order to leave her baby with a stranger. I don't know anything about her family situation, but it's obvious she has no one else she can trust. Try to imagine how you'd feel if that were your predicament. She couldn't turn to her family or the baby's father, or even his family."

"Well, we need to find out who she is," Caron said coldly.

"And how should we go about doing that?"

Inez took a breath. "There has to be a birth certificate or something like that. The hospital has records. They put footprints on the birth certificates."

I nodded. "Indeed they do. Should we don ski masks and sneak into the hospital to riffle through the files?"

"We can make a print of Skyler's foot for comparison," Inez began enthusiastically, then paused to consider her plan. "We'll have to use bobby pins to pick the locks of the file cabinets."

"And we'll need stun guns for the guards," said Caron. "Maybe a helicopter to drop us on the roof of the hospital. And, if the employees are aliens from a distant galaxy, we'll have to disrupt their communication with the mother ship and locate their lasers before they can liquidate us. Quick, Inez, call Spielberg and tell him to bring a camera crew."

She folded her arms. "It was just a suggestion."

"Let's wait and see what happens tomorrow," I said. "Skyler will sleep in my bedroom tonight. He can hang out at the bookstore until his mother returns. The problem will be resolved."

"Yeah, right," Caron said in an exceedingly sour tone. "Why should we be worried about little Moses? We need to review binomials and all that crap."

I shooed them down the hall to Caron's room, then

sat back and tried to remember if the other two witnesses during the birth had said anything that might lead to the mother's identity. I knew one of their names, and would recognize the second if I happened to see her. If the mother didn't call or come by in a day or so, I could go by the homeless shelter in case any of the three was there.

My copy of Dr. Spock's essential wisdom had long since gone to a garage sale, but I presumed I could recall the basics. Babies of a certain age did little more than sleep, eat, fuss, and periodically require a fresh diaper. I could take him with me to the bookstore, where I had a distressingly ample amount of idle time to look after him. And then his mother would present herself, explain, and carry him away.

It didn't seem wise to involve Peter, who might feel that the scrawled note was not adequate to prove I had temporary custody. Cops can be sticklers. I considered calling Luanne, then decided to wait until the following day.

Moving gingerly, I carried the basket to my bedroom and set it down. I changed into nightclothes, noting the scratches and bruises on my shins that had resulted from my less than graceful encounter with the rope ladder. No other physical damage was visible, but I suspected a few muscles might make known their grievances in the morning.

Skyler was lost in infantile dreams. I left him there and knocked on Caron's door. The conversation, which had been more centered around names than binomials, broke off as I went into the room.

"I'd better take the diaper bag," I said.

Inez gazed solemnly at me. "To make sure I didn't

overlook a vital clue? I looked very carefully, Ms. Malloy."

"To make sure I can warm up a bottle in the middle of the night," I said, then looked at my daughter, who was cross-legged on the bed and hunched over an open textbook. "I left a six-pack of sodas on the back porch."

Caron did not deign to respond. I picked up the denim bag and took it to the living room. The contents were as meager as Inez had reported. The nipple on the plastic bottle looked worn but functional. The nightgown, socks, and diapers were tiny, but so was Skyler. The bag lacked so much as a monogram, which wouldn't have been much help, anyway.

I made a cup of tea and took to the sofa to read a dated mystery novel while keeping one ear attuned for a wail from my bedroom. An hour later, just as the lady of the manor had discovered her lordship's body in the conservatory and the butler was dashing off to find smelling salts for the anorexic niece who'd dropped by unexpectedly in hopes of a substantial loan to pay off her gambling debts, Inez came down the hallway.

"Good night, Ms. Malloy," she murmured.

"Did you and Caron conquer binomials?"

"I suppose so. Are you going to need any help with Skyler? I can leave after fifth period tomorrow. Mr. O'Nally, the Latin teacher, is having some sort of creepy surgery on his toenails and gave us passes to the library."

"That's very kind of you, Inez. I don't think I'll need any help, but if you'd like to come by the Book Depot, you can take Skyler outside. A little sunshine might be good for him."

"You said his mother's my age?"

"Thereabouts."

"Is she married?"

I put down the book. "I don't think so. From what I was told, she was kicked out of her home and was living on the streets."

Inez thought this over. "Do you think she was going to Farberville High School before she got pregnant?"

"Probably, but I can't give you a decent description of her beyond medium height and long, dark hair. Can you think of a girl who dropped out before Christmas?"

"No one in any of my classes. Shall I ask around?"

"It can't hurt," I said, "although she may be from one of the little towns around here or even another state. Twenty dollars will buy a bus ticket; no passport required."

"This is so sad," she said, her lenses fogging up.

I went over to her and squeezed her shoulder. "Skyler is safe, Inez. We'll look after him and make sure that nothing bad will happen to him. If his mother is unable to convince me that she can take care of him, I'll call social services. They don't have metal cribs these days, and they're not brawny sadists. Their job is to do what's best for children in harmful situations."

"But what if his mother shows up and just takes him away? The police can't arrest her, can they? You can't stop her."

I pulled off her glasses and dried them on my shirttail. Settling them back on her nose, I lapsed into the maternally obdurate voice I usually reserve for Caron when she wheedles for an advance on her allowance or forgets to take out the garbage. "I will stop her, if I have to tie her up and read self-help books to her until the authorities arrive."

Inez sniffled, then slung her backpack over her shoulder and went downstairs.

I waited for a moment to see if Caron might come

padding down the hall to second Inez's apprehensions, then sighed and resumed the position on the sofa. The lady of the manor dithered for another page or two, but she no longer held my attention. I checked on Skyler, then reminded myself that I had yet another rock-a-bye baby, in this case literally in the treetop. Randy had not called, but it was possible the scrap of paper with my name and number was in the first wastebasket he'd encountered inside Koenig Hall. Even if his intentions had been honorable, he might be having problems getting a ride back to Oakland Heights, Phase One.

After a few minutes of wrinkling my brow and gazing blankly at the wall, I remembered his last name and opened the telephone directory. There was only one Randy Scarpo. I dialed the number, hoping he'd been so dumbfounded by whichever vectors had been differentiated that he'd forgotten to call me.

A woman answered. I asked to speak to Randy in what I thought was a modulated and polite voice.

"Who's this?" she said shrilly, as if I'd hissed an obscenity.

"Is this Jillian?"

Her decibel level rose. "Why are you calling? Where did you get my name? I don't know you!"

"Well, no, you don't." I went on to offer a somewhat coherent explanation for the purpose of my call, then added, "I'm worried about Miss Parchester. Some of the sightseers were hostile."

She calmed down, although there remained an inexplicable edge in her tone. "I understand why you're calling, Ms. Malloy. It's just that Randy's not home yet. He should have been here half an hour ago. I don't like to be here by myself at night."

"But"—I racked my mind for a moment—"Connor's there with you, isn't he?"

"He's been in bed since seven o'clock. Cars are still coming and going in the parking lot, and there's been shouting. It sounds like a movie company is filming a mob scene. Connor was so agitated that I had to put his crib in the back room so he could get to sleep. I'm afraid to go into the living room. What if these people are armed? What if they decide to burn down our building in protest? I still have nightmares about the fire last year. The three of us could have died from smoke inhalation."

"Isn't there someone in the complex who can stay with you until Randy gets home?"

"Not really."

And on that note, she hung up.

CHAPTER THREE

I didn't have much hope that Jillian would remind Randy to call me, since we hadn't exactly hit it off like, well, peanut butter and rye. If I called again, she might very well report me to the police for harassment. Peter would not find it endearing.

I was going to have to come up with an explanation for his abrupt ejection earlier. The truth did not seem prudent. Although I was convinced that I wasn't violating any laws, I didn't want to press my luck and end up having to hire a lawyer. Their meters never stop running.

At ten o'clock, I turned on the local news to find out if Jessica had a late-breaking story. After the mundane car wrecks and liquor store holdups, we were once again treated to a view of her unflagging radiance.

"This is Jessica Princeton, live"—it was hard to imagine her saying otherwise—"from the site of the confrontation between environmentalists and those who support property development as a sign of a healthy local economy," she said. "As you can see, most people have left. One member of the Farberville Green Party is seated on a camp stool beneath the tree, but has said he will be leaving shortly to prepare to go to court in the morning in hopes of winning an emergency injunction. Retired schoolteacher Emily Parchester remains on the platform, where she has vowed to stay as long as bulldozers threaten the trees. Despite KFAR's repeated requests, she has refused to make any further statements."

She almost frowned when she was handed a piece of paper, but only a single nerve twitched her eyelid as she read from the note. "This just in: Tomorrow at noon, Anthony Arm-strong will hold a press conference on the steps of the courthouse. Please join us then so we can hear his side of the dispute. This is Jessica Princeton for KFAR."

An irate cry from my bedroom ended my quest for news. I stopped in the bathroom to fetch a washcloth, then brought Skyler back to the couch and changed his diaper. I did so with amazing adeptness, considering I hadn't practiced in fourteen years. This did not quite seem to satisfy his demands. Cradling him in one arm, I heated a bottle of formula and returned to the living room, wishing I had a rocking chair—wishing, too, if for only a moment, that he was mine and we could spend the summer at the park marveling at the butterflies.

Eventually, Skyler went to sleep, and shortly thereafter, so did I.

Caron staggered into the kitchen the following morning. "I hardly got any sleep last night," she said as she rooted through the refrigerator. "I do have a test today, you know."

"Small babies need nourishment every few hours," I said, waiting for coffee to trickle into the pot.

"That is so fascinating. Why is the bread blue?"

"It was depressed when I bought it. However, you'll

be delighted to know that I'm going to drive you to school after we make a quick stop at the grocery store. Do we need milk?"

Caron stuck a bagel in the toaster. "You never drive me to school unless it's raining."

"I don't want your knees to be trembling when you take your algebra test."

"And you need to buy formula and diapers."

"Caron," I said as I poured a much-needed cup of coffee, "what I need is your cooperation for the next few days. If I take Skyler with me inside the store, I'll undoubtedly run into someone I know. I won't be able to pretend I found a baby under a cabbage leaf in the produce department. If I hedge, the assumption will be that it's yours. If I explain, Peter will show up at the bookstore within an hour."

"Mine?" she squeaked.

"It does happen."

"Well, it won't happen to me!"

She was still deeply upset, although I wasn't sure why. I decided it might be wise to give her some time to sort through her feelings before I made an effort to talk to her. "As soon as you're ready, we'll go. Skyler will be asleep in the basket in the backseat. You can study while I grab the necessities."

"What if he . . ."

"I'll change his diaper and give him a bottle while you're getting ready. I realize you felt as though he cried all night, but he's actually rather peaceful most of the time, like an elderly relative dozing on a porch swing."

She banged her plate in the sink. "I probably cried all the time, didn't I? You were so tired that you had to drop out of grad school. If I hadn't come along, you could have finished your dissertation and be teaching at some ivy-infested college, publishing tedious papers and speaking at colloquiums in Paris and Oxford. You'd have tenure by now, as well as a comfortable retirement plan. Instead, you were stuck with me."

"I wasn't stuck with you," I said gently.

"Did Dad feel the same way. Is that why he—"

"No, of course not." I was very sorry I'd discarded Dr. Spock's book, even though I doubted it had covered topics such as this. "Go take a shower and get dressed, dear."

She left the kitchen, and minutes later slammed the bathroom door. I fetched Skyler, who was awake and appeared to be interested in whatever he'd overheard. He seemed a bit young to assimilate it, but I wasn't sure. I gave him a sponge bath, then warmed up the last of the formula and held him as we both enjoyed the morning's libations.

Caron had her nose in her algebra book as we arrived in the grocery store parking lot. I grabbed my purse and said, "This shouldn't take more than ten minutes."

"Yeah, right," she muttered.

I glanced at Skyler, who was sucking his fist, then went into the store and tried to remember if I'd ever gone down an aisle stocked with diapers and little jars of strained things. I took a few wrong turns, but eventually found the appropriate aisle and stopped my cart in front of a vast display of disposable diapers. I'd preferred cloth diapers when Caron was a baby, although I had resorted to the politically incorrect ones in a pinch. I'd made my selection based on price. Now I was bedazzled by the options: pastels, gender, prints that changed colors when the diaper had served its purpose. Elastic or plain. Velcro or tape. Age, weight, level of mobility. No wonder Jillian Scarpo was in the grip of postpartum stress.

I was so caught up in my search for the perfect box that I was unaware a cart had stopped next to mine.

"Claire," said Sally Fromberger, "why ever are you buying diapers?" Her beady gaze shifted to my waist for a few seconds, then returned to my face. She clearly expected an explanation.

And I was clearly pinned between her cart and the Pampers until I offered one to Farberville's most dedicated busybody. "I was just . . . looking," I said, cursing myself for such a lame response. "What about you?"

"One of my cats is refusing to eat, so I thought I'd tempt her with strained liver. I'm afraid she has another impacted tooth." She paused, then said, "Just looking at diapers?"

I could almost hear Caron hissing in the car. I blindly grabbed a box of diapers and dropped it in the cart. "A cousin is coming to visit, so I thought I'd pick up a few things. If you'll excuse me, Sally, I need to drive Caron to school before the first bell." I tossed in a six-pack of the same formula that had been in the diaper bag. I had adequate supplies for the day, and when Inez came by after school, I could leave Skyler with her and shop in a store at the edge of town. Or in another county.

Sally deftly swung her cart in front of mine. "How old is Caron these days? Sixteen, isn't she?"

I resisted the urge to ram her cart and send her stumbling into the strained liver, beets, peas, carrots, and whatever designer vegetables were being strained these days. "Yes, she's sixteen, and she's also about to be late to algebra. I hope your cat recovers."

"I'm sure she will, in due time."

I received a few curious glances as I waited in line

at the checkout counter, taking some comfort in the fact I did not have the matronly aura of a grandmother. And, yes, I realize some grandmothers run marathons, dance until dawn, oversee megabuck businesses, and have seats in the U.S. Congress or cells in federal penitentiaries. An eclectic group.

Skyler was watching the sunlight on the upholstery when I arrived at the car. Caron ignored me. I dropped her off at the high school, then continued to the Book Depot. I parked behind the store and carried the basket through the back door. Discretion rather than cowardice, I told myself as I made sure Skyler was content.

I'd barely started making coffee when the telephone rang. Despite my reluctance, I answered it with a timid hello.

"What is going on?" demanded Luanne, wasting no time with conventional greetings. "Are you plotting to kidnap the sole heir of a wealthy stockbroker?"

"Know any?"

"That is not an answer."

"It's a response, though."

Luanne took a deep breath. "Why were you buying disposable diapers this morning? Most of us tend to equate diapers with babies. Have you opened an infant day-care center in the back room of the bookstore?"

"In a way," I admitted, then told her the whole story from Skyler's first appearance to his most recent one.

"Oh, dear," she said at last. "Oh, dear. You have no idea who the mother is or why she left the baby on your porch?"

"How could I? I suppose I might try to track Arnie down, but he's more likely to be on a freight train to Topeka than in a local shelter. The other witness had a car and an attitude. I don't have a clue where the mother's been staying for the last month. It's not that much of a crisis, Luanne. I'm looking at a couple of days of diapers and formula, not the specter of athletic shoes, college tuition, and future in-laws."

"Sally is convinced that he's Caron's child."

I would have uttered an Anglo-Saxon expletive had Skyler not been observing me; I did not want to be responsible if his first utterance was indelicate. "Sally dealt with Caron and Inez five weeks ago, for pity's sake! She knows perfectly well that Caron wasn't wearing pants with an elastic waistband and a maternity blouse."

"She was rather puzzled," said Luanne. "So, are you going to Anthony's press conference?"

"I don't see how I can."

Luanne rumbled for a moment, then said, "I'll find a stroller and a car seat at the thrift shop, and pick up you and your ward at eleven-thirty. If you're afraid of gossip, I'll push the stroller."

I was interested in hearing what Anthony Armstrong had to say, as well as what action he intended to take. Mr. Constantine, the Greens' lawyer, was shuffling his notes outside the courthouse, so we could expect to learn if he'd been successful in his plea for an injunction. And of course, Skyler was not too young for his first foray into the machinations of local politics. The one person who would have enjoyed it most was oak-bound.

Parking was scarce near the square, but we found a space behind a defunct department store that had succumbed to the mall. The KFAR van had the prime spot in front of the two-story granite courthouse. Jessica was nowhere in sight, but a cameraman was tinkering with his equipment. A substantial crowd had gathered. Finnigan Baybergen and his followers milled about, their signs held high and their voices strident. A few college students in T-shirts and ripped jeans raised clenched fists and chanted slogans that were artfully rhymed but also obscene. The rednecks were not present, which meant they were either working or had lost interest. Two uniformed officers stood on the opposite side of the street.

Several strangers paused to make nonsensical noises at Skyler. Luanne smiled modestly and avoided answering questions. I didn't know if Sally was there. She took an interest in all matters civic, but she was short enough to be hidden by the crowd. If she approached us, I would come up with a more elaborate lie about the cousin's arrival and desire for a nap.

A few minutes before noon, Jessica emerged from the van and took her position in front of the camera. She did not smile, but it was clear she was elated to be going "live" with a potentially rowdy audience. With a bit of luck, violence might ensue and her clip would make the national news.

At high noon, so to speak, the front door of the courthouse opened and a man dressed in a somber suit took a position on the steps. He had clipped silver hair and the genial expression of a politician who'd smoked a lot of cigars behind closed doors. He was more than stocky, and his chin was already showing symptoms of wattling, but he was no doubt a formidable presence on the golf course (and in the clubhouse bar). I could easily imagine him issuing an order to raze a hospice or an orphanage to create space for a gourmet coffee shop. We would never be friends. His loss.

Behind him came a bristly man with a briefcase, followed by a woman who looked to be in her early twenties, with flawless ash-blond hair and muted makeup. She wore a floral print ensemble that I assumed was de rigueur at country club luncheons and charity style shows. Despite her determined smile, she looked extremely bored with the melodrama of the moment.

Jessica assessed her for a moment, then looked into the camera and said, "This is Jessica Princeton, live from the steps of the Farberville courthouse. Anthony Armstrong, developer of the controversial Phase Two of Oakland Heights, has called this press conference to tell us his side of the story. Mr. Armstrong?"

"Thank you, Jessica," he said in a voice as facile as hers. "Before I proceed, let me say I'm a big fan of yours. Adrienne and I make a point of watching you every night. Isn't that right, honey?" The blond woman obligingly nodded, although she appeared more the type to fret over her nail polish than get mired in local news. I could see that Jessica and Adrienne would never play on the same side of the net at the club tennis tournament.

Armstrong continued. "For those of you who are concerned about Miss Emily Parchester, rest assured that I am equally concerned for her physical well-being. Professor Baybergen provided me with a list of the names of the Farberville Green Party, and a security officer made sure no one else except those listed approached the tree after eleven o'clock last night. I personally spoke to Miss Parchester this morning. She acknowledged that she had not slept well but was looking forward to a cup of tea."

Finnigan and his followers offered a few catcalls, but subsided when Jessica glowered at them. "So why is it necessary to remove this particular stand of trees, Mr. Armstrong?" she said.

"I have only one acre, the minimum for twenty-four additional units, for which I am required to provide parking spaces. I have spent six months and more than fifty thousand dollars with an engineering firm. I have filed the necessary papers with the city planning board, the landscape department, the streets and sewers commissions, and the tree preservation subcommittee. I have provided everything that is required by all the boards and commissions."

"And you were given permission to go ahead?"

Armstrong gazed solemnly at the camera. "That's correct, Jessica. I presented a plan that indicates which trees are to be removed, and the quantity to be replaced after construction is completed to meet the requirements of the city ordinance."

"How much did you pay under the table for the variance?" shouted Finnigan.

The man with the briefcase stepped forward, but Armstrong blocked him.

"I suspect my lawyer would like to explain the concept of slander, but we all need to act in a spirit of cooperation, not contentiousness. The head of the tree preservation subcommittee reviewed the plan in detail and agreed that I could reduce the canopy by an additional four percent in order to avoid problems that came to light with the grading plan and drainage calculations."

He went on, but I stopped listening as I spotted a figure standing behind one of the elm trees that ringed the courthouse. "Luanne," I whispered, elbowing her in the ribs for good measure, "look over there. It's Skyler's mother!"

Her face jerked around. "Where?"

I realized the girl must have seen me staring at her, because she had vanished in all of a few seconds. "I'm going to see if I can catch her. Wait here for me."

I strolled to the corner, hoping I looked nonchalant, then found the place where she'd been. It was hopeless to pursue her; there were stores ringing the square, and the courthouse had an entrance twenty feet away. I could not see myself bursting into every shop, office, and restroom in a three-block radius.

"Did you find her?" Luanne asked as I rejoined her.

I shook my head. "Did I miss anything?"

"A judge is hearing a request for a temporary injunction as we speak, and will rule this afternoon. Shall we go?"

Once Skyler was strapped in the car seat, I said, "Why don't we pick up some sandwiches and have a picnic at Phase Two? Miss Parchester might like to hear about the press conference."

Luanne agreed, and Skyler offered no objection. We stopped at one of the sandwich shops on Thurber Street, then made our way through the noon traffic and headed east.

"Why do you think Skyler's mother was there?" I asked. "She's likely to have more pressing problems than the deliverance of a stand of trees."

"Are you sure it was her?"

"I got a good look at her. She's thin, but her clothes and hair were clean." I thought for a moment. "If she'd figured out I wasn't home, and then seen that the Book Depot was closed, she might have taken a chance I was at the courthouse."

"And wanted to speak to you?"

"Most certainly not that," I said ruefully. "She bolted like a cat confronted with a hose. If she'd wanted to ask me how Skyler was, all she would have had to do was wait where she was."

Luanne raised her eyebrows. "So she might be a fugitive?"

"She can't have done anything more serious than

shoplifting or I'd have seen a mention in the local paper. If she'd allowed social services to take Skyler shortly after birth, and subsequently changed her mind and snatched him away from foster care . . ."

"It must have happened yesterday. Would it be considered kidnapping?"

"I don't know," I said, "and I can't call the department and ask them without tipping my hand. I suppose it would depend on whether or not she signed papers granting custody to the state." I twisted around to smile at Skyler. "I don't suppose you're going to tell us, are you?"

He had fallen asleep. When we arrived at Oakland Heights, I transferred him to the basket while Luanne juggled the sandwiches and cups of iced tea. The curtains were drawn in the Scarpos' condo, which was of no consequence since Randy had failed to call me and Jillian might appear with a steak knife if I knocked on their door.

"Miss Parchester!" I called as the three of us approached the oak. "It's Claire. I've brought Luanne Bradshaw and a wee visitor. May we offer you a chicken salad sandwich and iced tea for lunch?"

Her face appeared. "What a lovely surprise, Claire. I regret to say there's insufficient room for all of you up here, and of course I couldn't come down even if I wished. Is that an infant?"

"Yes, a cousin and all that sort of thing. Very complicated. If you drop the ladder, I'll bring up your lunch."

"That won't be necessary," she said as a basket attached to a length of twine nearly hit my head. My shoulder was less fortunate, but I'd survive. "Miss Peterson thought it might be expedient to utilize this if I needed something not too heavy, such as batteries or a newspaper. She's the chairperson of the hospital auxiliary and quite astute in foreseeing problems."

The sandwich and cup were dutifully sent up. I set Skyler's basket in the shade, then Luanne and I made ourselves as comfortable as we could on the rocky ground.

"Have you heard what took place at the press conference?" I called, craning my neck to stare at the bottom of the platform.

"No," she answered, "but I would be surprised if Mr. Armstrong said anything he hasn't already said at countless planning commission meetings. They brought to mind all the mindless faculty meetings after school, in which each person felt obligated to repeat whatever point had already been made. I used to sit in the back and crochet doilies. Do you crochet?"

"I do," Luanne said. "Soothing, isn't it?"

While they chatted about various patterns and thread weights, I thought about the girl who'd been introduced as Wal-Mart. She'd left her baby on my porch the previous evening and tracked me down at noon, probably to make sure that the situation was under control. I couldn't remember anything she'd said that might help me find her.

Luanne and I were packing up the remains of our lunch when the security officer came puffing up the incline.

"You gotta go," he announced.

"And we will, when we're ready," I said sweetly.

"You gotta go right now. You're trespassing on private property."

Miss Parchester's face appeared. "Now, Howie, these are my guests. It's rude of you to speak to them that way. I hope you remember that conversation we had several years ago after you accused Dibbins of stealing your jar of rubber cement. Where was it, Howie?"

He turned red. "In the supply cabinet, Miss Parchester."

"And what did I advise you to do?"

"Apologize. But this is different. These ladies are trespassing. Mr. Armstrong said I should call the police if anyone refuses to leave. He's gonna have somebody put up signs this afternoon."

"Is he worried that we're going to dig up the tree and transport it to a safe haven?" I inquired. "Arboretum Anonymous?"

"Or perhaps," Luanne added tartly, "he's now so concerned about the environment that he's afraid visitors will leave litter. He may intend to donate the land to the city for a quaint little park. A few picnic tables and barbecue pits will really lend charm."

Howie was still red, but he held his ground. "All I know is that nobody's allowed to come any closer than the edge of the parking lot."

"What if Miss Parchester needs food, water, or even medication?" I asked.

"I'm just following orders," he mumbled. "Otherwise, I'll get fired."

"Howie, Howie, Howie," Miss Parchester said with a discouraged sigh. "I doubt you will ever amount to anything with that attitude. Most of the atrocities against humanity were committed by those who claimed to be following orders." She looked at me. "I have everything I need, and I have mastered the cell phone. Your little friend appears to be stirring. You run along. Thank you ever so much for the sandwich and tea."

I shot Howie a cold look as Luanne and I went by

him and returned to her car. Only when Skyler had been buckled in the car seat and we were driving away did I find my voice. "That Armstrong is a scumbag! An hour ago he was blinking back tears as he told us how worried he was about poor Miss Parchester. He must have forgotten to mention he was cutting off her supplies. I'm sure Finnigan and the others assumed they could bring whatever she might need on a daily basis."

"I can't see them crossing the line and risking arrest."

"Or putting on camouflage and scuttling between the trees in the middle of the night," I said. "You, on the other hand, look quite fetching in olive green and matching greasepaint."

"So do you."

We arrived at the Book Depot, transferred Skyler to the basket and the car seat to my car, and wished each other improbably profitable afternoons. No customers were jostling for position underneath the portico as I took the Closed sign out of the window and unlocked the door. I poured out the morning coffee and utilized a pot of hot water to warm a bottle of formula.

This baby business wasn't that complicated, I told myself as I settled Skyler in the office for a nap, then went to peruse the self-help rack for anything that might be useful. I sat down on the stool behind the counter and thumbed through a developmental guide, even though I knew I wouldn't have him long enough to see much progress.

I was in the fourth month (sitting up, reaching for toys) when the bell above the front door jangled and Peter came inside. I hastily stuffed the book in a drawer.

"I brought you a cappuccino and a cookie," he said. "I came by earlier to see if you might go out for lunch, but you weren't here."

"Luanne and I went to the press conference at the courthouse. Did you hear about it?"

"Only that he seems to believe he has the law on his side and the planning commission in his back pocket." He put a sack on the counter and produced two paper cups with plastic lids. "Chocolate chip cookies okay with you?"

He was trying hard to pretend I hadn't booted him out the door the previous evening. I found it so endearing that I leaned over and kissed him.

"I'm sorry about what happened," I said. "Caron, uh, met a boy and it upset her. She was desperate to talk about it. Every now and then she really does want my advice. It happens so rarely that I can't put her off."

His eyes had a libidinous glint. "Then odds are good it won't happen any time soon. Why don't we go out to dinner tonight, then go to your place, open a bottle of wine, and watch a movie featuring a sheik and a voluptuous harlot draped in scarves?"

Oops.

CHAPTER FOUR

Lying to Sally was a mentally stimulating exercise in mendacity, but I wasn't comfortable having to lie to Peter. We'd had our differences, certainly, but he was damn close to everything I desired in a relationship that just might last for a very long time. Physical appeal aside (and that was not insignificant—I am not yet over the particular hill in question), he was amusing, warm, sensual, and sensitive. He called my bluffs, as I did his. When it came to tidying up investigations of a felonious nature, he had his officious position, but I had my wits and perspicacity. Caron was fond of him; she would never refer to him as "Father," but she would be thrilled if and when the day arrived that she would ask him to escort her down the aisle.

I paused to sniffle at the notion, then reminded myself that I had a responsibility to my guest in the office, whom I dearly hoped was sound asleep, or at least entranced by sunlight glinting on the cobwebs. Vowing to be more truthful as soon as I had disposed of the dilemma, I said, "I think I'd better be there for Caron tonight." I folded his arms around me. He was a few inches taller, requiring me to gaze up at his generous lips and disarmingly boyish dimples. "Rain check?"

Peter was not quite as overcome with sentiment as I was, and, in fact, had the audacity to sound somewhat suspicious as he said, "You're not planning to camp out under an oak tree, are you? Armstrong called in some favors, and the area is now off-limits. The uniformed guys are going to be patrolling nearby, prepared to haul in trespassers."

"Camp out?" I said. "Do I appear to be in need of a merit badge?"

"If you get arrested, you'll end up in a cell for the night."

I toyed with his earlobes, which usually distracts him in ways best left undescribed. "And you won't post bail?"

"No, but I'll leave instructions that you're to have our finest accommodations."

I did my best to pretend I wasn't listening for a plaintive noise from the office as we drank cappuccinos and nibbled on cookies. To my relief, my science fiction hippie wandered in, which prompted Peter to leave with a promise to call me in a day or two. Filing a complaint for shoplifting was time-consuming and hardly worth his energy.

"Keep your hands in view at all times," I called as I crumpled cups and dropped them in the wastebasket.

"Like, wow, is he that cop?" came a voice from behind the fiction rack.

"Like, wow, he is," I said, "and he left his X-ray vision goggles behind."

"Cool."

"If you bolt for the door, I'll tackle you."

His furry face appeared. "Promise?"

We bantered for a while, then I frisked him and let him depart, as our daily ritual demanded. I was quite sure he had successful days, but he was no worse than the faculty wives who tucked lurid romances into their purses—and their spouses, who did the same into their briefcases. English lit professors of both genders were the worst, but I could not risk offending them since they were kind enough to supply me with their upcoming semester's reading lists. Chaucer and Dante were not best-selling authors, but a sale equated cents on the dollar and I didn't have to shelve them in the travel section.

The bell jangled so violently that I worried about its well-being as Inez stumbled into the bookstore shortly after two o'clock. "Is everything all right, Ms. Malloy?" she asked between gasps. "You still have Skyler, don't you? You can't let his mother just take him away. He might end up with drug dealers or alcoholics who live in a trailer park."

"Sit down and catch your breath, Inez. Skyler's asleep in the office." I realized that telling her whom I'd seen near the courthouse would only fuel her paranoia—and to some extent, she had a point.

"What's more," Inez continued, "the word at school is that it's Caron's baby. Rhonda Maguire's mother was in the next checkout lane at the grocery store this morning. Rhonda heard about it when she called her mother after first period about a notebook or something. The principal might as well have announced it over the intercom."

"That's ridiculous. Did no one take into consideration that Caron was never pregnant?"

"Rhonda told everybody that Caron must have had the baby last summer and left it with relatives in another state. Then something terrible happened, like an earthquake or a hurricane, so the baby had to be sent back here. Mrs. Maguire didn't see the baby, you know; she just saw you buying diapers and stuff."

I hesitated, but finally forced myself to ask, "And how is Caron taking this?"

Inez blinked at me from behind her thick lenses. "Not very well. She asked to be excused in the middle of the algebra test. I couldn't find her at lunch. Kerry and Aly said she was so listless in English that Mrs. McLair sent her to the nurse's office. I don't think anybody saw her after that."

Now it seemed I had two basket cases. At this rate, I might be ordering wicker in bulk.

I'd planned to leave Inez in charge of both Skyler and the bookstore while I picked up more baby supplies, but I could foresee problems if Caron, any of her classmates, Peter, or even the elusive mother appeared in my absence. Inez had told a few whoppers in her time; however, at the moment she was too agitated to think clearly.

"Here's what I need you to do," I said as I took some money from the cash register. "Put Skyler in my car and go to the discount store in Waverly. Buy two six-packs of formula, diapers, baby wipes, plastic bottles, a package of T-shirts, and a couple of cotton blankets."

"What if somebody sees me?"

"Quite a few people will see you, Inez, but they'll be strangers. That's why I suggested Waverly. When you're finished shopping, go to the park and let Skyler enjoy some fresh air. Come back here at five."

"Then what?"

"I'll think of something."

I made sure she knew how to operate the buckles of the car seat, then watched them drive away. As I went back inside, I wondered what I would do if the mother showed up and demanded the return of her child. Before I complied, I would have to hear a satisfactory explanation for her recent erratic behavior, as well as assurances that Skyler would be in a safe environment. But could I legally stop her? Did I have a moral obligation to do so anyway? How fine were the jail's finest accommodations?

Several customers wandered in over the remainder of the afternoon. Sally Fromberger walked by the store several times, covertly checking for signs of a bassinet or a playpen. A trio of high school girls, all unfamiliar, came into the store, giggled as they pretended to browse, and then fled after I stalked them down and offered to help with their selections.

During a lull I called the campus switchboard and requested to be transferred to Finnigan Baybergen's office. He answered with a terse, "Baybergen. Who's this?"

"Claire Malloy, Miss Parchester's friend. You and I exchanged some remarks last night."

"Oh, yes. I saw you today at the press conference. Someone mentioned you have a little bookstore here in Farberville."

I let the disparaging remark slide by. "Afterwards, Luanne Bradshaw and I went out to Phase Two to take Miss Parchester a sandwich. Are you aware that Armstrong has instructed the security guard to allow no one to go closer to the tree than the edge of the parking lot?"

"Of course I am. Louis Ferncliff was arrested several hours ago. He spent a very uncomfortable hour at the police station before he was allowed to post a fifty-dollar bond and leave. The Margolises have suggested we solicit contributions to assist those who commit acts of civil disobedience for the greater good. May we count on a check from you?"

"I'm afraid my 'little bookstore' doesn't generate much in the way of profits. So the police are cooperating with Armstrong?"

He exhaled noisily. "According to Louis, an officer arrived five minutes after the security cop called the station on his cell phone. I haven't heard of anyone else being arrested thus far."

"What are you going to do about Miss Parchester?"

"She has plenty of food and water for another few days, and she's adamant that she will not be driven out of the tree because of Armstrong's petty ploy. She's convinced he'll back down after the media exposes him. I wish I were as certain."

"So do I," I said. "Any news about the injunction?"

"Constantine's still at the federal courthouse, waiting for a ruling. If you'll excuse me, I need to keep the line free."

"One more thing. Is it true that you have the only key to the padlock that prevents Miss Parchester from leaving the platform?"

Baybergen did not answer immediately. I was on the verge of repeating the question when he said, "Good point. I'll go out there this evening and have her lower the basket so I can send up a newspaper. Taped to it will be a copy of the key. If I am arrested, so be it. Maybe I can teach in a community college in Costa Rica. The rain forests are extraordinary, I've been told. Goodbye, Ms. Malloy."

"Adios, Assistant Professor Baybergen," I said to the dial tone. I replaced the receiver, then fuddled about, selling a few books, dusting the stock, and glumly flipping through invoices. Caron did not appear. I was not yet alarmed, although I was a bit worried. We were going to have to sit down and sort all this out, despite the convolutions and complexities. I doubted she knew why she was reacting so emotionally, and I wasn't sure I did, either. Dr. Spock wasn't available, and Mr. Spock would not beam me up.

Inez appeared at five o'clock. Skyler was fast asleep, no doubt worn out from his encounters with butterflies at the park.

"He is such a good baby," Inez whispered.

"But not ours," I reminded both of us as I locked the front door and prepared to leave.

"Did Caron come by?"

I shook my head. "She's probably at home. Do you want to come along?"

"I don't know what to say."

"Neither do I," I acknowledged while we transferred Skyler once again to the car seat. "I suppose I could call Rhonda's mother and offer some sort of glib excuse for being caught in the act of buying diapers. What do you think?"

Inez handed me some change. "Rhonda's mouth runs in only one direction, and that's downstream."

"Well, then," I said inanely. We drove to the duplex. Caron was in her room, with music resonating so loudly that I hoped we would not hear complaints from the androgynous downstairs tenant. Inez pounded on the bedroom door while I settled Skyler on a blanket on the sofa, then poured myself a drink. It had been a stressful twenty-four hours. Skyler seemed to be the only one who was oblivious.

Inez came into the living room. "She won't let me in."

"She'll come out sooner or later. Go on home."

"But I feel as though I should—"

I gave her a kiss on the forehead. "We both do, but we'll have to wait for Caron."

Inez left. Skyler slurped down a fair amount of formula, observed me while I changed his diaper, and then seemed reasonably agreeable to watching the local news. Jessica's segment was a replay of the noon press conference interview. Mr. Ferncliff would have to wait until ten o'clock for his fleeting moment of fame.

Caron emerged an hour later to stick a frozen entrée in the microwave. "You heard?" she said from the kitchen as she punched buttons.

"Inez told me."

She came into the living room. "What am I supposed to do? I can't tell the truth. If I do, the police and social services will get involved, and Skyler will be whisked away. On the other hand, if I keep my mouth shut, every last person at the high school will think he's my child. Any Ideas, Mother?"

"Can you hang in another day?" I asked her as she sat down across from me.

"And sacrifice my chances of being a cheerleader? Whatever will happen to me?"

"I never envisioned you with pom-poms. The moment I laid eyes on you, I assumed you'd be a rocket scientist or a brain surgeon. Well . . . or at least a cancer researcher or a marine biologist out to save the dolphins. Watching you do cartwheels on a football field never entered my mind."

"You could call me in sick."

I resisted the urge to mention the dreaded algebra test, which she would have to make up in the next day or two. "Is that what you want?"

"As opposed to listening to whispers and snickers

when I walk down the halls? Gee, tough decision."

"If you'll look after Skyler."

"I suppose so," she said. "Did you talk to Peter?"

I gave her a report of all that had happened, tactfully omitting the three girls who'd come into the Book Depot. Caron listened, but she was too distracted by her own problems to do more than nod occasionally. I let her go to her room, then settled down next to Skyler and tried to immerse myself in a novel. I had marginal success, since I couldn't prevent myself from listening for someone coming through the front door and tiptoeing up the stairs to my landing. Or gypsies sneaking up the back steps. Or trolls scaling the back side of the house to wait in the attic until we'd fallen asleep.

I finally put down the book and went into the kitchen to make a cup of tea. As I put fresh water in the teakettle, I realized it was beginning to rain. Poor Miss Parchester, I thought as I took out a mug and a spoon. Not only was she sitting alone in the tree, she was in for a decidedly uncomfortable night. I hoped Papa was proud of her, wherever he was.

I knocked on Caron's door the following morning. "You need to get up, dear. I've called the school. Skyler has been bathed, dressed, and fed."

She opened the door, her expression wary. "What if somebody shows up while you're gone? What am I supposed to do?"

I couldn't advise her to spend the day at the park, since rain was still coming down. I doubted babies were welcome in the college library. The mall was not an option, since it was likely that more than one of her classmates would be playing hooky.

"Keep your music low, and the same with the volume

on the television. I'll be at the Book Depot as usual, so no one will come looking for me here. Don't answer the phone. If you start getting stir-crazy, call Luanne. The car seat will be on the back porch. She can take you and Skyler out for a hamburger or something. Just don't drive by the high school—I told them you'd be in a parenting class all day."

"How thoughtful of you, Mother. I must think of a way to return the favor one of these days."

"Skyler's on a blanket on the living room rug. Call me if you have any problems."

I drove to the bookstore, made a pot of coffee, and sat down behind the counter to read the newspaper. I was still perusing the front page when the phone rang. Praying Caron was not already in crisis after a scant half hour, I picked up the receiver.

"Have you listened to the news on the radio this morning?" demanded Luanne in her charmingly brusque fashion.

"No. What happened?"

"Anthony Armstrong's dead. There wasn't much of a story, just that his body had been found around midnight last night. Foul play is suspected."

"Murdered?" I said with a gulp.

"It comes to mind. That's all the announcer said, except that detectives were investigating. Peter will be in charge, won't he?"

"That doesn't mean we can buy him a beer and hear all the details. He seems to have a misconception that I meddle in official investigations, which we both know is completely fallacious. We'd have better luck with Jessica."

"Or Finnigan Baybergen, although it's hard to imagine his gang of senior citizens committing mayhem of this magnitude. Now, if somebody had let the air out of the tires on Anthony's Mercedes or canceled Adrienne's hair appointment . . ."

"I wonder what this will mean in Miss Parchester's case," I said. "Surely Phase Two will be in limbo for a long time."

"I have no idea," said Luanne. "I assume you have Skyler with you. Do you want to bring him here at noon so that we can watch the news? I'm sure Jessica will be standing under an umbrella, coming to us live with all the latest hearsay and speculations."

I explained the situation, adding, "I think I'd better stay here and visible. I don't want someone going to the duplex to look for me. If Caron calls you, put her off until after you've watched the news and called me."

She agreed and hung up. I tried to read the newspaper, but my mind refused to focus on national politics and international civil wars. Anthony Armstrong's death could be the result of an unwise decision to investigate a burglary in progress in his house. He could have slipped while going downstairs. He could have come home inebriated and inadvertently taken too many pills. It could have been a coincidence.

And I could have failed to notice I was pregnant and given birth to Skyler while reading a mystery novel.

The morning crawled by minute by minute. A few students purchased the slim yellow study guides that just might get them a passing grade in their lit classes. A sorority girl admitted she had no idea what was on her reading list, so I loaded her up with paperbacks that she would never read. Sally Fromberger went by twice, dressed in a utilitarian raincoat and a plastic bonnet.

By half past twelve, I was staring at the telephone. Anthony Armstrong's death was none of my concern. I was worried only about Miss Parchester, whose sturdy shoes might begin to squish as the rain continued, but all I wanted to hear was that she'd come down from the tree and gone to her house in a quaint neighborhood in the historic district. Finnigan Baybergen had sworn he would send her up the key.

The telephone finally rang. "What?" I said as I snatched up the receiver.

"Breathe deeply," Luanne said, then refused to answer my disjointed questions until I subsided. "Jessica doesn't know much. Adrienne found Anthony's body when she arrived home last night at midnight. He'd been shot twice in the chest. She called 911. We may or may not hear the tape on the six o'clock news, depending on the whim of the prosecutor's office. She has been questioned, as has another family member. Jessica's hair, by the way, looked as though she'd draped a weasel over her head."

"Another family member?" I said.

"That's about it."

"And Miss Parchester?"

"None of that came up. Adrienne choked out a few sentences, then dashed away when her mascara began to dribble."

"Why did she come home at midnight?" I asked.

"She didn't say," Luanne said with an exasperated sigh. "Don't you have enough to deal with as it is? You are not Nancy Drew."

I gazed at the rack of mystery novels. "I could have been, if I'd had a blue roadster and a boyfriend named Ned Nickerson."

"Why don't you worry about a boyfriend named Peter?"

"One of these days, I will," I said uncomfortably. "Have you heard from Caron?"

"Six times, thus far. Is this the first time she's ever laid eyes on a baby? I used to baby-sit every weekend before I went off to boarding school. The pay wasn't much, but the perks were good once the brats were in bed. I experimented with every brand of makeup available in the poshest department stores, as well as a few outfits. Some of those silk negligees were downright scandalous."

"I'm one hundred percent cotton," I said. "Can you see after Caron and Skyler?"

"Cheeseburgers and shakes in half an hour. We'll have a diaper drill before we go. Listen, Claire—Anthony Armstrong's death is none of your business. It's likely that Miss Parchester will come down from the tree now that the project is halted until all this is resolved."

In that I can be a patient woman when I choose, I waited forty-five minutes before I hung up the Closed sign and drove to Phase Two. The KFAR van was not present. A few unprepossessing cars were parked in the lot. Signs alerting us that we were trespassing had been placed along the back of the parking lot. The rain had stopped, but the sky remained gray and unfriendly.

"Miss Parchester?" I called as I approached the tree. "How are you?"

Howie emerged from behind a building and cut me off. "Don't make me have you arrested," he said. "Everybody gets mad at me, especially Miss Parchester. I'm just doing my job, you know."

"And how many noble souls have been arrested thus far?"

"One yesterday afternoon, and three more later. I was

warned to expect a lot more today. I guess the rain's been keeping them away."

"But Anthony Armstrong is no longer issuing orders," I pointed out.

"The word I got is to keep seeing that trespassers are arrested and taken to the police station," he said. "Mr. Armstrong's wife showed up about nine o'clock this morning. She told me what was going on, then said to follow orders. Miss Parchester and me talked about it, and she seemed to think I should do what I was told. I'm making twice minimum wage for doing nothing more than patrolling the area."

"Twenty-four hours a day?" I asked.

"Naw, I leave at midnight and come back at eight. Nobody's supposed to know that. Every couple of hours, I go over to the construction shed and take a break for half an hour or so. It ain't like commandos are crawling up the bluff or anything. If they were, Miss Parchester would take care of them."

"Then why don't you take a break while I visit her?"

Howie studied the ground for a moment. "I wish I could oblige, but what with Mr. Armstrong's death and all, I'm kinda nervous. The last thing I want to do is get fired."

"Did Mrs. Armstrong seem upset?"

"Her eyes were red and her face was all puffy like she hadn't gotten any sleep. I don't see how she could have, with police in the house all night. She said they were still there and driving her so crazy that she was going to her athletic club for an hour just to get away. Can't blame her."

I opened my wallet and took out a ten-dollar bill. "Howie, why don't you take a hike around the perimeter in case Jessica and her cameraman are sneaking up through the woods?"

"I'll be back in five minutes," he said as he put the bill in his shirt pocket.

I did not point out that I had surely purchased ten minutes, but instead waited until he'd trudged around the corner of the condos and out of sight. I headed for the tree at a brisker pace.

"Miss Parchester?" I called.

She peered down at me. "Why, Claire, how nice to see you so soon. I hope you don't feel as though you must bring me lunch every day. Some degree of deprivation strengthens my will to maintain the vigil. The rain was a bit much, I must admit, but as you can see, I'm still here."

"Did you hear about Anthony Armstrong?"

"Only a brief report on the radio. How distressing for his family."

"Howie said that Adrienne Armstrong was here this morning," I said, hoping the crick in my neck was temporary. "Did she speak to you?"

"Only to Howie, and they were so far away that I couldn't hear them. It does seem that Phase Two may still be ongoing. Mr. Constantine was able to get an emergency injunction, but the judge has scheduled a hearing in five days to make a final ruling."

"You can go home until then. Wouldn't you like a nice hot bath and dry slippers?"

Miss Parchester gave me a disappointed look. "You haven't thought this through, have you? If I were to leave the tree, I would be prevented from returning should the ruling go against us. No one has actually seen a migratory hawk in this area. Mr. Constantine is relying on an Audubon guide and EPA regulations regarding endangered species. Our case isn't very strong."

I heard Howie whistling loudly as he came in our direction. "I'd better go," I said. "Is there anything you need?"

"It's very kind of you to inquire, but I'm reasonably content. Run along before Howie gets here. I'm afraid he fancies himself to be a bounty hunter."

I waggled my fingers at her, then went to my car. Since I was no longer in the commission of a misdemeanor, I sat and thought. Why had Adrienne Armstrong instructed hapless Howie to continue his vigilance when it might very well be months, or even years, before probate issues could be resolved and Phase Two continued? I'd seen their lawyer at the press conference the previous day, but his name had not been mentioned. Adrienne was long gone from the athletic club by now, and I was aware that I might not be welcome at the crime scene.

I had not come up with a plan of action (except, perhaps, buying a sandwich on the way back to the Book Depot) when a chubby young woman came out of the Scarpos' unit. Her shirt and jeans were baggy, her brown hair uncombed, her eyes narrowed with muted hostility.

"Are you Claire Malloy?" she demanded.

"Are you Jillian?"

She came over to the car. "So where's Randy?"

I resisted the urge to put up the window before she did something that might prove painful. "I have no idea whatsoever where Randy is," I said. "I have neither seen him nor spoken to him since I gave him a ride to campus the other night. As I told you, I'd asked him to call me to report on Miss Parchester, but he never did. Why would you think I know where he is?"

"I'm sorry," she said, beginning to snivel and, thankfully, backing away from the car. "I just thought after

you called, that—well, that, I just thought . . ." She
wiped her nose on the back of her hand. "I'm sorry. I
can see now that you're not what I suspected."

Which I interpreted to mean that I was entirely too
old to engage in frivolous romps with graduate students,
which I most certainly was—but only because I found
them tedious and pretentious now that I had achieved
some degree of maturity. In our day, Carlton and I had
swilled red wine and read poetry aloud on the banks of
meandering creeks. We'd gone to parties where the favorite parlor game had been deconstructing innocent authors.

"Is something wrong?" I asked Jillian.

"No, everything's okay. Randy left early because he
had a meeting with a professor, and then he was going
to the library. I gave him a shopping list, but he left it
on the kitchen table. He'll probably remember to pick
up most of it before he comes home."

"You don't have a car?"

She managed a wobbly smile. "We can't afford a second one until Randy has a real job. He's already been
approached by several companies, but he wants to finish
his degree before he considers the offers. I don't mind.
Connor and I keep each other company. It's not like we
have anything else to do."

I gestured at the signs warning trespassers to stay
away. "But I guess you can't take the stroller too far
until this is resolved."

"We don't go outside much," Jillian said. "Connor's
got all these allergies, and he had an asthma attack a few
weeks ago. The doctor didn't act like it was serious, but
Randy and I agreed that we shouldn't take any risks.
Connor's very delicate. He only weighed six pounds and
seven ounces when he was born. I was in labor for sev-

enteen hours. The doctor wanted to give me an epidural, but I refused because natural birth is so much better for the baby."

"So I've been told," I murmured. "I really must be going, Jillian."

"Wouldn't you like to come inside and see Connor? He's napping right now, but we could have coffee."

"Thank you, but no. I have a business to run."

I felt like a coward as I drove back to the Book Depot, having left a lonely creature standing in the parking lot of Oakland Heights, Phase One. A better person than I would have admired the slumbering baby, sipped coffee, looked at countless photos, and tweaked a little cheek when the time came. But I had another cheek to tweak when the desire came over me, as well as problems of my own.

No one of any import came into the store the remainder of the afternoon. Luanne called to say that she, Caron, and Skyler had enjoyed their outing, and that Caron had broached the situation at the high school. When pressed, Luanne admitted that she'd offered little in the way of concrete advice. Neither of us could come up with a way Caron might quash the gossip without resorting to the truth.

Caron and Skyler were asleep on her bed when I arrived home. I retreated to the kitchen, poured myself a drink, and sat down on the sofa to hear what Jessica had to report.

She had the lead spot, and she would have been salivating had it not been unsightly. "This is Jessica Princeton, live from outside the Farberville Police Station." She glanced over her shoulder, then gave us a recapitulation of what had been reported earlier, which amounted to nothing I hadn't heard: Anthony Armstrong, shot twice, his body discovered by his wife, detectives investigating, and so forth. "Stay with me," she commanded, perhaps not only to her viewers but also to the news director in the studio. "A police vehicle is pulling up behind me. Getting out of the vehicle are two uniformed officers."

The camera shifted as figures emerged. The first two were as Jessica had said. One of them opened a back door and gestured for its occupant to climb out.

Skyler's mother stared into the camera.

CHAPTER FIVE

Once the officers and the girl were inside the police station, Jessica Princeton squared her discreetly enhanced shoulders and resumed. "That was Daphne Armstrong, daughter of slain developer Anthony Armstrong. We don't know yet if she's been charged with anything or has simply been brought in for further questioning. Lieutenant Peter Rosen, who was at the scene last night, has refused to comment. KFAR has been able to determine that Miss Armstrong was taken into custody this afternoon at the home of her mother, Sheila Armstrong, who was divorced from Anthony Armstrong three years ago. She also declined to speak to us."

I must have resembled a pop-eyed koi as I gaped at the television screen. Skyler's mother, taken into custody to discuss Skyler's grandfather's murder?

Jessica was running low on late-breaking news, but she continued to command the camera. "Daphne Armstrong is said to be eighteen years old and a former student at Disciples Christian Academy. Administrators at the academy did not return repeated calls. At this moment, officers remain at the scene of the crime, searching the yard, outbuildings, and nearby woods, presumably for the weapon. Let's go to Chuck, who's standing by on the road at the edge of the property. Has anything been uncovered at this hour?"

Chuck, who apparently had a fondness for pizza, beer, and pink shirts with tight collars, appeared on the screen. Behind him was an expanse of lawn, and beyond it a sprawling house with peculiar Italian accents, as if it had been transported under cover of darkness from Tuscany to the sylvan hills of Farberville. No one had thought to bring along an olive grove.

"Thank you, Jessica," he said. "Things here are quiet at this hour. Documents at the county courthouse indicate Mr. Armstrong's house is situated on more than three acres of mostly unimproved wooded hillsides, adjoined on the south by Oakland Heights and the proposed expansion. Officers continue to search for evidence, but thus far we've had no indication that they've found anything of significance. Mrs. Armstrong, her sister Chantilly Durmond, and the family lawyer are inside the house. No one has agreed to speak with us."

I wondered if Mrs. Armstrong and company were having fettuccine primavera and a nice bottle of Chianti. But there was another Mrs. Armstrong, the mother of Daphne. For all I knew, there was yet another Mrs. Armstrong, the mother of the deceased, or a bevy of sisters-in-law with the same title.

Coverage returned to the studio for the forecast of impending rainy weather for the next few days. I stared with minimal comprehension until Caron came down the hall, Skyler tucked in her arm.

"What's wrong?" she said.

"Everything."

"Should I start packing?"

"I don't think so," I said. I left her standing in the middle of the room and went into the kitchen to pour myself a significant amount of scotch. When I returned to the living room, she'd put Skyler on a blanket on the rug and was sitting cross-legged next to him. Her eyes were intent on mine.

I sat down on the sofa. "You'd better know what's going on."

It did not take me long to relate what I knew. When I'd finished, she looked up and said, "So what are you going to do, Mother?"

"I wish I knew," I said, keeping my voice even so as not to disturb Skyler—or send Caron thundering down the stairs to the nearest safe house (which would be Inez's, where she could have halibut on a weekly basis). "Daphne wouldn't have been taken into custody if the police didn't have some reason to believe she killed her father. She might be released in an hour, held as a witness, or charged."

"Skyler's not a witness," said Caron. "He has an alibi. Why should he have to suffer because of this?"

I propped my elbows on my knees and rubbed my face with my hands. That which had been perplexing, bemusing, intriguing, even amusing, was now deadly serious. Someone had murdered Anthony Armstrong, and the police had indicated that it might be Daphne Armstrong. At the moment, only three other people knew I had her baby in my care, but quite a few more people must have known of his existence. And my foray into the grocery store had not gone unnoticed. Even Sally Fromberger and Rhonda Maguire's mother might begin to piece it together—along with the entirety of the Farberville High School community, upping the count to well over five hundred. Keeping a secret in a town the size of Farberville was, in my experience, harder than slogging in a scholarly fashion through James Joyce, Henry James, or even James Fenimore Cooper and every last one of his blasted Mohicans.

"Did they say she did it?" asked Caron, interrupting my addled thoughts. "Are they sure?"

"No, but she was brought in for questioning, and that's a bad sign."

"So call Peter."

"And tell him what? I'm concerned because I've put down a deposit for a time-share in Phase Two?"

Caron, who had been convinced only a day ago that the universe existed solely for her personal gratification or aggravation, with an emphasis on the latter, said, "You can't tell him everything, but you could find out what he knows. Daphne didn't kill anybody, especially not her father. She wouldn't have done that."

"How do you know?"

"I just know. Maybe you can try to talk to her."

"I'm not her lawyer."

The following morning I once again called Caron in sick, but warned her that this would be the last day of malingering and made her promise to get her assignments from Inez. Then, dressed in the navy suit that I wore to funerals, and carrying one of Carlton's battered briefcases, I went into the Farberville Police Station, nodded politely at the officer at the desk, and said, "I'm here to see Daphne Armstrong. I understand she's been detained and has asked for counsel."

"Your name is . . ."

"Ms. Miranda."

No bells or whistles went off. The officer, who looked as though she should have been in classes with Caron, asked me to sign my name on a clipboard and gestured for me to follow her. The corridor was humid and reeked of misery muted by disinfectant. The cell doors were slabs of steel with openings large enough for only trays of food and periodic supervision.

"Do you want to talk to her in the conference room?" the officer asked.

"I'd prefer to see her in her cell. Please hurry; I'm due in court in half an hour." Where, at some time in the future, if I failed to pull off this ploy, I would be consigned to one of these cells to sleep on a thin mattress and survive on baloney sandwiches and powdered fruit drinks. I wondered if I should have tucked my toothbrush into the briefcase.

"Up to you. Holler when you're ready to leave."

Daphne Armstrong was hunched on a corner of her cot, her hair brushing her bony knees. She flushed as she recognized me, and then averted her face. "Go away. I don't have to talk to you."

"Don't you want to know how Skyler's doing?"

She looked up. "Is he okay? He was getting a diaper rash, but I put some antibiotic cream on it and it was getting better. The tube was empty, or I would have left it in the diaper bag."

I sat down next to her. "He's fine. You, on the other hand, are not."

"It's not so bad here," she said, ignoring the implications of my remark. "The food's okay. We had beans and cornbread last night."

"Have you been charged?"

"Right now I'm what they call a material witness, but that detective seems to think I did it. You have to believe me, Mrs. Malloy—I didn't shoot my father. I may have wanted to, and I may have been there, but I couldn't

point a gun at him and pull the trigger. He just refused
to understand, and Adrienne made it worse. She kept
telling me that we should be friends, but she's the kind
that never bothered to look at me in the hall at school.
She was a cheerleader, naturally, and the homecoming
queen. She has all these albums with pictures of her
sitting on the back of a convertible, wearing a rhinestone
tiara. Like I was supposed to deal with a stepmother
who's seven years older than I am? She was in first
grade when I was born."

My time was too limited for family counseling.
"Where have you and Skyler been living since his
birth?"

"We went to the shelter, but they started bullying me
to contact social services. We stayed at my mother's
place for a couple of weeks. I was thinking it might be
okay, but it didn't work out. I didn't want Skyler to live
on the streets, so I wrote that note and left him on your
porch. You aren't mad, are you?"

"No," I said, squeezing her distressingly limp hand,
"I'm worried about you. Will you tell me what happened
last night?"

"I went to the house about eleven-thirty. The Mercedes wasn't there, so I thought they were at one of their
fancy parties at the country club. I let myself in the back
door and went upstairs to get some of my things. All of
a sudden, I heard two gunshots. I crouched inside the
closet for maybe five minutes, hiding behind some winter coats. When I didn't hear anything else, I crept downstairs and saw my father sprawled on the rug in his
office. His shirt was covered with blood."

"Did you see a gun?"

"Yeah, it was by the doorway. I know I shouldn't
have touched it, but I heard a noise somewhere in the

back of the house, maybe the kitchen or dining room, and I was too scared to think straight. I grabbed the gun and went out the front door. That's when a car drove up. I just kept running." She hesitated for a moment. "If I'm sent to prison, will you keep Skyler? He's not much trouble."

"Do you want me to help you, Daphne? I'm not a lawyer, but I can ask questions and try to get to the bottom of this so that you and Skyler can be together again."

"It's not like I'm going to college. My son doesn't deserve to live under a bridge and scavenge through garbage cans for food. He should go to kindergarten. Maybe when he's in elementary school, he can play soccer and take piano lessons. Even if I get out of this mess, I can't provide any of that with a minimum-wage job." Tears began to leak down her cheeks. "You keep him, Mrs. Malloy."

"Why wouldn't your father help you?"

Daphne stared at her feet. "When I told him I was pregnant, he told me to have an abortion so I wouldn't hurt his precious reputation. He was on the board of directors at Disciples, a deacon at church, and president of some civic club. The governor wanted him to serve on some stupid state commission. The country club had just elected him chairman of the membership committee. I said some nasty things and walked out, but that was when Joey still had his apartment and job."

"Joey would be the father of your child?"

"He was the only one. We were planning to get married. I knew he had a temper, but he'd never been violent before. I guess the stress was too much for him."

"Violent?" I repeated weakly.

"He's not like that. He had a basement apartment and

a job at a garage, but then he got into this fight at a bar and was sentenced to six months in the county jail. His landlord made me move out. I was sleeping in a storage shed in the alley behind Thurber Street when Arnie rescued me, and you know the rest of it. Joey got out last week, but he can't find a job. Up until a couple of days ago, we were sleeping in his car. It wasn't too bad, but then Skyler got the diaper rash and it all started falling apart."

"Why didn't you stay at your mother's house?"

"She has problems." Her voice was flat, as if she'd said it many times before.

The cell door opened. "And so does Ms. Miranda," Peter said as he joined us in the six-by-eight-foot concrete shrine to claustrophobia. "She's here under false pretenses, unless she attended law school and passed the bar in the last week."

"I never said I was Daphne's attorney," I said stiffly. "It is possible my remarks were misinterpreted. They often are."

He grimaced as he looked at my admittedly atypical attire. "Why don't you come with me and we'll see if the community theater is conducting auditions?"

Daphne put her hand on my arm as I started to rise. "Don't get my mother involved in this, please," she whispered. "She's barely making it now, and it won't take much to send her flying out an attic window."

I patted her shoulder, then joined Peter in the hallway. "A cup of coffee might be nice."

"So would an explanation."

"Regular or decaf?"

"Claire," he said—or growled, depending on one's interpretation of the guttural noises he was making under his breath as he escorted me to his office—"you can't poke your nose into every case that comes along."

I sat down in the chair opposite his desk. "Why would you assume I have a personal interest in this? Perhaps I was worried that Legal Aid had not yet arrived to help this young girl. She's not much older than Caron. I'd like to think the maternal community has a responsibility to make sure that offspring are protected when the long arm of the law snatches them up. What sort of a case do you have?"

"Go sell books."

"I intend to do so shortly," I said. "Have you found the weapon?"

"I find it difficult to believe that this so-called maternal community of yours monitors the local news and assigns caseworkers. If there's anything you should tell me, I wish you'd do it."

"She was seen leaving the scene of the crime by Adrienne, according to the news last night. What was the perfect wife doing out so late?"

Peter ran his fingers through his hair. His left eyelid twitched, but I was fairly certain he wasn't winking at me. "That is none of your concern—unless you want to tell me why you're here."

"Coffee, I thought."

"Not here in my office, damn it! Here in the police station, pretending you had a legal right to speak to Daphne Arm-strong."

"Oh," I murmured, wishing I had a jolt of caffeine. He wasn't buying 'Mom-Squad' explanation, obviously. I couldn't offer another one that did not include Skyler.

"Would you care to elaborate?"

"Why don't I just leave?" I suggested. "I won't make any further attempts to speak to Daphne without your consent."

"She'll be charged later today. Adrienne Armstrong and her sister saw Daphne run out of the house and down a path that leads to Oakland Heights. Another witness saw her drive away from the parking lot. Thus far, it's circumstantial, but we're hoping to find the weapon."

"Paraffin test?"

"Inconclusive."

"You didn't mention a motive."

Peter looked at me. "Nor did you. Is there a reason she would have killed her father?"

"How would I know?" I picked up the briefcase that might well have contained calcified egg salad sandwiches and memos regarding departmental meetings adjourned well over a decade ago. "Unless I am to be detained, I would like to leave now."

He cut me off before I could reach his office door. "This cop-boyfriend/amateur-sleuth thing isn't going to work indefinitely, Claire. You trot around getting people to spill their guts, and I always end up looking like a lamebrain."

"Not always," I said tactfully.

"We can talk about this in a more private setting, but I need to warn you that something's going to have to change. One of us is going to have to retire."

I wished more than anything that I could tell him the truth about Daphne and Skyler. He wasn't angry, but he was decidedly frustrated, as well he should have been—and his remark about past situations had validity. I had done my best to stay out of the limelight, but the media had not always cooperated.

I entwined my fingers behind his neck. "I just can't talk about this one. Give me a day or two, and then we'll cuddle on the couch and have a bottle of passable wine. You can choose the movie."

"Why are you involved in this?"

If only I could have trusted him not to call social services and have Skyler carted off. However, he operated by the book—and sometimes the book was not well written. Miss Parchester had espoused civil disobedience and taken a stand. Surely I could, too, if for no more than another day or so.

"I'm not really involved," I said.

"And I'm not really Tinkerbell, so there's no reason to clap."

"You do have such a way with words. I think it would be best for me to leave before either of us blurts out something worthy of regret at a later time. Daphne Armstrong told me nothing that you and KFAR don't already know. She said she didn't kill her father, but I'm sure you've heard that. She's frightened and upset. Is she on a suicide watch?"

"Every fifteen minutes," Peter said, his demeanor softening. "Is there anything else you should tell me?"

"I think not."

"You issued a rain check yesterday. How about dinner tonight?"

It might have worked, but he had a habit of inviting himself upstairs and suggesting we engage in adult behavior. When Caron was home, we restricted ourselves to discreet junior high school groping. When she was sleeping over at Inez's house, we widened our range to include my bedroom. Little did he know someone else would be in said room, albeit in a basket.

"Caron's still upset."

He gave me a perplexed look, as if he were a puppy that had been smacked with a rolled newspaper for the most minor of transgressions. "Did I say or do anything the other night? She seemed distressed when she opened the door, and she mumbled something that didn't make much sense before she scurried down the hall to her bedroom. Has our relationship become a problem for her? Should I try to talk to her?"

"It has nothing to do with you—or with us, for that matter. She's battling issues that involve her father. Give us a few days, okay?"

"Okay," he said as he glanced at the hall, then pulled me behind the door and kissed me in a most unprofessional manner. "And you will mind your own business, won't you?"

"I promise," I said without adding that Daphne's impending charge for murder was most certainly my business—and that I intended to get down to it before I found myself with a foundling, so to speak.

Ten minutes later, I parked in front of Secondhand Rose and went inside.

"Well?" Luanne said.

"She didn't say much, but she swore she didn't kill him," I said as I sat down and repeated the brief conversation that had been so abruptly interrupted. "I don't suppose I expected her to say anything else. The baby's father is named Joey. He did time for assault but is back in town."

"Now, there's a clue. Should we open a bottle of champagne?"

"Give me a break, Luanne. All I know is that Daphne was seen leaving the house just before Anthony Armstrong's body was discovered. Her reason for being there didn't ring true. Why didn't she simply go by when she knew for sure that her father was away from the house? Adrienne wouldn't have prevented her from taking a suitcase of clothes." I began to pace between the rack of threadbare velvet gowns from the thirties and a display case with beaded purses and felt hats adorned with very tired feathers. "And she grabbed the gun," I added, picking up my pace. "Peter thinks it's possible she might have fired it. Has the girl never watched a cop show on TV? Rule number one is don't pick up the gun!"

Luanne cut me off before I floundered into the merchandise. "But she swore she didn't do it, and her story makes some sense. First, an unauthorized entry, key or not. A gunshot, and her father on the rug, bleeding. She heard a noise and panicked."

"I suspect her lawyer won't get anything else out of her. All she wants is what's best for Skyler, but she doesn't believe she can provide it—or anything else. She might be able to if she inherits some money from her father's estate."

"If she didn't kill him," Luanne said dryly.

"Well, there's that."

"And that would require you to come up with someone else who happened to have been seen running out of the house at midnight. Any ideas?"

"No," I admitted, "and she didn't really explain why she went to the house. Her father threw her out when she announced she was pregnant and refused to have an abortion. I don't know what part in this Adrienne played, but I doubt Daphne was invited for dinner on a regular basis."

"And I doubt Adrienne is going to invite you for coffee and details."

"I don't even know where the house is, although I gather it's near Oakland Heights. Did you notice any formidable iron gates?"

Luanne shook her head. "There were some driveways, but I couldn't see the houses. Are you going to peddle paperbacks door-to-door until you find it?"

"I guess not," I said. "Have you heard from Caron?"

"Oh, yes. We've moved on to Burping 101."

I went to the Book Depot, made coffee, and spread the newspaper on the counter. Once again, it failed to engage me. My science fiction hippie showed up with a sack of week-old doughnuts, and we discussed alien transmutations until it was time for him to wander home and watch reruns of *Dr. Who.*

Daphne Armstrong was off-limits unless I scaled the exterior of the police station and whispered at her through the barred window. I had noted that Peter said Daphne had been seen driving away from the parking lot at Oakland Heights, but I had no idea how to pursue it. Joey, purportedly the father of her baby, had been turned loose on society and owned a car.

But what would happen if I tracked him down? Even if Daphne was charged with the murder of her father—which seemed likely—could I prevent Joey from taking Skyler? He was the biological father. I had no claim beyond the scribbled note.

I chewed on my lip for a long while, then found the telephone directory in a desk drawer and looked up an address for Sheila Armstrong. I hadn't promised Daphne I wouldn't speak to her mother, after all.

Sheila Armstrong lived in the same neighborhood as Miss Parchester. Here, houses were as much as a hundred years old, trimmed with gingerbread molding, rejuvenated with painfully authentic hues of paint and flower beds filled with fiercely dedicated perennials. Sheila's house was shabbier than those on either side, the lawn in need of a trim, the shutters in need of alignment, the garden in need of a backhoe. Those who strolled in the evening, as many of the residents surely did, no doubt tut-tutted and averted their eyes as they passed by.

I had not a clue what I would say as I knocked on the door.

"Yes?" trilled a woman as she flung open the door. "Are you the terminator? You don't look like a terminator, but of course the only one I've ever seen was in some silly movie!"

In that she was wearing only black cowboy boots, gossamer harem pants, and a red bra, I was taken aback, to put it mildly.

"Not the terminator," I said at last.

"I meant to say 'exterminator.' The termites are eating up the foundation and the flour beetles are making me crazy. Do come in."

Any sane person would have bolted for the sidewalk. I went inside.

All the drapes in the living room were drawn, leaving an eerie glow that suggested visitation at a mortuary. The furniture was an eclectic combination of battered wicker chairs, lumpy upholstered sofas, and stools from a long-defunct ice-cream parlor. The redolence was sour but bearable.

"You're Sheila Armstrong?" I said as I perched on what proved to be a precariously wobbly stool.

She draped herself across a chair, oblivious of her lack of clothing, and pushed a tangled mass of gray-streaked hair out of her face. Even in the gloom, her skin was so pale that I doubted she ventured out of her house until after sunset. Her makeup had been applied with a zealous hand. "Perhaps, perhaps not. Are you a terminator or an exterminator? I simply cannot make plans for the rest of the day until you explain your motives."

"I was hoping we could talk about Daphne."

"Yes, Daphne." She lit a cigarette and blew a stream of smoke that seemed to swirl in the sunlight coming through a gap in the drapes. "She was here when they came looking for her yesterday. I told her to hide under the bed or in the attic, but she just sat and waited. She used to be high-spirited, but her father systematically broke her as one would a wild pony. She didn't even protest when he forced her to attend that dreadful church school. If he had listened to me, none of this would have happened."

"The murder—or the baby?"

"None of it," she said emphatically. "Would you like some vodka?"

When I shook my head, she went into another room and returned with a glass filled to the brim with a colorless beverage that was not likely to be water. She took a drink, and then a long drag on her cigarette. "Just who are you?"

I told her my name and vaguely alluded to the bookstore. "Daphne came to my apartment several days ago because she needed help. She was worried about Skyler."

"She should have been more worried about that boyfriend of hers. They should have kept him locked up for the rest of his life. After I met him, I warned her that he was disaster in the making. There she was, dating a boy nine years older who worked as a mechanic, when she could have been doing her schoolwork and thinking about college. That's when Anthony sent her to that school, where they wear prissy uniforms and recite Bible verses every morning. A course in sex education would have been more pragmatic, wouldn't it?"

I wasn't sure what to make of her, dressed as she was

in expectation of the arrival of an exterminator. The vodka was being consumed with practiced efficiency; the glass was already half empty (or half full, if she was an optimist). She hadn't shown any concern for Skyler's whereabouts or well-being. Or Daphne's, for that matter.

"She lived with you for a time, didn't she?" I asked.

"That was several weeks ago. She seemed more like a feral cat than my little girl. I kept expecting her to hiss over table scraps. The infant screamed night and day. It was simply too stressful for me. Do you have children, Mrs. Malarky?"

"Malloy," I murmured, although I doubted it would penetrate her haze. "Yes, I have a daughter. I would do whatever was required to stop her from living on the streets."

"Anthony's problem. He wanted custody, and I never contested it. My share in the divorce settlement was laughable. He's played golf with every lawyer and judge in the county for twenty years. Most of them have invested in his developments and come away with a profit. He built three quarters of the apartment and condominium complexes in Farberville, as well as several residential developments. His corporation owns dozens of rental houses. I accepted this one as part of the deal, since I knew I wouldn't be able to afford anything better. Unfortunately, I'm finding it difficult to afford utilities."

"But Daphne would have been better off living here," I said.

Sheila snorted. "She was very angry at me after the divorce, and hasn't gotten past it. I tried to continue our relationship, but she criticized me relentlessly. Our visitations became so antagonistic that I suggested she come less often and only stay for an hour. I hadn't seen her in more than a year when she showed up on the doorstep with a newborn baby, if you can imagine. Suddenly I was supposed to live with dirty diapers and constant crying? When Daphne was born, I had full-time help to handle the more bothersome aspects of mothering. That was in Tunica, though, and help was affordable as long as one wasn't too picky about references or prison records. Are you sure you wouldn't like some vodka, perhaps with a splash of cranberry juice?"

The non sequitur, as well as her casual recitation, left me dumbstruck for a moment. "So you kicked her out, just as her father did?"

"He was the one with the grandiose house and fat income. He could have at least let her live in one of his apartments on the south side of town. It would have cost less than Adrienne's athletic club membership or the lease payments on her Jaguar."

"How long had they been married?" I asked cautiously.

Sheila stubbed out the cigarette in an overflowing ashtray and lit another one. "They started sleeping together the day after she came to work at his office about four years ago. Anthony was ripe for a mid-life crisis, and darling Adrienne smelled the money and the possibility of more plastic surgery for the few body parts yet to be lifted, tucked, or vacuumed. Six months after that, Anthony filed for divorce, and the day after the decree was final, they left for Tahiti on their honeymoon."

"How did Daphne feel about it?"

"She didn't say anything to me, and I didn't ask. In their absence, I gather she found the key to the wine cellar and hosted a few parties. Poor Anthony must have been furious when he discovered his coveted vintages were depleted. He was always obsessed with serving the perfect bottle to those who could appreciate its cost. I myself preferred vodka, although a pricier brand than what I've been reduced to."

"But he didn't throw her out then?"

"She told me that Adrienne convinced him not to despite the damage to the house and the theft of several of his rifles and shotguns. Anthony always tried to be the epitome of a macho man, even though he loathed the hunting and fishing trips with his cronies. He would have much rather played poker at the country club." She drained the glass. "He was fonder of waiters than waders."

I realized I'd better get to the point before she got back to the bottle. "Do you have any idea why Daphne went to his house two nights ago?"

Sheila blinked at me. "How would I know? Until she showed up a few days ago, I hadn't seen her in weeks. At least she didn't have that baby with her. I do hope no one's going to expect me to take it while she's in prison. I can't stretch my meager resources to cover diapers and that sort of thing." Her eyes widened. "Anthony's death won't affect my alimony checks, will it?"

"Surely not," I said soothingly. "What did Daphne say when she arrived here yesterday? Did she say anything about what happened?"

"Not that I recall. She was surly when I attempted to make conversation. She asked if she could have something to eat, and I told her to look in the refrigerator. She'd just finished the piece of chicken I was saving for my dinner when the police arrived."

"And you didn't know what had happened to Anthony?"

"I had no idea. My television is broken, and I keep the radio tuned to NPR while I do my yoga exercises."

An authoritative rap on the door halted our conversation. Sheila wobbled to her feet and smiled at me. "The exterminator. I hope you won't mind leaving, whoever you are. There's nothing I can do for Daphne or her baby."

"So I heard," I said acerbically.

She threw open the door to both usher me out and usher in the exterminator. On the porch stood Sergeant Jorgeson and two uniformed officers.

"We have a search warrant," he began, then spotted me hovering behind her. "Oh, dear, Ms. Malloy."

Likewise, Jorgeson.

CHAPTER SIX

It seemed like the time to beat an auspicious retreat, but Jorgeson did not step aside. "Whatever are you doing here, Ms. Malloy?" he asked in a discouraged voice, as if, perchance, we'd had this exchange before. Despite his vaguely deferential demeanor, I've always suspected he's more dangerous than Peter. Distracting him with a kiss was out of the question; I couldn't remember ever so much as shaking his hand, and if he had a first name (which he most likely did), I didn't know what it was. He had the tenacity of a bulldog, but also, unfortunately, a latent resemblance.

"Comforting my friend Sheila," I said. "Whatever are you doing here, Sergeant Jorgeson?"

"We have a search warrant. This is a homicide investigation, and we do that sometimes."

"Still no weapon?"

As I'd hoped, I was dismissed with a flip of his hand. Sheila was cooing in his ear as I got in my car and drove back down Thurber Street to my bookstore. All I'd learned was that Daphne's mother was flakier than a stale croissant—and less appealing.

I fumed while I drank a cup of coffee, then worked off my anger by attacking the paperback racks with a feather duster until I was sneezing so violently that I had to go out to the portico and mop my nose with a tissue.

At which time, my life being congested with coincidences the past few days, Sally Fromberger came ambling up ever so casually, just as if she hadn't been lurking in the municipal parking lot across the street. I wondered if she had binoculars in her ecologically-correct woven handbag.

"I was surprised to find the Book Depot closed," she said.

"Morning sickness!" I snapped. "The obstetrician thinks it'll be twins this time."

Sally's perpetually jocular expression faded. "Are you implying that you . . ."

"You can't believe the track and field team finds me desirable? Is that what puzzles you? I used to hurdle in high school." I dried my eyes on my jacket cuffs. "I just wasn't prepared for twins. The father will be graduating soon, and he's taken an entry-level job in Atlanta. I'm counting on you, Sally Fromberger, to help me through this. I just can't face the bookstore right now. Will you keep it open for me while I go home and eat crackers?"

"Yes, of course," she said nervously. "Is there anything else you want to tell me?"

I forced myself to give her a hug. "I knew I could count on you. What are dear friends for, after all?"

"But you're coming back?"

"As soon as my stomach has calmed down. You won't tell anybody about this, will you? I have to think of my reputation."

Sally most certainly was thinking of nothing else.

"Please don't worry, Claire. I want to help in any way I can."

"I know you do," I said humbly, then hurried through the store, grabbed my purse, and went out to my car before she came to her senses. She might call Luanne, but she couldn't lay her hands on my high school yearbooks to discover that I'd been no more involved in track and field than I'd been a cover girl on *Field and Stream*.

Perhaps it was the time to find Joey, although I had no intention of telling him anything more than necessary. Daphne and Skyler had been living in his car until a few days ago, when she'd decided to go to her father's house. If Joey had kicked her out, she could have become desperate enough to beg Anthony for help. But she'd been seen driving away from Oakland Heights, and I couldn't imagine Sheila allowing her to borrow her car. If Sheila even owned a car. It was not the time to swing back by her house and ask.

I decided to stop by Oakland Heights to visit Miss Parchester and find out if she'd seen Daphne running to the parking lot. Howie would have to be bribed, I supposed, but I would insist on a fair return for my investment this time.

"Hello, dear," she trilled as I came up the slope of the parking lot. "Such excitement these last few days, don't you think? I do believe that television reporter—Jessica, her name is—would have climbed up here to interview me if I'd permitted her to do so. I was obliged to threaten her with the thermos before she retreated."

"Where's Howie?" I called softly.

She blushed. "I think he went to the shed for personal reasons. Why don't you scurry up here before he returns? He won't be able to see you from the ground."

My eggplant-hued bruises said no, but I nodded and
watched as the rope ladder plummeted down. I scrambled up and then helped her retrieve the ladder before
Howie appeared.

"How are you doing?" I asked between gasps.

"Very nicely, thank you. I'm out of lemons, however.
Can you drink tea without it?"

"I'm not in the mood for tea, Miss Parchester. Have
you been listening to the local radio station?"

She opened a tin and offered me a brownie. When I
shook my head, she put the tin aside and said, "I'm
afraid I have. First this murder, and now little Daphne
under arrest. I can hardly believe it. I only hope that I
am not in some way responsible. As a staunch supporter
of the Green Party, I volunteered to do this in order to
save trees, not destroy lives."

"You aren't responsible," I said, surprised. "How
could you be?"

"I may have given Daphne poor advice."

I stared at her. "You gave Daphne advice?"

"Poor advice."

"So you said. I didn't realize you knew Daphne."

Miss Parchester sighed as she nibbled on a brownie.
"A year or two ago, I saw her stumbling down the sidewalk and invited her inside for a cup of cocoa. She'd
just come from her mother's house, and the visit had not
gone well. She had no other adults with whom to talk.
I listened to her that day for more than an hour, and
again on subsequent afternoons. I could offer no solu-
tions, but I could provide her with a sympathetic ear and
a few words of wisdom. Neither of her parents was the
least bit concerned about her feelings. Divorce is hard
on adolescents as well as younger children."

"And you've spoken to her recently?"

Miss Parchester held a finger to her lips as we heard the sound of shoes crunching on dried leaves. "Howie," she whispered melodramatically. "He mustn't see you."

I flattened myself on the platform, my head resting on the brownie tin and my knees drawn up. I'd never felt quite so silly, hiding from someone not yet old enough to frequent a bar. But Howie could have me arrested and hauled to the jail, where further complications might arise.

"Everything all right, Miss Parchester?" he called.

She hesitated, then said, "I did hear some clomping about and voices in the direction of the bluff. I should think those dedicated members of the Green Party whom you had arrested yesterday are out on bond. They very well could be attempting to bring me fresh supplies. I wouldn't tell you this if I weren't concerned about you, Howie. If the site is infiltrated, you will be fired."

I giggled, then clamped my hand over my mouth until Howie's footsteps retreated. "It's hard to picture Finnigan scaling the bluff with a bag of lemons clenched between his teeth."

"You may be underestimating his degree of commitment," Miss Parchester said with a reproachful frown. "His younger sister was living at Oakland Heights last year when there was a fire. She suffered serious medical problems."

"Was Anthony Armstrong responsible? Didn't he comply with all the building codes?"

She gazed at the valley below. "Yes, he did, but Finnigan has learned from a colleague in the geology department that this development is situated on a fault. In states such as California and Utah, where earthquakes are a factor, more stringent building specifications are mandated."

I held my breath for a moment, waiting to see if the tree would begin to sway as the ground shook beneath us. "We're on a fault?" I squeaked.

"Supposedly an inactive one, although it's possible that even a minor shifting could have caused gas lines to rupture in proximity to a pilot light of a hot water heater or furnace. Finnigan suspects Anthony was aware of this and constructed the condominiums despite the remote possibility that there might be consequences."

"Does Finnigan have proof of this?"

"No, he merely thinks evidence would have shown up on the topographical survey. Having never seen one myself, I have no opinion. He has many opinions, of course."

I propped myself up on one elbow. "And his sister?"

Miss Parchester sighed again. "I gather from what he's said that she is recovering but unable to resume her education. I'm not sure if he's dedicated to the environment or to vengeance."

"Oh, dear," I said rather inadequately.

"You'd best be on your way. Howie may return soon."

"I will, but let's talk about Daphne for a minute. What precisely did you advise her to do?"

"Let's continue this later, Claire. I do not want to be responsible for your arrest." She dropped the rope ladder. "And do look after Skyler, please."

"You know about him?"

"I'm living in a tree, not in a cave. Run along now. Howie's likely to be testy when he comes back from the bluff, having found nothing but chipmunks."

I reluctantly made my way down the ladder, watched as it was jerked up, and went to my car. The situation had become murkier. I had no idea what advice Miss

Parchester had given Daphne. I could only hope that it had not been to take no prisoners.

As I sat, tossing around idle thoughts, Randy and Jillian came out of their condo. Both were visibly upset. I briefly debated the wisdom of interfering in a marital spat, then got out of my car and approached them.

"Claire Malloy," I said. "I gave you a ride the other night, Randy."

"Yeah, sure. Can I do something for you?"

"Such as?" Jillian said, sneering at him. "You don't need a ride right now, do you? You're going to take the car and go to work. What time will you be home, Randy? Midnight again?"

"You know we need the money," he said to her, then looked at me, mutely asking for moral support.

I saw the anger etched on Jillian's face, the lines too deeply drawn to have come from the current argument. I instinctively stepped back, then said, "I could give Randy a ride if you need the car, Jillian."

"Why would I need the car? Where is it I'd go?"

The door slammed behind her as she went into the condo. Randy and I looked at each other for a long moment. He must have realized I had more sympathy for Jillian than for him, but it was already clear that he was a less than perspicacious young man. I had no idea what he would say.

"Yeah, a ride," he muttered. "I'd appreciate it. Jillian might need to go to the grocery store."

I gestured for him to follow me back to my car. Once we'd pulled out of the parking lot, I asked him where he wanted to go.

"The Farberville Fitness Center, if it's not too inconvenient. I work the desk, run loads of towels, clean the showers, put fresh rolls of toilet paper in the stalls. Jillian seems to think I lounge in the hot tub with sorority girls."

"She seems to think she's stuck at home with a baby," I said dryly.

"So what am I supposed to do? We don't have to worry about rent, but we have other expenses. Jillian just doesn't understand that the pissant stipend I receive as a graduate assistant won't cover groceries, doctor's visits, medicine, utilities, gas, cable—"

"I get the point."

"We were doing okay until Connor came along," he said, ignoring me. "Jillian's parents helped with her tuition, and she had a job at the library. I was being considered for an internship with a software company that would have guaranteed me a job after graduation. So, out of the blue, she gets pregnant."

"I presume you were in some way involved in that, Randy."

"She said she was on the pill. We'd agreed to wait until I had a good job and she'd finished her degree."

I braked at a stoplight. "So you're punishing her?"

"No, I'm taking a full load, teaching two undergraduate classes, and putting in thirty hours a week at the fitness center. She's changing diapers and watching soap operas all day. She doesn't read, cook, or even take Connor out in his stroller. I've given up trying to have any conversations with her."

This was not a situation in which I wanted to become involved. I had a good idea where it would go, but I doubted a lecture from me would deflect the sad resolution. As we neared the fitness center, I said, "Did you happen to hear anything the night of the murder? There's an unconfirmed story that someone saw the girl drive out of your parking lot."

"That was me. Connor had colic, and I was walking around, jiggling him and praying he'd go to sleep, when I glanced out the window. Things are pretty quiet after midnight, so it was unusual to see someone running across the lot. She jumped in a car and drove off."

"Did you notice the color or model of the car?" I asked as I stopped in front of the center.

"No, I just heard the car door slam and the engine," he said. "Thanks for the ride. I'll have to hope Jillian will have calmed down enough to pick me up after my shift. Guess I'll find out when the time comes." He shrugged, then got out of the car and entered the building.

I watched the stream of impeccably clothed men and women, most of them in their twenties and thirties, as they went inside to grunt, grimace, and otherwise regenerate themselves on a daily basis. Adrienne Armstrong would have fit in perfectly, and it seemed likely that she had as recently as the morning after she'd discovered her husband's corpse.

My dress was inappropriate, but I decided to give it a shot. I pulled a few oak leaves out of my hair, then conscientiously locked my car (as if it might be the prime target in a metallic sea of Mercedes, Porsches, Jaguars, and SUVs large enough to haul soccer goalposts, twenty screaming children, and the odd umpire or two) and went inside.

Even these paragons of physical vitality sweated, I realized as I wrinkled my nose. The carpet looked as if some of them had come directly from the polo field. I wandered down a hall, keeping an eye out for Randy, and ducked around a corner when I heard his voice. The only door opened onto an expanse of six tennis courts, all occupied by players dressed in white and making primitive noises as they slammed their rackets against pastel-colored balls. Adrienne Armstrong was not among them.

I retreated, then paused to listen for Randy's voice from what I presumed was a reception area. As I may have mentioned in the past, I go to extremes to avoid even the mildest glint of perspiration. Life's too challenging to inflict intentional discomfort. I therefore did not frequent athletic clubs, and would have been equally as familiar with the facilities of, shall we say, the Kremlin or a Klingon battleship.

I peered around the corner at the main hallway. Two women dressed in designer exercise attire came by, both carrying monogrammed bags and chatting about a fundraiser. I smiled as best I could, causing no more than one well-drawn eyebrow to rise, then waited until they were out the front door before proceeding into the labyrinth, where I might encounter dragons, ogres, and aerobics instructors.

Eventually I went into what proved to be the ladies' locker room. Half a dozen women were in various stages of putting on or peeling off Spandex shorts, socks, pricy athletic shoes, and halters.

One of them, a peppy thing with wide brown eyes, looked up at me from a bench. "First time?" she asked.

"In a manner of speaking," I said. "Is this where Adrienne Armstrong comes?"

"Wasn't that the most awful thing! I could have cried when I heard about it on the news. My husband, Bradley, said it was all the fault of that group of crackpots who want to prevent progress in Farberville. This community is growing, and people have to live somewhere, don't they?"

"Indeed they do," I said, sitting down beside her.

"Have you seen Adrienne since this happened?"

The woman shook her head. "She missed our Tae Bo class this morning. She's usually the first one on the floor, and I don't think any of us could stop staring at her usual spot over in the corner. Bradley had his secretary send flowers to her house, but I'm thinking I ought to go by and see how she's holding up. Such an awful thing!" She finished lacing up her shoes and slipped terrycloth bands on her wrist. "Are you a friend?"

"Not a close one. How often does she work out?"

"She just puts all the rest of us to shame. She comes for the Tae Bo class every morning, then does the weight machines for an hour. To be honest, my muscles are screaming so bad that it's all I can do to make it to the whirlpool to soak. Some evenings, if she doesn't have a function, she'll come back to run laps in the gym or play racquetball. I don't know how she does it at her age."

"Which is?" I inquired.

"She has to be at least twenty-five, but she's got the tightest butt out here. Just ask Bradley, who was thoughtful enough to share that with me while we were vacationing in Aruba over Christmas. Like I wanted to hear that!"

"Did Anthony come here, too?"

She pulled her hair into a ponytail and secured it with a matching terrycloth band. "Yeah, but not so much anymore. He used to play tennis a couple of evenings a week, but then he started canceling dates at the last minute. Too strenuous at his age, I guess." She stuffed her purse and bag into a locker. "Kimberlee's my personal trainer, and she doesn't like to be kept waiting. Will I see you again out here?"

"Probably not," I said. "I just dropped by because I'm

worried about Adrienne. Such an awful thing, you know."

"Do I ever!" she said, clutching my hand for a brief moment. "Everybody feels so bad, especially the staff. Adrienne spends more time out here than most of them. She has her charity work, of course, and volunteers at an elementary school, tutoring little minority children. I wish I had as much time as she does, but Bradley's just now getting his firm on its feet and I work at the reception desk three days a week. Do you have an accountant?"

"Yes, but I'll keep Bradley in mind if the situation changes."

I gave her a weak smile, then left the locker room and made it to my car without encountering Randy Scarpo. I'd hoped I might run into Adrienne Armstrong, but in that I had no idea what to say to her, it was just as well. Any mention of Daphne would be awkward.

Hoping that Sally could hold down the fort for a while longer, I resolved to find Joey. There were a few challenging aspects: no last name, no residence, no current employment, no clue to his whereabouts. Then again, Farberville did not have a limitless number of garages.

I decided to start with the garages I'd driven by over the years, and then, if necessary, consult the yellow pages for the more remote ones. Sally might be driving off whatever hapless customers came into the Book Depot, but they would return. And until I helped Daphne, I had custody of her baby.

Asking innocent questions of those who worked in garages proved more frustrating than I'd anticipated—when I could find anyone who would listen. The hierarchy was impossible to determine when all the men wore grease-stained jumpsuits and refused to stop making deafening noises with various pneumatic tools. Although they seemed comfortable standing under vehicles on racks or sliding beneath same held aloft by flimsy jacks, I did not. I'd mouthed my query at six or seven places before a guy jerked his thumb and shouted for me to go into the office.

The older woman seated behind a desk piled high with papers and folders looked up as I closed the door behind me. She had a helmet of bleached hair and serious purple eye shadow, but her smile was amicable.

"Help you, honey?" she said. "Car trouble?"

I sat down across from her. "I'm looking for a mechanic named Joey."

"Nobody named Joey here, but Mort ought to be finishing up that valve job before long and he can take a look. He's been working here for eight years, and before that he was over Cannelletti's shop out towards Farmington. Real dependable, Mort is, and damn smart at pinpointing the problem. No complaints all the time he's been here."

"It's not about my car, although I'm sure it could use some attention from someone as skilled as Mort. This Joey is in his mid-twenties, and he was working in a garage until about six months ago, when he was sent to jail for assault. He was released a few weeks ago."

"No last name?" she asked with such sympathy that I refused to imagine what she was thinking. "Cute guy, huh?"

"I've never met him," I said evenly. "I'm trying to help a friend locate him."

"Of course you are. I wish I could tell you something, but nobody named Joey has worked here for the last fifteen years. A few years back there was a guy named

Joseph, a real hell-raiser with the ladies, but he was in his sixties and wasn't what you'd call attractive unless you were blind in one eye, which he happened to be, too. He left town after he was caught peeping in sorority house windows—and some fraternity houses as well. The city prosecutor personally drove him to the bus station and bought him a one-way ticket to Alabama . . . or was it Mississippi?"

"Thanks, anyway," I said as I stood up.

She gnawed on her lower lip. "There was a fellow out at Cannelletti's earlier this spring, name of José. That's kinda like Joey, ain't it? I heard he got into some trouble with the police. You want I should call out there and ask?"

"Out toward Farmington, you said? No, please don't bother to call. I'll go by and see if they might have any information."

"Are you a lawyer, honey? You got that look about you."

I'd forgotten that I was still wearing my navy suit. "No," I said, "I'm not a lawyer. Just helping a friend, that's all."

"Right," she said. "Well, I hope you find this fellow. You sound kinda desperate."

I could see that she wanted me to drop back onto the chair, burst into tears, and tell her the wretched truth about my lust for a muscular young mechanic who'd rotated my tires more than once.

I left her to her fantasies and once again went out to my car. The afternoon was dwindling, as was Sally's goodwill. But I finally had a lead, or at least an intimation of one. Someone named José could certainly have Americanized his name. Or not, I thought glumly as I drove past the stadium and out toward Farmington, keeping an eye out for a garage named Cannelletti's.

A sloppy pyramid of tires almost obscured the faded sign in the window of the squat, concrete-block building. Several cars beyond redemption in anyone's lifetime (including Mort's) were parked in the weeds on either side. I would not have been surprised to see buzzards circling overhead.

I parked and went into the office. A bald man with a bristly gray mustache was glaring at an invoice and mumbling under his breath. It was just as well that I couldn't understand his words.

"Hi," I said. "I'm hoping you can help me."

"I wish I could say the same."

"Are you Mr. Cannelletti?"

"Are you mistaking me for the pope?" he said as he put down the paper and stared at me. "Do you think I got a flock of cardinals out there doing lube jobs?"

"The thought never crossed my mind." I sat down on a stool across the counter from him. "I'm trying to find someone who may have been working here up until six months ago."

"The warranty's only good for thirty days."

"Oh, nothing like that," I said, doing my best to envelop him in a warm glow of camaraderie. "It's a personal thing."

"What those jerks do on their own time is none of my business. I make it clear when I hire them that there's no point in calling me for bail. Better they should call the archbishop. Same fat chance."

There was a hint of amusement in his eyes, however, so I persevered. "I'm looking for a man named Joey, or perhaps José when he worked for you. All I know is that he's about twenty-seven years old and was sent to the county jail six months ago. He was released a week ago."

"Calling himself Joey, is he?"

I leaned forward. "So you know him? Do you have any idea where I can find him?"

"You his probation officer?"

It occurred to me that the day might have gone more smoothly had I changed into jeans and a T-shirt, rather than running around dressed like little Miss Perry Mason. "No, I own a bookstore in Farberville. It's important that I find Joey. Can you help me?"

Mr. Cannelletti studied me for a long moment. "The best way I can help you is to not help you. He's bad news, this Joey. What with the way he used to do drugs, I was always worried that he'd cause an accident out in the bays. I was about to fire him when he took care of the problem himself."

"But you know where I can find him, don't you?"

"He came here last week, looking for a job. I told him I couldn't take him back on account of having hired somebody else. The truth is I'm shorthanded and he probably knew it, but he just shrugged and drove off."

"You didn't answer my question, Mr. Cannelletti."

"I don't guess I did. Okay, you look old enough to know your own mind. There's a bar in Waverly, just past the first stoplight. That's where he used to hang out, and where he got himself arrested. Mostly punks, bikers, and prostitutes. It's no place for a lady, especially an unescorted one. I'd go with you, but Mrs. Cannelletti would get all kinds of ideas and I'd be sleeping in the hammock until the first freeze. I'll tell you the name of it if you promise you won't go there by yourself."

He was a rather sweet old man, and I felt a twinge of guilt as I showed him my palm and said, "I promise."

"You'd lie to Saint Peter, wouldn't you?" he said, sighing. "You'd better be real careful, lady. The name of the bar is Dante's. Joey, or José Guilerra, as he used to call himself, drives an '89 Trans Am, bright yellow with black racing stripes. He seemed sober enough when he was here last, but I wouldn't count on it if you chase him down. What's more, you walk in that place dressed like you are right now, they're all likely to think you're from the INS and all hell's gonna break loose. Green cards are scarce in there."

I got off the stool. "Thanks, Mr. Cannelletti. You've been a great help."

"I just hope you heard what I said. Joey was a fairly good mechanic, but he's real tightly wound. I can't imagine why you're looking for him, but the best advice I can give you is to forget about it."

"I wish I could," I said truthfully. "Did he ever bring a girl named Daphne out here?"

"That pathetic little thing. Sometimes she'd come along while he was working and offer to clean the restrooms or make coffee. She was real eager to talk to someone, even if just about the weather. A couple of times my wife took her around to yard sales to buy clothes. Joey didn't much like it and stopped bringing her. Is she doing okay?"

"Not exactly," I said, then left before I blurted out the truth. After all, he might as well see it on KFAR at five o'clock, or at ten.

So Joey hung out at a bar named Dante's, which was not a comforting name in that the volume of the trilogy we are all most familiar with included the word *inferno*. And what I expected to say to him if and when I found him was not glaringly obvious. Asking him if Daphne had borrowed his car to drive to Oakland Heights and shoot her father might not prove to be an interesting hypothetical, especially for someone who used drugs and had been described as "tightly wound." I doubted six months in jail had mellowed him.

But, I thought as I drove in the direction of the Book Depot, he was the only lead I had. Daphne had offered nothing more than a hackneyed plot seen on TV dramas weekly, if not daily. Daphne's mother had told me nothing whatsoever. Peter would not be enlightening me any time soon. Adrienne would be buffered by her family and her lawyer. Unlike Miss Marple, I could not stop by the vicarage for cucumber sandwiches and village gossip.

I parked behind the bookstore and went inside. Sally was reasonably civil as I thanked her for minding the store and assured her that I felt well enough to handle the infrequent customer who might wander in. Although I could see she was salivating for details of my delicate condition, I shooed her out, stuck the flyspecked Closed sign in the window, and called Luanne.

"Hey, biker chick," I drawled, "wanna go for a pitcher of beer?"

CHAPTER SEVEN

"Would it be your first pitcher of beer today?" asked Luanne, not altogether facetiously. "Sally called earlier. She wants to organize a baby shower. Gurgles from a baby are charming, but gurgles from someone with Sally's girth are—"

"It's complicated," I said, "but I need your help."

"To browse outlet furniture stores for matching bassinets?"

"I had to tell her something," I muttered, then added, "Will you meet me at my place in half an hour? Wear something . . . well, casual."

"Pink or blue?"

"Damn it, Luanne! I have a lead on Joey. If I don't find him, you may find yourself feeding strained beets and spinach to Skyler until he graduates to pizza. Caron will drop out of school and join a punk band crisscrossing the country in an old school bus adorned with satanic images. In the meantime, I'll be at the women's prison chopping cotton—or, if I'm lucky, working in the laundry room. Sweat will be streaming down my face and Big

Bertha will be ogling my comely backside. Sooner or later she'll pull a shiv on—"

"A what?"

I realized I was getting carried away and tried to temper my tone. "A weapon made from a spoon or, in this case, maybe a barrette."

"Big Bertha's going to pull a barrette on you?"

"And it won't be pretty," I said. "Now, are you coming with me or not?"

Luanne was silent for a moment. "Dressed as a biker chick?"

"If I knew what biker chicks wear, I'd tell you," I said testily. "Come by in half an hour."

"And then we steal Harleys? Do you know how to operate one?"

I replaced the receiver and went home to rid myself of my prim suit. I was not surprised to find Inez in the kitchen, heating a bottle in a saucepan of water.

"How's Caron doing?" I asked as I peeled off my jacket and hung it on a chair.

"Fine, I think."

"You brought her assignments?"

"Oh, yes, Ms. Malloy. All of her teachers were really nice about it. Mrs. McLair said Caron doesn't even have to write the paper on *Macbeth* that's due on Monday. We read the first act today. I suppose it's all really symbolic and deep and stuff, but I thought it was creepy."

"It is, Inez. Where are Caron and Skyler?"

She lowered her voice. "Skyler's in the living room. Caron's in her room, talking on the phone to Merissa. Rhonda the Rottweiler just won't let go of this. This morning she was conducting a lottery on who everybody thought was the father. Tickets cost a dollar."

I shuddered. "And you told Caron?"

Inez took the bottle out of the pan and squirted a few drops of formula on her wrist. "I didn't, but you can be sure Merissa has by now. I wish there was something I could do, Ms. Malloy, but I don't know what it is."

"Nor do I." I went into the living room and squatted next to Skyler. "You got any ideas, kid?"

When he failed to offer any, even after I'd tickled his toes, I continued to my room, changed into jeans and a black T-shirt, and emerged as Caron came out of her room. Her demeanor was that of a tropical storm soon to be upgraded to a hurricane, with torrential rain and winds strong enough to spew tornados at every trailer park within a hundred miles.

"Did Inez Tell You?" she said.

"She mentioned something about the paper on *Macbeth*."

"Like I should be worried about that old crap? I'll get my GED and join the army. Khaki is not my color, but I can deal with it, and then I'll be stationed in someplace like Azerbaijan. Or maybe I can join the Peace Corps and teach hygiene to primitive tribes in Zimbabwe. In any case, I am never setting foot in Farberville High School again. Never!"

I dragged her to the sofa and forced her down. "Luanne and I are going to see if we can find Skyler's father. He may be able to help."

"And ruin Rhonda's lottery? According to Merissa, odds are three to two on Waylan Pulaski, this major geek who hangs out in the custodian's closet sniffing cleaning compounds. I think I spoke to him all of twice last year." She flopped against the cushions. "What have I done to deserve this? I brake for squirrels in the street, I put coins in the Salvation Army kettles at Christmas, I do my own laundry sometimes. But now I'm the gigglebutt of Farberville High School! Just one little blip on Rhonda's radar screen and my life is ruined! It's Just Not Fair!"

"No, it isn't," I said, "but life's not too rosy for Daphne Armstrong, nor for Skyler."

"I suppose not," she agreed sullenly.

"After Skyler's been fed, why don't you and Inez put him in the car seat and go for a drive? You've been cooped up all day."

Inez came out of the kitchen. "My mother's been trying to get me to go out to my aunt's house in Hasty and pick up some old magazines. We could do that."

"Be still my heart," Caron said. "I feel a myocardial infraction coming on any minute."

"I think it's called a myocardial infarction," Inez offered.

Caron shuddered. "That is so gross. Do you remember when that sophomore boy with the dirty blond hair ripped one off in the cafeteria last Friday? I thought I was going to toss my burrito. Rhonda brayed, but she was looking a little green. Wouldn't her pom-pom teammates have been amused if she'd barfed all over the table?"

Opting not to delve into high school cafeteria decorum or medical terminology, I patted her knee. "And then you can have dinner at Inez's before you come back and tackle your assignments. Inez, can you convince your mother that you're baby-sitting for a friend of mine?"

"Probably. She's not as suspicious as you are, Ms. Malloy."

"I am not suspicious; I merely have a vigorous imagination," I said coolly. "What's on the menu, Inez?"

"This tofu lasagna thing my mother makes when she's

mad at my father. It's not as nauseating as it sounds."

"How could it be?" Caron said as she stood up. "Okay, we can go get the magazines, but I'm not eating any tofu lasagna in this lifetime. Let's pack up Skyler and go somewhere. Anywhere."

I went into the bathroom and applied industrial-strength makeup, then used Caron's mousse to slick down my curly hair. I contemplated drawing a tattoo with an eyeliner pencil, then discarded the idea. Since *National Geographic* had never done a feature on biker chicks, I could only wing it.

When I returned to the living room, the girls and Skyler were gone and Luanne was sitting on the sofa. "What's wrong with you?" she asked, her eyebrows raised indelicately. "You look as though you were mugged by a tar salesman."

"Shall we go?"

Luanne was wearing leather boots, black jeans, and a hot pink shirt that barely covered her navel. I handed her the eyeliner as we went down to her car.

"This is an undercover operation," I said. "We have to blend in, ask seemingly innocuous questions, and find this guy."

"Aren't we a tad old for this kind of thing—say, twenty years?"

"Are you amenable to having Skyler every other weekend and six weeks in the summer, as well as baking cookies for Daphne and visiting her at the women's prison? Or, worst case scenario, trying to figure out how to mail me a metal nail file so I can tunnel out of maximum security?"

"Feel free to elaborate on what exactly we're supposed to be doing," Luanne said as she slathered on the eyeliner, handed it back to me, and started the car.

Dante's Lounge proved to be a minor eyesore, a brick building with a neon sign in front and a plethora of motorcycles and rust-tainted pickups parked around it. No yellow Trans Ams were among them.

We were cut off at the door by a bearded man pushing a stroller. The child was clad in pink, suggesting a gender. Luanne and I made appropriate noises, then held open the door and followed them into a brightly lit room with pool tables, stools lining a bar, minimal smoke, and several other babies in strollers parked at the perimeter of the room. The jukebox was playing what might be described as elevator music.

"Infant happy hour," said the gray-haired bartender as we approached the bar. "Cal over there suggested it. We're having a cookie exchange on Saturday if you ladies are interested." He looked at us. "Or not."

I wished I could have licked my eyelids, but, unfortunately, I could not. "We're looking for Joey. I think his last name is Guilerra."

"Never heard of him."

Luanne picked up a cue stick and gazed at the handful of patrons sitting at the bar and around Formica-topped tables. "Anybody want to play a little eight ball? Five bucks?"

A chunky young man with a wisp of hair on his chin stood up. "Yeah, I'll play. Who are you?"

"Farberville Fats," Luanne said as she racked the balls. "Are you the reigning champion of infant happy hour? Does the trophy have a nipple?"

"You're not fat."

"Too bad you can't say the same about yourself."

She began to rack the balls. The young man was smirking, either at the wittiness of his retort or at the thought of tucking a five-dollar bill into his back pocket.

His smirk would soon be fading; Luanne is a woman of many talents. Mansions in Connecticut have billiard rooms next to the libraries, only a floor or two above the wine cellars and family vaults.

I took a stool at the bar and asked for a beer. As the bartender set down a mug, I said, "Joey, or maybe José, has a yellow Trans Am with racing stripes. His girl-friend, Daphne, may have come here with him."

"Why are you looking for him?"

"Daphne's in a lot of trouble, and I think Joey might be able to help her."

He lowered his voice. "She the one who shot her father the other night?"

"The police seem to think she did, but I'm not so sure. I'd like to ask Joey what she told him before she borrowed his car and went to her father's house, or if she saw him afterward."

"You aiming to get him in trouble, too?"

I was, but opted to shake my head. "Daphne won't tell me why she went there or much about what happened. She may have told him. I just want to talk to him for no more than ten or fifteen minutes. Do you have any idea where I can find him?"

I heard an explosive expletive behind me, indicative that the five-dollar bill had gone into Luanne's pocket.

The bartender raised his voice. "Leon, I told you not to use that kind of language when the babies are here! Now, you take your sorry self out of here and don't come back for a week. I'm writing it down on the cal-endar, so don't think you can come crawling in before then." He looked at me. "Leon fancies himself to be a pool shark. He's good, but not half as good as your friend over there. Think she'd like to play in one of our monthly tournaments? The winner gets a case of beer and a free tune-up."

"I'll ask her," I said. "What about Joey?"

"Hang on." He went along the bar, refilling mugs, fishing pickled eggs out of a gallon jar, and snapping cellophane packets of potato chips and beef jerky off metal racks. Once everyone was superficially content, he came back and put a slip of paper on the bar in front of me. "Like I said, I never heard of the guy."

I picked up the paper, nodded at him, and turned around to watch Luanne run the table while her next victim shifted from foot to foot. Once she'd finished, I motioned for her to retire her cue and leave with me.

When we were in her car, I unfolded the slip of paper. On it was written "Pot O' Gold trailer park." Directions were not included.

"Have you ever heard of it?" I asked.

"I've seen it," she said, frowning. "It's in one of the little towns around here, the sort where the dogs are safe sleeping in the middle of the road. I can't quite remember which one."

"Why were you in any of them?"

"Back when I was involved with the virile young man with the impressive biceps, we'd go on picnics. Fried chicken, potato salad, and sex under the benevolent eyes of Mother Nature. It was always his idea, of course. My idea of roughing it consists of a hotel without room service." She chewed on her lip for a moment. "I think I know where it is, but it's at least twenty miles away and it's possible Joey won't be home."

"Let's go see if we can find it," I said. "If he's not there, maybe one of the other residents can tell us something. At least I'll know where it is in case I need to go back there on my own tomorrow."

Luanne pulled out of the parking lot. "This is a fool's errand. You have no idea if he'll agree to talk to you, or even if he happens to know anything. Which he may not. From what you've heard about him, he sounds like the type to open the door with a gun in his hand. Caron will be Very Deeply Annoyed if she has to go into an orphanage. She still has scars from reading *Oliver Twist* at an impressionable age."

"Just drive—okay?"

"As madam wishes," Luanne murmured as she turned on the radio.

We arrived at the little town half an hour later. Luanne squinted at the various intersecting roads, then came to a decision and turned right at an unmarked corner. "This seems familiar," she said, "but I could be wrong. It does happen every once in a while."

I pointed at a weathered wrought iron arch spanning an entrance. "There it is. Let's drive around and see if his car is here. Do you know what a Trans Am looks like?"

"Only if it's yellow with racing stripes and has a vanity plate with the name Joey on it. If we actually spot this vehicle, what are we going to do?"

"As you said, he's probably not here, so we don't have to do anything whatsoever. If he is, I'll think of something."

"Oh, my gawd! There's a cop car behind us. With your grotesque sense of fashion, you look like one of the usual suspects. The cop no doubt thinks we're here for a drug deal. Now what?"

My mouth went dry as I imagined myself in a cell in this forsaken town, beating off rats with my belt—if I was allowed to keep it. Caron would be more than Very

Deeply Annoyed if I called and asked her to bring bail money.

"Keep driving," I said in a shaky voice, "and turn into the trailer park. We aren't breaking any laws, you know. We're merely looking for a friend of a friend. If the cop continues to follow us, don't stop. We can come back later."

"I hope we're allowed to share a cell, because I'm going to pass the time plucking out your gray hairs, one by one. After that, your eyelashes." She drove under the arch and followed a dirt road that meandered between rows of trailers that were so battered and beaten that it looked as though the park was a primary target for hailstorms. "The cop car didn't turn in after us," she said. "Now all we have to worry about is being shot."

Frayed shirts and dingy bras hung from clotheslines. Ditches alongside the road were filled with sluggish brown water that would have appalled Walter Reed. Children dressed in ill-fitting clothes played in front of some trailers; in front of others, men in undershirts sat on aluminum patio chairs, drinking beer or undisclosed beverages in paper bags. No one waved, or even bothered to look at us. The few trees were stunted and diseased.

"Can we go now?" Luanne said as she braked to allow a feral cat to dart across the road.

"Okay, this is crazy," I admitted. "Even if we saw the Trans Am—and there it is!"

"Even if we saw it, we wouldn't stop?"

"Stop! We have to think."

Luanne obediently stopped. "Let's think about picking up Chinese and going back to your apartment to make charts and maps and diagrams and time lines of everything we know thus far. This, in my humble opinion, might be a better plan than getting out of the car and approaching that trailer. If ever I saw a structure more likely to house the unindicted members of the Manson family . . ."

I stared at the trailer with the bright yellow car parked beside it. Joey had to know something, and possibly what he could tell me might help Daphne. I wasn't sure what I would tell him. I certainly did not want to consign Skyler to such an environment, should his mother be convicted of murder. If Joey wished, he would be in the strongest position to demand custody. And then Skyler, with his penetrating stares and fleeting smiles, would grow up with mangy dogs, potentially abusive adults, and very few chances. As much as I loathe the word *destiny,* this might be his.

Luanne handed me a tissue. "Okay, I'll be right behind you, Kimosabe. Don't mention the baby."

I blew my nose, then opened the car door and approached the trailer. Before I reached the door, a woman with a simian forehead, thick lips, and brassy red hair came out and pointed at me.

"If you're from the collection agency, I already told you I mailed the check on Thursday." She tossed her not insubstantial bosom, barely constrained by a halter. "What's more, the roof leaks and the toilet keeps backing up. I should be suing you!"

"I doubt that," I said. "Is Joey here?"

"You doubt that the check's in the mail or that the roof leaks? You come any closer and you sure as hell won't doubt the whole place stinks."

I gave her a steely look. "I doubt that I care about any of that, or about your threat to sue me. I shall repeat the question in case you weren't listening: Is Joey here?"

"Who wants to know?"

Luanne nudged me aside. "It's possible his probation officer does. Why don't you go inside and let him know that we're here?"

"You don't look like no probation officer."

"We're undercover," Luanne said, advancing. "If we find any illegal substances inside, both of you are likely to do hard time."

The woman made an obscene gesture, but then went back into the trailer.

"Hard time?" I whispered, trying not to snicker in a manner ill-becoming of an undercover officer of the court. "Are we going to send them up the river, or up the creek, anyway?"

Luanne pinched my arm. "This is your idea, not mine. I would much rather be eating egg rolls and watching the news, but—no, you wanted to come all the way out here in case Joey finds the need to fall to his knees and confess that he shot Anthony Armstrong and somehow framed Daphne. He will then meekly climb into the backseat so that we can deliver him to the Farberville authorities, with only a brief stop at the television station so that Jessica will have the scoop."

A young man, barrel-chested and adorned with multicolored tattoos down both arms, emerged from the trailer. His dusky face was round, almost cherubic, but his eyes were cold. "Who're you?"

"I'm a friend of Daphne," I said.

"She needs one," he said. "I saw the news. So whatta you want from me? If you're looking to raise bail money, I got about seventeen dollars."

I resisted the impulse to sputter an apology and retreat. "I know that Daphne was kicked out of her home after she told her father that she was pregnant with your baby. She lived with you for a while, then ended up homeless. After Skyler was born, she made an attempt to stay with her mother, but it was a disaster. You, she, and Skyler were living in your car a week ago. Now she's in jail for murder. What I want to know is what really happened."

"So do I," he said, then glanced over his shoulder. "Bocaraton's having a bad hair day. You wanna buy me a beer?"

Luanne glared as I gestured for him to get in the car, but said nothing and allowed him to give her directions to a painfully pink bar and grill. Once inside, we settled in a back booth and ordered a pitcher of beer from the proprietress, whose stare made it clear we'd be very sorry if we attempted a hold-up.

I waited until a pitcher and three mugs were banged down in front of us, then said to Joey, "So how did you and Daphne meet?"

"A party at some guy's house out by the lake," he said. "I don't know how or why she was there. I could tell right off she was a little princess, but she was doing everything she could to prove something to somebody. I hauled her off before she got herself in real trouble. After that, well, she and I, you know, saw each other."

"And you got her pregnant," I said flatly.

Joey filled a mug. "Yeah, I suppose. She swore she hadn't slept with anyone else. When she told me, I wasn't real excited about getting married, but I told her I'd take care of her." He took a gulp, wiped his lips, and tried to smile. "I guess I thought her parents would relent and take her in, or at least give her enough cash to get by on. Turned out her father was a tight-ass and her mother was—and still is—a friggin' nutcase."

"So you abandoned her and the baby?" Luanne said in a disturbingly conversational tone.

"I didn't dump them," Joey protested. "Once I got out, I couldn't find a job. I heard about a garage up in Joplin, and decided to go see if they'd take me on. Daphne had me drop her and Skyler off on Thurber Street, saying she'd apply for a waitressing job and then stay with her mother until I got back. I told her nobody was gonna hire a girl hauling around a baby, but she wanted to try."

I moved the pitcher out of his (and Luanne's) reach. "This was the day before her father was killed. Joplin's not that far, Joey."

"Maybe an hour and a half, something like that," he said. "After I got back, I went by her mother's house, but neither Daphne or Sheila would let me inside or even see Skyler to make sure he was okay. They were both acting crazy, saying they were going to be rich. They wouldn't tell me anything except to say I was"—he groped for the word—"superfluous. I guess I should have been flattered. I don't know what it means, but it sounds cool."

"And it is," Luanne cooed.

I gave her a hard look, then turned back to Joey. "So that's the last time you saw her? You didn't let her borrow your car the next night?"

"She doesn't even know how to drive a stick shift."

"So she never drove your car?"

"No," he said with such conviction that my hypothesis dissipated along with the foam in the beer pitcher. "I tried to teach her once, but she damn near stripped the gears."

"Does her mother have a car?"

"Yeah, a big clunker out in a garage behind her house, but I don't know if it still runs. She can walk to a grocery store and a liquor store, which is about all she ever goes to. She's a real crazy bitch."

"Who thinks she is going to be rich," I said. "Did she find a Picasso in the attic?"

"Picasso who? I knew a guy back in Mexico named Picasso, but we called him Pico. What would he be doing in her attic?"

I tried not to sigh. "Did she or Daphne say anything that might have indicated why they expected to come into some money?"

"I don't think they were planning to hold up a convenience store or a bank, if that's what you're thinking. There were some photo albums on the table when I was there. Maybe she remembered she was the daughter of the king of England or something like that. Whatever it was, Daphne was buying it. She shoved me out onto the porch and slammed the door in my face. I would have kicked down the door and slapped the shit out of her, but I'm on probation."

Luanne refilled his mug. "So how did you end up out here with that woman?"

"Bocaraton? She's okay, just kinda protective. She was at Dante's the other night, and offered to let me stay with her until I find a job."

"Two nights ago?" I asked.

"Yeah. I was really pissed at Daphne, so I went for a beer. Bocaraton got to feeling kinda . . . frisky, and we left about ten. I haven't been out of the trailer park since then, except to buy beer and pork rinds. Bocaraton keeps whining at me to go apply for a job at the poultry plant where she works, but I ain't the kind to yank guts out of dead chickens."

"I gather you didn't get the job in Joplin, then?"

His jaw tightened. "No. Soon as the jerk heard I'd

been in jail, he hustled me out and told me not to come back."

I was surprised to hear he'd found the need to share the less savory details of his personal life. "Then why did you mention it?"

Bocaraton was not the only resident of the Pot O' Gold adept at whining. "It's on account of being on probation," he said. "If my probation officer agreed to let me move out of state, I'd have to have a letter from the boss that said I really did have the job and what the pay was. If I just split, the first time I got stopped for speeding, I'd end up back in jail. Buncha crap." He chugged what beer remained in his mug. "Yeah, buncha crap."

"Aren't you interested in Skyler?" asked Luanne.

"I figure the state has him in foster care, which is a lot better than sleeping in a car. Besides, Bocaraton ain't exactly what you'd call motherly." He gave us a lopsided grin. "You girls ready for another pitcher? Maybe a little dancing?"

"Perhaps another time," I murmured, then dropped a dollar tip on the table and left with Luanne. "It sounds as though our boy has an alibi," I said as we climbed into her car. "And not much of a motive, for that matter."

Luanne pulled out in time to avoid being trapped behind a tractor inching down the middle of the road. "If he was telling the truth, he didn't have any idea that Daphne was going to the house."

"She and her mother told him they were going to be rich. Maybe they let drop something that led him to believe he could steal something of value."

"There's been no suggestion of robbery."

I rubbed my temples. "So he waited until Bocaraton passed out, which is not improbable, then went to Armstrong's house. Unaware that Daphne was upstairs, he confronted Armstrong and shot him. He fled out the back door. Daphne made the unfortunate decision to go out the front door just as Adrienne drove up."

"Or," said Luanne, always pragmatic, "he and Daphne arranged to meet there at half past eleven. While she was searching upstairs, he went into the office and ended up killing Armstrong. She realized the gun would incriminate them, so she snatched it up. Adrienne didn't see Joey because he wasn't gallant enough to pause and help Daphne down the front steps. Which means she lied to you, but stranger things have happened."

"But Randy Scarpo saw her get in a car and drive away." I mentally replayed what he'd said. "No, he saw her run by and then heard her get in a car and drive away. Joey could have made it to the car a minute or two earlier and waited for her. He could be the one who actually drove away, with Daphne as a passenger. She didn't want to incriminate him because . . . well, because he's Skyler's father and she's the most fatalistic creature I've ever met. She's docilely accepted everything that has happened to her as though she deserved it. She needs a transfusion of Caron's blood. Even Inez has more spirit."

"Or she could be telling the truth," said Luanne, "as could Joey."

I caught her wrist before she could turn on the radio. "I'm going to have to talk to Daphne again, but I don't know how to get past Peter. The dispatcher's probably still smarting from the lecture he must have given her, and will not give me a warm welcome."

"You could tell him the truth."

"I'm not prepared to do that just yet." I thought for a long moment. "I could get a wig and sunglasses, and claim I'm Daphne's mother. I'm fairly confident Sheila hasn't visited her, or will anytime soon."

"The dispatcher most likely has your photo tacked on her bulletin board. Nothing short of cosmetic surgery is going to get you past her or any of the other dispatchers."

I gazed at pastures dotted with blissful bovines. "You could get away with it, Luanne. As long as Peter and Jorgeson are out—"

"I am not about to get myself arrested for impersonating Sheila. I may be a crazy bitch, but I'm not certifiable. And why do you think Daphne would tell me anything? I don't exactly inspire confidence in grocery checkers, bank tellers, and store clerks. The missionaries won't even knock on my door anymore. My clientele is discerning but wary. Daphne's more likely to spill her secrets to Jessica than to me."

"Well, then, what are we going to do?" I demanded plaintively. "Kidnap the delightful Bocaraton and threaten to shave her underarms until she repudiates Joey's alibi? Are there any iron cots in the basement under your store? Can we pick up handcuffs at the thrift shop?"

"Bocaraton undoubtedly shaves her underarms with a switchblade and gives herself manicures with a hedge trimmer. What about talking to Adrienne?"

"She has no reason to let me in her house, much less answer any questions."

Luanne glanced at me. "I have one tiny suggestion, but you're not going to like it."

"Don't even bother to say it," I said with a groan.

CHAPTER EIGHT

The following morning after I'd fed and bathed Skyler, I called the Farberville Fitness Center and inquired about trial memberships. I listened to a rote recital of all the seemingly endless packages and options, then at last was told I could have a free two-day pass.

"Do you have day care?" I asked.

"From seven in the morning until nine at night," the girl said proudly, "and it's only four-fifty an hour. Once you're enrolled as a premium member, it's a dollar an hour. We also have special classes for mothers and toddlers, and gymnastics classes for school-aged children if you purchase the inclusive family fitness plan."

I let her prattle on for a few more minutes, then ended the conversation. As I went past the bathroom, I could hear the shower running. I could not hear what its occupant was saying, but that was just as well. She'd certainly aired her grievances at length the previous evening. I'd offered my entire arsenal of sympathetic platitudes to no avail. She'd stomped up and down the hallway so many times that the downstairs tenant must have thought we were training horses (and not the type one whispered to). I had remained firm, but I was a little bit worried about Rhonda's future well-being.

I'd changed into a T-shirt and shorts, and was putting on my less than fashionable sneakers when Caron marched into the kitchen and yanked open the refrigerator door with enough vehemence to cause the pickle jars to clink.

"Where's the orange juice?" she snapped.

"On the counter by the sink. I made some toast for you."

"Doesn't the death row inmate get to choose what he or she wants as a last meal before being subjected to a Lethal Injection of Humiliation?"

I finished tying my shoes but remained where I was. "It's not going to be that bad, dear. Your friends know you couldn't have had a baby. If someone says something snide, just say the baby belongs to my cousin, who's visiting us. Second cousin Connie from Cannes, or Helga from Helsinki. Inez is the only person at Farberville High who knows the truth."

Caron came to the doorway with a glass in one hand and a gnawed piece of toast in the other. "So you're telling me I should lie?" she said, her nostrils quivering.

"At times it's necessary. I've never blatantly lied to Peter, but I've had to omit information or misrepresent things just a tiny bit."

"God, I hope I don't turn out like you," she said as she went to her room and slammed the door.

I decided it might be wiser to let her walk to school in hopes she might burn off some of her fury before she went into the high school and a misbegotten soul said something imprudent. I put Skyler in the basket, grabbed the diaper bag, took him downstairs, then conscientiously strapped him in the car seat. Madness, I told myself as we drove toward the fitness center. I owned no sleek Spandex shorts, no terrycloth sweatbands, no designer shoes. My last attempt to participate in an aerobics class had left my internal organs begging to be put out of their collective misery.

"Skyler, my buddy," I said as I pulled into the parking lot, "I hope you'll remember this when you're a CEO of a multinational conglomerate. You owe me big time."

I carried him inside and found the desk. "I called earlier about a trial membership," I said to a girl with choppy purple hair and abnormally bright eyes.

"We are so glad to see you! I just know you're going to love it here. Why, I'd sleep here every night if they'd let me, but Randy—he's my boss—makes me leave at ten. Of course it's pretty quiet by then, but you know what I'd love to do? Run a marathon on the treadmill while listening to Hawg's Breath on my headphones. He is so phat!"

"Then he should run with you," I said. "Do you want me to fill out a form?"

"That is the most darling baby I've ever seen! Boy or girl?"

For the sake of expediency, I resisted the urge to say neither and picked up a pen. The girl crouched over Skyler and cooed at him while I tackled several pages of questions more intrusive than a medical history or a tax return. I did not see a need to answer truthfully.

When she rejoined me, she gave me a schedule of classes and offered to show me around the sprawling facility. I allowed her to escort us to the day-care room, where a middle-aged woman with less-alarming hair seemed reasonably pleased to add Skyler to the roster for what I promised would be only an hour. He could use a brief spot of socialization, I told myself with a pang of guilt as I handed the basket and diaper bag over to a stranger who could very well be a psychotic kidnapper who prowled neonatal wards, as well as day-care rooms.

I bit back the urge to demand the woman's references and allowed my purple-haired Sherpa to lead me to the weights room. After ascertaining that Adrienne was not there, I shooed her away and wandered down various hallways until I once again found the tennis courts.

Adrienne was seated on a bench, her left foot on her right knee so that she could massage her ankle. Beside her was a young woman of a similar age, putting away her racket in a canvas bag that undoubtedly murmured of money to those with keener ears than mine.

"Adrienne Armstrong?" I said as I approached them.

"Yes," she said, "I am. And you are . . ."

I held out my hand. "Claire Malloy. I wanted to tell you how sorry I was to hear about what happened to Anthony. It must be a nightmare for you. Your husband killed, and then your stepdaughter arrested."

Her eyes narrowed as she touched my hand. "Do we know each other?"

"Oh, I'm afraid not," I said with a little laugh. "Anthony was a dear old friend, although we hadn't seen each other since my husband's death so many years ago. At the time, Anthony was there for me. I don't know how I could have coped without his wise advice."

She remained leery. "Were you also friends with Sheila?"

"Sheila? Not my cup of tea, I'm afraid, although Daphne always seemed like a nice girl. You must be very concerned about her."

The second woman stood up. "Adrienne is terribly concerned about Daphne, but there's not much she can do. I'm Chantilly Durmond, Adrienne's sister."

There was a strong resemblance. Both had blond hair, vaguely feline facial features, blue eyes, and wide mouths. It was hard to tell which one was older, and I doubted either would admit as much.

I squeezed her shoulder. "Isn't it wonderful that you can be here for Adrienne during this dreadful time. I would have given anything to have a sister to shield me from the reporters and bolster my spirits in the evening. Do you live nearby?"

Adrienne handed her racket to Chantilly. "Be a dear and leave this at the pro shop to be restrung. I'll meet you in the locker room in five minutes." She waited until Chantilly left, then looked at me with decidedly cool eyes. "Anthony never mentioned you."

"This was years ago," I said dismissively, or so I hoped. "I'm so glad to find you here so that I can offer my condolences."

"But you said that you and Anthony were close friends."

"Perhaps I should have said associates. My husband dabbled in rentals around the campus." That much was true, if somewhat euphemistic.

"Oh, really," she said as she resumed massaging her ankle. "You must excuse me, ah, Ms. Malloy. I'm going to have to get ice on this before it begins to swell. It's been weak since I sprained it in high school, and I wish I'd had enough sense not to risk an injury now. I have so many things to see to, what with the funeral and all. I anticipate at least five hundred people at the church, and then eighty at the luncheon afterwards—and what a circus that's going to be. Anthony's sister and her husband are vegans. His uncle is strictly meat and potatoes. His secretary is allergic to gluten, mushrooms, and dairy

products; and his lawyer will go into anaphylactic shock
if a bee so much as looks at him cross-eyed. His grandmother, who must be a hundred and sixty years old,
starts in with her gin at nine in the morning. How am I
supposed to arrange this? It's going to be a disaster, the
talk of the town for the next ten years."

I picked up her gym bag. "Let me help you, Adrienne.
Chantilly and I will get you home and settle you in with
a nice cup of tea and an ice pack, then start making
phone calls."

"Do you really know how to do this?" she asked tear-
ily. "I could, but my husband's been murdered and the
police are crawling all over the yard. Reporters are lined
along the driveway like starving hyenas. That woman—
that dreadful woman—that beastly woman—"

"Jessica Princeton?"

"Yes!" Adrienne said as she grabbed my arm and
pulled herself to her feet with only a genteel grunt. "Can
you believe she had the audacity to show up here, my
one haven, and pretend she was a member! Sucking up
to me, trying to trick me into"—she gulped loudly—
"telling her things about my private life with Anthony.
Is there no decency in this world?"

"Outrageous," I said.

"So you will come by and help? Chantilly simply has
no idea how to put on a luncheon of this magnitude.
When your husband died, you must have gained some
experience."

"Some." I saw no reason to elaborate. After Carlton's
funeral, about a dozen of us had gone out for pizza. Out
of respect for his memory, we'd eschewed anchovies.
Carlton had always turned up his nose at anchovies, so
it was the least we could do. He wasn't fond of black

olives, either, but we were willing to make only so many concessions.

"I will be so grateful," Adrienne continued. "You are such a dear friend . . . ah?"

"Claire," I supplied. "I have a small complication, but I'll come over to your house in an hour. I hope we'll have a chance to talk further."

Chantilly joined us in the hall. "I left your racket, and they promised to have it in a week. Adrienne, you absolutely must go home and lie down. The reverend is coming by at eleven to discuss the service, and the funeral director is asking all these ludicrous questions. I cannot cope with either if I don't have a stiff Bloody Mary. When Mother and Daddy died, Aunt Beebie and the church ladies took care of everything. When my goldfish bellied up, I flushed it down the toilet. I don't know what to say to all these reporters and detectives. I don't even know what to say to the damn florist!"

Adrienne touched her sister's lips. "Claire has agreed to supervise things."

I did the best I could to keep the panic out of my eyes. "I'll be at the house shortly. Please instruct the police to allow me inside."

"You can't come now?" asked Chantilly.

Not with Skyler. "No, but I'll be there as soon as I can," I promised.

Once they'd gone outside, I fetched Skyler, paid the four-fifty minimum, and drove to Luanne's store. Ignoring a small bevy of sorority girls pawing through molted fur coats, I pulled Luanne into the back room, told her what had transpired, and said, "You've got to watch Skyler."

"Do you really think Adrienne will recognize Skyler?"

"I don't think I can explain why I have an infant in my care. What's more, I'm putting on a luncheon for a hundred people, and I won't have time to warm up bottles and change diapers."

"So how many crab rolls will you be ordering?"

"Just stay by your phone," I said with some degree of urgency. "When we get around to ordering quantities, I'll need you. Skyler, on the other hand, needs you now. His diaper was not changed at the fitness center. I think I'll cancel my membership in the morning."

"You didn't buy a membership."

"Whatever." I swept past the sorority girls and went outside, gazed sadly at the Book Depot down the street, where no lucrative financial transactions were taking place, then drove home to change into slacks and a blouse in order to fend off funeral directors, florists, caterers, and reporters. Maybe. Medieval literature was my forte, popular culture my frailty.

I was heading out the door when the phone rang. Envisioning scenes of a SWAT team on the roof of Farberville High School, I snatched up the receiver.

"Claire," Peter said.

"Name," I said, "but rank and serial number unknown, having been issued neither. Social Security number, possibly. License plate number if you want to hold while I run down and look."

"It's been two days."

"Two days since you made dire threats at the police department?"

He took a deep breath. "Is something going on? I thought we'd gotten past the situation with Leslie and were moving ahead. Now, you won't see me. Jorgeson told me that you were at Sheila Armstrong's house only hours after you promised me you'd stay out of this case.

You've been evasive, and I don't know what it means. I'm a guy, after all. Show a little compassion."

I wanted to collapse in a puddle, babble endearments, and suggest that we meet at a sleazy motel for a steamy afternoon romp. However, circumstances precluded such a thing. "I did go by Sheila's house to ask her about Daphne. She didn't say anything useful. Did Jorgeson do any better with her?"

"Not really. She acknowledged that Daphne moved in with a boyfriend last summer, but she didn't know his name and Daphne won't tell us. We'd like to talk to him, but we have no way to find him without more information."

"Surely he'll come forward," I said. "I'm sorry, but I was on the way out the door for an appointment. We can continue this later."

"An appointment?"

"Not with a neurosurgeon or anything like that. I'll call you this evening and we can talk. It's complicated, Peter."

He exhaled loudly. "Tracking down potential suspects, I assume."

"I have to go now," I said, and then replaced the receiver. I did not allow myself to consider the implications of my actions as I grabbed my purse and went out to the car. But as I drove to Anthony and Adrienne Armstrong's house, it was challenging not to remember my sanctimonious remark to Caron only an hour or so earlier. Oh, no, I never lied to Peter; I merely hedged. And her parting shot had hurt. I put it on the list of things we'd have to discuss in the future.

I found the road to the Armstrong house without problem, and parked next to a police car. I reluctantly acknowledged my name to an officer, who looked at a notebook and then waved me up the sidewalk. Chantilly opened the door before I reached the porch.

"This is so super of you," she said as she caught my hand. "I just really don't know how to do this sort of thing. I can book a European tour or a Mediterranean cruise, but I am not a party person. It's all I can do to buy a veggie platter when I have people over."

"So you're a travel agent?"

"In Atlanta. Would you like a glass of iced tea?"

"I'd love one," I said, then followed her across an artfully decorated living room cluttered with potted plants and flowers, and into a kitchen that would cause many a chef to weep. Double this, double that, an island to rival Capri, an extensive range (on which the deer and antelope actually could have played), ice maker clunking steadily, dozens of cookbooks neatly aligned on hardwood shelves above a desk with a telephone and a small television.

"Goodness," I said as Chantilly took a pitcher out of a dauntingly large refrigerator that might have contained a couple of corpses. "Does anyone cook?"

"I don't think so. Adrienne certainly doesn't. Sugar or lemon?"

"Neither, thank you. She and Anthony were married three years ago?"

Chantilly handed me a glass, then sat down on a stool. "Something like that. They took off to an exotic island without telling anybody except Daphne. Well, he must have told his secretary, and Adrienne left a message on my machine. It's not like any of us were invited, though. Strictly romantic."

"Had you met Anthony before they were married?"

"Claire!" Adrienne said as she came into the room, limping just a bit. "I am so glad you came. Why don't we all just settle down right here and get to work? Chantilly, would you be a sweetheart and get me a glass of tea? I've been on the phone with some newspaper reporter, and my mouth is so dry I could spit cottonseeds. Claire, look in that drawer in the desk and find us some paper and something to write with."

I did as instructed, reminding myself that I was on a mission of significance. Adrienne's limp was unconvincing, but I was not a physical therapist qualified to diagnose the extent of her injury—if any.

"Thank you, sweetie," she said as I produced a pad and several pens. "There's so much to be done, and I just won't be able to hold my head up if this luncheon is a disaster. Mary Margaret is going to propose my name to Junior League next fall." She paused to blot her forehead with a napkin. "Unless, of course, she thinks this business is too sordid. Poor Anthony, killed by his daughter's hand. It's like one of those tacky daytime soap operas."

I saw a tiny slit. "And you drove up just as Daphne ran out of the house. Did you wonder what had happened?"

"I was simply bewildered," Adrienne said, shaking her head. "Chantilly, I'd like just a squirt of lemon in my tea, if it's not too much trouble. I'd do it myself, but my ankle's swelling up like a ham hock."

"No trouble at all," said Chantilly. "Why don't we all go out to the conservatory so you can elevate your foot? I'll bring an ice pack."

Adrienne allowed me to cling to her arm as she hobbled through the living room and out to a glassed enclosure filled with wicker furniture and well-doctored houseplants. "I know you think I sound callous," she said as she lowered herself onto a sofa. "I'm still in shock. Anthony and I loved each other very dearly. I fell for him the day he hired me, and I guess I didn't hide it well. He was so smart, so savvy, so much more mature than the jocks I dated in high school. He knew everything about fine wines and gourmet food. I was just a kid with a degree in communications, hoping to find an office job to pay the rent. When I saw what was going to happen between the two of us, I should have quit and left town. But I didn't, obviously. Do you think I'm a terrible person?"

"He *was* married," I pointed out quietly.

"And miserable. His wife drank to excess, communicated with spirits, ran around the property stark naked, and had been arrested for shoplifting the week before Anthony hired me. He said they'd had separate bedrooms for ten years. It wasn't much of a marriage."

"What about Daphne?"

"Anthony really believed that she and I could be friends and that I could steer her in the right directions. Her mother had neglected her. Even before Anthony filed for divorce, I tried everything to convince Daphne to trust me."

"Daphne's a disaster," Chantilly said as she came onto the porch with a pitcher of iced tea and an ice pack. "If you step back, she's not all that unattractive. With a decent haircut, makeup, clothes from someplace other than a Dumpster, she might not look like something no respectable cat would drag in. I suppose if I'd been sent to that puritanical academy I'd slink around and whine, too."

"And get yourself pregnant?" added Adrienne. "If I'd had any idea she was sexually active, I would have hauled her off to a gynecologist."

I pulled over an ottoman and eased Adrienne's foot

onto it. "Did you and Anthony ever meet Joey?"

"Was that his name?" she said, wincing as Chantilly settled the ice pack on her ankle. "I don't think I even heard that much. When Daphne and Anthony had the blowup, I retreated to the bedroom and stayed there until he came upstairs. He was so angry that I didn't dare ask him what had occurred until the next morning. He felt betrayed by her irresponsible actions. Even in my role as the wicked stepmother, I did, too. If she had only come to me instead of her father, I could have helped."

Chantilly put the pad and pens on the glass-topped table in front of the sofa. "I don't think we can serve peanut butter and jelly sandwiches tomorrow."

Adrienne smiled wanly. "No, I suppose not. Claire, if you don't mind too dreadfully, would you please call the caterer, run through the menu, and remind him that we'll need ten tables and eighty chairs to be set up in the backyard tomorrow morning by nine o'clock? Table-cloths, linens, utensils, glassware, and so forth. Tell the florists we prefer centerpieces to those dreary arrange-ments. Randy Scarpo has agreed to bartend, but he'll need the necessary paraphernalia. The liquor store will deliver, but they must absolutely be here by ten and not one minute later. We'll need plenty of ice, as well as limes, lemons, olives, and all that sort of thing."

"Sounds like we're set then," Chantilly said. "The reverend should be here in an hour. Why don't you rest?"

I trailed her back to the kitchen. "Do you have the names and numbers of all these people I'm supposed to call?"

"They're in here." She gave me a leather-bound ad-dress book. "Adrienne's already made the arrangements, but she doesn't quite trust them—or anyone else these days. She cried all night after we found Anthony's body. I finally had to force her to take a sedative."

"You were with her?"

Chantilly nodded. "I came last week to stay for a few days. We were supposed to meet at this fabulous resort in Cancún, but she decided at the last minute not to leave Anthony on his own. He could get so caught up in his business affairs that he'd forget to eat without her around to nag him. She was devoted to him." Her voice dropped. "I've always wondered if he was kind of a father figure. Our parents died while we were in elementary school."

"And the night you two came home and saw Daphne . . ."

"Adrienne insisted that we catch a late aerobics class at the fitness center. Afterwards, we stopped at a Mexican restaurant and had margaritas. When the waiter started mopping the floor under our feet, we figured out that it was time to leave. Even though she left a ten-dollar tip, the manager positively glowered at us. It wasn't even midnight, if you can believe it. Clubs in Atlanta stay open until two. This town is so provincial."

"That it is." I began to flip through the notebook. "Do we need eight tables with ten chairs each, or ten tables with eight chairs each?"

"I don't think it matters. If you don't mind, I'm going to dash upstairs and take a shower. The telephone's been ringing off the wall. Just keep a list of everyone who calls to offer condolences. If a delivery boy shows up with a plant or arrangement, stick it in the dining room and jot down the name on the card. Tell anyone who shows up with some gawd-awful casserole that Adrienne's resting and can't see visitors." She surprised me with a quick kiss on the cheek. "You are such a wonderful friend, Claire."

What I was, I told myself as Chantilly left the kitchen, was such a wonderful hypocrite, even worse—I gulped—than that Princess of Facetiousness, Jessica Princeton. Unfortunately, it did seem that Adrienne and Chantilly had alibis for the time of the shooting. Daphne had said that she found the body, then raced outside as their car came up the driveway. The surly staff at the Mexican restaurant would be able to supply a fairly precise time for their departure, which Peter or Jorgeson would have already confirmed. The medical examiner would have been able to rule out a much earlier time of death.

I looked at the list of calls to be made. Dealing with the caterer was too daunting, so I opted for the liquor store. Adrienne's name was enough to give me quick access to the manager, who seemed to know exactly what was expected. I then called the three florists listed and requested centerpieces rather than funereal displays. Although I could see their eyes rolling, all acquiesced. I had a feeling we might be able to grace more than eight (or ten) tables.

I was trying to find the nerve to tackle the caterer, one Jacque Chambrun, when the doorbell chimed. Most likely the reverend, I assured myself as I went to answer the door. He could be ushered to the conservatory. Well-meaning friends would require more tact. If Mary Margaret had proposed me for Junior League and I'd gone to their boot camp, I might have felt more confident. I was well out of this league.

I pasted on a sad smile and opened the door. On the porch stood Assistant Professor Finnigan Baybergen, tweedy hat in hand.

"You?" he said, stepping back. "What are you doing here?"

"Same question. You go first."

"I came by to offer my condolences."

"I came by to call the caterer," I said. "I thought Anthony Armstrong was your avowed enemy, the despoiler of the forests, the ruination of the quasi-bucolic ambience of Farberville."

Finnigan regarded me without much warmth. "I would like to speak to Mrs. Armstrong and assure her that the Farberville Green Party is appalled by this senseless act. Violence is in violation of our basic tenets."

"Miss Parchester has a gun."

"Only to protect herself. We condemn all acts of aggression that do not infringe on our civil liberties."

"Don't start reciting the Constitution," I warned him as I stepped aside. "Adrienne is resting. Why don't you come into the kitchen and have some iced tea? Your face is flushed."

"This isn't easy for me," he said. "Armstrong and I were avowed enemies, as you suggested. I've been informed that the development will continue, despite any complications of probate. It seems Mrs. Armstrong is a full partner in Oakland Heights, Phase Two."

"Did you come to offer condolences or to try to persuade her to call off the project?" I said as we went into the kitchen. "Which is it?"

He sat down on a stool. "Both, I guess. Today is Miss Parchester's fifth day on the platform. We have been able to get necessities to her, but none of us can afford to keep getting arrested. Bail is one hundred dollars for the second offense, and five hundred for the third."

"Is there anything critical that she needs?"

"By tomorrow she'll be running low on food and water."

I poured him a glass of tea. "Bribe Howie to look the other way. That's what I've been doing."

Finnigan gave me an embarrassed look. "Howie's not fond of me. After our conversation three days ago, I realized I had to get the key to Miss Parchester. He objected, and I'm afraid I took a swing at him. I'm not very good at that sort of thing, as you may have guessed, but I managed to connect with the tip of his nose. He pushed me hard enough to send me sprawling in a thicket. If Mr. Constantine hadn't been there to argue with the police officers, I might have been charged with assault."

"Oh, dear," I said, trying not to giggle as I envisioned the bout of playground bluster. "But you did get the key to her?"

"Yes, and was arrested shortly thereafter." He took a swallow of tea. "Maybe we should talk her into coming down. I don't want to be responsible for endangering her health."

I did not point out that it was a bit late to be locking the barn door. "I saw her yesterday, and the only thing she needed was lemons for her tea. I'll go by later and check on her."

"If you're as concerned about Miss Parchester as you've been professing for the last four days, what are you doing here? Anthony Armstrong deserves full responsibility for this situation. If he hadn't cozied up to the planning commissioners, inviting them to watch football games from his skybox and arranging deep-sea fishing trips in Baja, do you honestly believe he would have gotten the variances? That was how he operated."

"That was not how he operated!" said Adrienne as

she came into the kitchen. "Anthony never invited anyone who was not a close personal friend. Business was
never discussed. Should we have lived in a social cocoon
on the off chance we might run into a city official? This
is a small town, Mr. Baybergen. You and your kind may
be content to sit around and whine about petty politics,
but Anthony and I preferred a more sophisticated life-
style." She shot me an icy look. "I have no idea why
Claire allowed you in my house, but I would like you
to leave. I am mourning the loss of my husband, and I
will not tolerate insinuations about his character."

He stood up. "I just wanted to offer the Green Party's
condolences, Mrs. Armstrong, and assure you that we
had nothing to do with this."

"Of course you didn't," she said. "Anthony's daughter shot him. I really would appreciate it if you'd leave
now. Claire will show you out." She turned her back on
us and opened one of the refrigerator doors.

Finnigan and I retreated to the front door. I was going
to suggest we have a few words on the porch, but it
occurred to me that the police officer at the end of the
walk might mention it to Peter.

"How did you get past the officer outside?" I asked
him. "I have a feeling your name's not on the list."

"Hardly. I told the young man that it was an oversight
but I was willing to accept an apology. He stammered
something and waved me by."

I wondered if I could have utilized his approach and
saved myself a trip to the fitness center. At least I hadn't
been dragged into an aerobics class or dunked in a hot
tub. "I'd like to ask you something, Professor Baybergen," I began tentatively. "Someone told me that your
sister was living in Oakland Heights last year and was
injured in the fire. Has she recovered?"

He stared at me. "Who told you that and why is it any of your concern?"

I ignored the first half of his question and said, "I've always been afraid of fire. As a child, I was unable to toast marshmallows and was expelled from my Girl Scout troop. She must have been terrorized."

"Traumatized is a more apt description. She awoke to discover her bedroom was filled with smoke. She had to stumble downstairs in the dark. The front door lock was jammed, so she had to find her way out the back. The smoke was so thick that she collapsed on the patio and had to be transported by ambulance to the emergency room. Damage to her lungs requires her to utilize an oxygen tank most of the time."

"Claire!" called Adrienne. "Did you confirm my hair appointment?"

Although I wanted to continue talking to Baybergen, I opened the door for him. "I'm really sorry about your sister. I hope she does better."

"I'm really sorry about Armstrong, but I hope he rots in hell," he said, mimicking my tone of voice, then went across the porch and down the steps.

I returned to the kitchen and found Adrienne arranging a plate of fruit and cheese. "I wasn't aware of the hair appointment," I said. "Shall I call now?"

"That would be so sweet, but could you please carry this out to the conservatory first? Oh, and a pitcher of fresh tea and a glass for the minister. Perhaps I ought to offer him something more substantial, like sandwiches. There's a package of smoked salmon on the bottom shelf in the refrigerator, and cucumbers in one of the drawers. Please cut the sandwiches in quarters and trim the crusts, and be sure to cover them with a damp towel so they won't be too dry."

"Certainly," I said as she limped out of the room. The minister wasn't scheduled to appear for an hour, however, and I did not want to be accountable if the sandwiches were the slightest bit stale. I perched on a stool and sipped tea, trying to determine if there was anything more to be learned from Adrienne, Chantilly, or even from the house itself. But first things first, I told myself as I found the leather address book and flipped through it until I chanced upon the caterer. Said gentleman sounded more like Brooklyn than Breton, but he decidedly knew his business and was offended when I dared to mention crab rolls. The hairdresser's receptionist confirmed the three o'clock appointment. Between the calls, the telephone rang several times with well-wishers asking if there was anything they might do. Two floral arrangements arrived and were carried mutely to the dining room, where a botanical garden was taking shape. A woman came to the front door with a platter of cookies from, as she told me at length, the distressed office staffers. Two minutes later, a third delivery boy from a florist arrived with a four-foot-high banana tree. I wearily pointed at the dining room.

I peeked at Adrienne, who appeared to be dozing, then glanced at the staircase to the second floor. Chantilly was up there somewhere, drying her hair and applying makeup. Daphne had returned here the night of the murder, but I doubted that she had crept in to snatch a pair of pajamas or a bottle of conditioner. Could whatever she and her mother had told Joey might make them rich be just above my head?

I decided to find out.

CHAPTER NINE

I took the receiver off the hook, then cautiously went upstairs. No step dared to squeak in Anthony Armstrong's custom-built house, but I had no idea where Chantilly might be. The second problem was that I had no idea what I was looking for or even which of the rooms beyond closed doors might have been Daphne's before she had been tossed out onto the streets. It did not seem likely that she had squirreled away a chest containing the crown jewels or an Egyptian sarcophagus that would cause hearts to pound wildly at the British Museum. Scrapbooks and bald Barbie dolls seemed more probable.

The room nearest the top of the stairs was clearly the master bedroom, replete with a king-size bed, puffy satin bedspread, window treatments, inset shelves with small pieces of pottery artfully lighted, an afghan ever so casually draped on an easy chair that no one would be so presumptuous as to sit in, and depictions on the walls of Venetian canals and Tuscan landscapes. Even the silk nightgown on the bed looked as if it had been placed for effect.

Resisting an admittedly foolish impulse to turn down the bedspread and leave a chocolate on the pillow, I roamed onward. The room across the hall appeared to be Chantilly's; clothes were heaped on all available surfaces and I could hear a hair dryer in what I supposed was a bathroom. I closed the door and tried the next, which appeared to be an uninspired but serviceable guest room. I was getting uneasy, in that someone could ring the doorbell at any moment. My absence would be conspicuous. Adrienne's ankle problem had already shifted from left to right more than once, and I knew she would be able to come looking for me. While I was looking for whatever. Wherever.

The last door on the left opened onto a room that only a teenager could love. Posters of leering rock musicians decorated all four walls, while angelic teddy bears grinned from the canopied bed. A television, VCR, and elaborate stereo system were ensconced in a customized cabinet with shelves for many dozens of CDs and cassettes. A computer and printer were collecting dust on a desk in one corner. The top of the dresser was bereft of anything more than a small lamp and a glass vase with silk flowers that matched the prissy floral print of the wallpaper. I went into the room and looked in a closet filled with pleated skirts, blazers (school uniforms, I cleverly deduced), and modest dresses. Pairs of sensible shoes were aligned on the floor. Another door led to a bathroom with a stall shower. Pastel towels were draped over rods. No makeup or hair paraphernalia sullied the cabinet surface. The bar of soap, no doubt scented, awaited inaugural use.

Adrienne's doing, I thought as I idly opened a drawer, definitely not Sheila's. Sheila would have preferred gaudy beach towels and a futon in the middle of the bedroom, ringed by candles. I continued poking around, but found nothing that might be redeemable at the bank.

I was in the hallway when the doorbell rang. I scurried downstairs, hoping to beat out Adrienne. I was not surprised to see she was still in the conservatory, both feet on the stool, her head back, arms draped gracefully on throw pillows, eyes closed. A classic vignette of a mourning widow, I thought rather sourly as I opened the front door and eyed an elderly man with a bulbous nose, thin white hair, and an ill-fitting suit.

"Yes?" I said, trying to catch my breath.

"I am here to see Mrs. Armstrong," he said. "We have an appointment."

"You must be Reverend Simpleton," Chantilly chirped from behind me. "Do come in, you darling man. Adrienne's expecting you." She nudged me aside and took his arm. "She's holding up well, considering the circumstances. I just feel blessed to be able to be here to help her. Please let me show you the way. Claire, be a dear and see to the refreshments."

I waited until they went past me, then closed the door and reminded myself that I was in the presence of clergy. Acerbic comments would be inappropriate, especially from the help—and in my case, indentured.

In the kitchen, I replaced the receiver, started the kettle to make fresh tea, and rooted through the refrigerator until I found the smoked salmon et al. Ten minutes later I took the pitcher and a platter of sandwiches to the conservatory and smiled apologetically as the three of them looked up at me as if I'd barged into a top-secret Pentagon briefing. No wonder kitchen maids in crime fiction kept bumping off their employers, I thought as I tiptoed out of the room.

I decided to stay until the session in the conservatory

was concluded, then pass the mantle to Chantilly. A few more visitors showed up over the next hour; all retreated gracefully (or gratefully) when I informed them with undue gravity that Adrienne was in consultation with the minister, whose name I'd already forgotten. Two more floral arrangements were delivered, both potential centerpieces if everyone at the table was seven feet tall.

During a lull, I crept out of the kitchen and went searching for Anthony's office. I knew from what Daphne had told me that it was on the first floor. I found it down a hallway past the bottom of the staircase. No officious yellow tape forbade me from entering the room, although I suspected the Farberville CID would be less than pleased that I was violating the sanctity of the crime scene. As I stood in the doorway, I saw a dark stain on the oriental rug in front of the desk. I was almost surprised Adrienne had not instructed me to arrange to have the rug steam-cleaned before the funeral because of some relative's delicate constitution. Perhaps the decorator was scheduled to show up in the morning with a replacement.

The floor-to-ceiling bookshelves were filled with sets of expensively bound classics chosen more for their complementary hues than their content. On the wall near two leather chairs and an antique globe was a gun case. Behind the glass cabinet doors were a few handguns and hunting rifles. The locks showed no signs of tampering. If Daphne had indeed fired a gun, she had not taken it from the case. She could have taken one from Joey—or stolen it from him, I amended. But she'd claimed to have been upstairs when her father was shot, and I desperately wanted to believe her.

Even though I knew the police had already searched every centimeter of the room, I went behind the desk

and began to ease open drawers. The quantity of paperwork was impressive. Among manila folders dedicated
to projects past and future were copies of city ordinances
for everything from utilities to storm drains, and, of
course, tree preservation. The pens in the middle drawer
were not plastic and could not be purchased at a discount
office supply store. A half-empty roll of heartburn mints
indicated Anthony was not always as self-assured as
he'd presented himself to be in front of the camera. At
the back of the drawer I found a file of Daphne's progress reports from the Disciples Academy. I popped a
mint in my mouth as I skimmed through them. Said
progress had been minimal, if not minuscule, and she'd
been close to expulsion at the close of the last spring
semester. Which conceivably had been her goal—which
she'd achieved by conceiving, inadvertently or otherwise.

I was pawing through another drawer when I heard
the telephone ring in the kitchen. I hastily replaced
everything and hurried out of the room, feeling like a
game show contestant trying to beat the clock. Alas, I
did not. Chantilly was already in the kitchen, receiver to
her ear, chattering cheerfully about the comparative vir-
tues of Farberville's hotels (both of them) and motels
(many, mostly squalid). When she spotted me, she asked
the caller to wait for a moment, then covered the mouth-
piece with her hand and said, "That man is wolfing down
sandwiches as if anticipating the advent of Lent in the
morning. Will you please make another platter and take
it to the conservatory? Oh, and slice the lemon pound
cake in the refrigerator and take that, too. There are
plates and silverware somewhere. You'll have to look."

She resumed talking while I mutely followed orders,
then took the sandwiches and cake to the conservatory,

where the minister and Adrienne were regarding each other with mulish expressions. The tension between them would have been harder to slice than the pound cake.

"Claire," Adrienne said, managing a smile, "do sit down. We're having a minor disagreement about the service. As I'm sure you remember, Anthony disliked pomp. He appreciated simple things, like watching a sunset from the patio or doing the crossword puzzle on a lazy Sunday afternoon. He loved to make popcorn and watch John Wayne movies. I had to bully him into attending the symphony series, and he positively fidgeted the entire time. Don't you agree that he would have preferred only a few of his favorite hymns, a eulogy, and a brief graveside ceremony?"

Simpleton stuffed a sandwich in his mouth, swallowed, and said, "I do think it's important for me to share some philosophical observations and insights into the ephemerality of life and the specter of everlasting bliss. Many relatives and close friends find comfort in the spiritual message I offer them."

"There's a fifty percent chance of thunderstorms tomorrow afternoon," Adrienne said as if she wanted to cram a slice of lemon pound cake up his nose. "Hello? I have eighty people coming after the service."

"A sermon offers solace," he intoned, keeping an eye on her in case she made any sudden moves.

I backed away for the same reason. "Adrienne, I wish I could stay, but I have obligations. I've reconfirmed all of the arrangements, including your hair appointment this afternoon."

She sniffled into a tissue. "You have been so wonderful to do all this, Claire. Can you be here by ten tomorrow to supervise everything? I'll be at the church and then at the cemetery"—she glared at the reverend—"until shortly before noon. Jacque is very, very good, but he's been known to fly off the handle if so much as a single sprig of parsley is limp. I don't know what he'll do should the skies turn cloudy."

Her spiritual adviser picked up another sandwich. "Anthony was a parishioner for more than thirty years, Adrienne. Although he did not attend services on a weekly basis, he was in his own way devout, and always generous with our parish projects. We cannot rush through this because of—"

I left the room and returned to the kitchen to collect my purse. Chantilly was seated on a stool, drinking what appeared to be a Bloody Mary with more vodka than tomato juice. She most likely would have gotten along quite well with Sheila, aka the first Mrs. Anthony Armstrong. It was difficult to judge how well she got along with the second one.

"Tired?" I said as I sat down beside her.

"It's driving me, like, totally crazy. I mean, I feel sorry for Adrienne and all, but she acts like she's the only one who's inconvenienced by this. I had to beg to take off the rest of this week. Justine, this python at my office, is probably putting the squeeze on all my regular clients—and she doesn't have a clue about first-class cabins. She probably thinks a porthole is a wine bucket."

"Daphne's in jail," I said. "That's inconvenient, too."

"Then she shouldn't have killed him."

"I suppose not." I waited for a moment as she sucked pensively on a celery stalk. "When you and Adrienne drove up that night, did you see or hear anything that made you wonder if someone else was here? A shadow, for instance, or footsteps moving in a different direction?"

Chantilly drained the glass. "The back door was open, but Daphne must have left it that way when she came inside."

"Then why would she run out the front door?"

"Because she panicked," she said as she replenished her drink. "How long are we to have the pleasure of Reverend Simpleton's company? Anthony's relatives will be descending like a tribe of baboons this afternoon. I really need to check in with my office before Justine filches all of my big accounts. What's more, I have nothing to wear tomorrow. I have a pink sundress, but it's strapless. Do you think I can get away with it if I wrap a dark scarf over my shoulders?"

I assured her that it would blend in well with customary dress at funerals in Farberville, in that I didn't care. Adrienne could deal with the aftermath at the country club, fitness center, and Junior League evaluation. I put away the remainder of the salmon and cucumbers, wiped off the cutting board, and after reminding her of Adrienne's hair appointment, hightailed it to my car.

Jorgeson stood beside it, shaking his head. "Ms. Malloy," he said, "once again we meet. Is there no place on this planet of ours where I might be confident of not seeing you?"

I considered his question. "You could be fairly confident at any football game, heavy metal concert, wrestling match, or proctologist's office. Other than that, Jorgeson, I don't know. What are you doing here?"

"Investigating a murder. And you?"

"Still no weapon?" I said as I leaned against the hood of my car. "I was thinking about that, Jorgeson. The weapon did not come from the gun case in the office. Where do you think she got it? It's a stretch to think her mother had one."

Jorgeson tugged on his chin. "We don't know as of yet, Ms. Malloy. Sheila Armstrong doesn't have a license for a handgun, but she's not the type to waste time with bureaucratic hurdles. Mr. Armstrong's weapons are accounted for. He kept a thirty-eight-caliber in a desk drawer. The lab determined that it has not been fired recently. We're still trying to find the boyfriend." He gazed over my head at the trees along the top of the hill. "The lieutenant seems to think you might be able to help us there."

"Me?" I said indignantly. "Why would *I* know anything?"

"He just said something to that effect, Ms. Malloy. I'm not a mind-reader. You, on the other hand, are doing a fine job of anticipating my moves. You could save me some time if you'd tell me what's on my agenda."

"When shall we two meet again? I have no idea, Jorgeson. I came by this morning to offer my condolences to Adrienne Armstrong. She and some minister are in the conservatory, debating the funeral service. He does not appreciate the need for expediency due to the weather forecast. She will be delighted if you interrupt them, and will offer you salmon-and-cucumber sandwiches, as well as iced tea and lemon pound cake. Bloody Marys are available in the kitchen."

"When you searched his office, did you discover anything we might have overlooked?"

I didn't bother to sputter a denial. "No, but I wasn't really looking for anything. Anthony was probably sitting at his desk when someone came into the office. He rose and came into the middle of the room. Then, well, the conversation was terminated. Did Chantilly tell you that the back door was open?"

"Meaning what, Ms. Malloy?"

"I don't know, Jorgeson," I admitted as I got into my car. I turned around and drove back to the road, but instead of fetching Skyler and opening the Book Depot, I pulled into the parking lot of Oakland Heights. Most of the spaces were unoccupied. I parked by the sign warning me not to trespass and waited for Howie to come thundering out from behind the shed.

When he failed to appear, I approached the platform. "Miss Parchester?"

"Good morning, Claire," she said as she peered down at me. "How are you today? Isn't the weather lovely?"

"Oh, yes. Where's Howie?"

"Do you promise that this will remain strictly between the two of us? Despite his inclination to bluster, he is a nice boy. I would be conscience-stricken if I were to cause him problems."

"Cross my heart, Miss Parchester. Where is he?"

"I sent him to do a little shopping for me. Is that all you wanted to know?"

I sat down where I could see her. "No, I would like to know about what you saw and heard the night of the murder. Three nights ago, around midnight."

"Nothing out of the ordinary, I'm afraid. I listened to a symphony on the radio. Professor Baybergen called at ten to ask if I was all right. I assured him that I was, then wiggled deeper into the sleeping bag. I really do recommend fresh air for a good night's sleep. When I return home, I shall make a point of opening all my bedroom windows before retiring."

"An excellent idea," I said. "On that night, Daphne parked a car in the lot over there and walked past the tree at eleven-thirty or thereabouts. Did either you or Howie see her then?"

"Howie had left for the night. He originally believed

he could sleep on a chair in the shed, but he has a certain condition—a delicate one that he shared with me amidst much stammering—that precluded it. I instructed him to go home, which he did. I myself saw no one in the immediate area."

"Were you awake?"

"Yes, I was," she said brusquely. "Howie may well return shortly. You'd best be on your way, Claire."

I looked up at her, surprised by her reaction. "Did you see or hear Daphne come back by here half an hour later? She's admitted as much, and she was seen in the parking lot."

"I did not see her, nor did I hear her." Her face vanished, although more abruptly than that of the Cheshire cat. What's more, she hadn't been smiling.

But Daphne had come by the tree, I thought as I stood up and brushed off my derriere. Could Miss Parchester have been tippling the elderberry wine to the extent that she'd been so soundly asleep that she'd failed to hear Daphne run by?

"Miss Parchester," I said, "please talk to me."

"I've already answered your questions. Run along before Howie arrests you. Louis Ferncliff says they are quite rude at the police station, and he was obliged to wait more than two hours before he was permitted to leave. Eliza Peterson threatened a hunger strike after three hours in a cell with a young woman of questionable virtue and an obvious lack of temperance."

I went to my car, then hesitated. Randy Scarpo had told the police that he saw Daphne, but he could not have seen more than a glimpse of a girl outside his condo. I forced myself to knock on his front door, aware that he was likely to be at the campus and I would find myself facing Jillian, who did not consider me her best friend.

He opened the door. "Ms. Malloy, I was just getting ready to go to class. Are you my designated driver?"

"I understand you'll be bartending at the Armstrong home tomorrow. Adrienne asked me to confirm everything."

"Yeah." He came out to the sidewalk. "Twenty bucks an hour, and I'm happy to help her out. Ms. Armstrong's a real go-getter at the center. Tae Bo, aerobics, weights, racquetball, tennis—you name it, she does it."

"Obsessively?"

"No, nothing like that. She just feels like she has to stay fit for the sake of her marriage. A lot of the ladies spend hours at the center. I have to run them off at ten o'clock every night."

"But you stay until midnight," Jillian said from the doorway.

Randy pushed back his hair. "Yes, I do. I do maintenance, work out, and study in peace and quiet. No one bitches at me. No one complains. No one spits up on my shoulder. I sit at the desk and grade papers, do my own assignments, and dread the time when I have to come back here. The fitness center smells like sweat, but this place stinks of urine and sour milk."

I truly did not want to be in the middle of this. "So you'll be there by eleven o'clock to slice limes?"

"For twenty bucks an hour, I'll start peeling olives at dawn," he said.

"Am I invited?" asked Jillian in a noticeably tight voice.

"I believe it's mostly for close friends and relatives," I said as I edged toward my car. "If you'd like to come— you and Connor, that is—you'll be welcome. You might find it boring, though. Since I hardly know anyone, I won't be able to introduce you, but the food should be excellent. The caterer's very confident."

Randy looked back at her. "Don't be ridiculous."

"Why not?" she said, then stepped inside and slammed the door.

I halted as I bumped against my car. "I'd like to ask you something, Randy. Was there any gossip about Adrienne at the fitness center?"

"Like having an affair? You have to remember that I'm just the guy who replenishes the toilet paper and makes sure the towels are stacked in the locker rooms. These people wouldn't recognize me in the grocery store. Why would they share gossip with me?"

"Does she have regular partners for racquetball and tennis?"

He shrugged. "Occasionally I've reserved court time for her. She plays with different people, mostly women. She doesn't much like playing against men because they have a better shot at beating her. She and her husband used to play mixed doubles in the evening, but he quit sometime last year. These days she plays with women who're married to lawyers, bankers, and doctors. Once in a while she plays with this guy who used to be the tennis coach at Farber College. He's in his eighties."

"Why did she ask you to bartend?"

"A couple of days ago she stopped at the desk, possibly because the police told her that I saw Daphne that night. We talked for a few minutes, then she said that I could make a hundred dollars or so by helping her out tomorrow afternoon. I get minimum wage at the fitness center."

I leapt on a long shot. "Are you sure you got a good look at the girl in the parking lot?"

Randy grimaced. "I wish I could say I hadn't, but Ms. Armstrong dragged her stepdaughter to aerobics classes several times. I recognized her. She ran across the parking lot, jumped in a car, and drove away. The police even asked me to identify her in a lineup yesterday. I told them the truth."

"And you didn't see the car?"

"Sorry," he said. "I think I'd better go inside now."

I nodded, and then sat in my car for a long while, trying to sort through recent information. Adrienne and Chantilly, armed with iron-clad alibis, had seen Daphne stumble out of the house. Randy had seen her get into a car. Howie had not been present. Miss Parchester had neither seen nor heard Daphne's hesitant approach or frantic retreat, which puzzled me.

But I had a month-old baby awaiting my tender mercies, as well as a much older one who might be holding the entirety of Farberville High School hostage as she barked demands on the intercom.

I parked in front of Secondhand Rose and went inside. Behind the counter, Skyler was asleep in his basket, his forehead puckered as he faced illusionary foes. Luanne came out of the back room. "It's about time," she said, her expression grim. "Peter called half an hour ago, looking for you. He did not sound happy when I told him I didn't know where you were. I suppose I could have told him where you said were going, but hearsay is unreliable."

"That's peculiar, since I talked to him earlier this morning. Did he say why he was looking for me?"

"I did my best, but he was in a foul mood. What did you and he have to say?"

"Nothing that should have set him off," I said, my brow as puckered as Skyler's, my foes somewhat less illusionary. I told her what had transpired since I dropped off Skyler. "Yes, Jorgeson was there when I came out of the house, but he failed to raise a ruckus. He and Peter both know I'm on the prowl. I wonder what's going on."

Luanne glanced at her watch. "It's nearly noon. Maybe Jessica can shed some light on this."

"Maybe," I said, "but I am not going to take any responsibility for gas station holdups, tornadoes, health department violations, check kiting—"

She steered me into the back room. "Peter's just annoyed because you keep stalling. Men's egos are like ostrich eggs—large and brittle. I'll keep Skyler tonight if you want to kiss up to Robo Cop."

"Let's just watch the news."

She turned on the portable TV she kept on her desk. I was prepared for a segment on some academic program recently introduced on the campus, or a scandal at one of the area county sheriffs' departments. Troublesome findings after an audit in a city department. A human interest feature about a chimpanzee that delivered Meals on Wheels and read to the visually impaired. Or a bomb threat at the high school.

"This is Jessica Princeton," said a familiar voice, "live from the second floor of the county courthouse. As you can see from all the activity behind me, there's a crisis and law enforcement agents are everywhere. I'm standing in front of Judge Derby Nott's courtroom, where earlier this morning several inmates from the police department were transported for arraignment. Sources tell KFAR that four men and two women were scheduled to appear before Judge Nott between ten and eleven. Two of the men have been charged with operating a meth lab in a warehouse at the edge of Springville, one with possession of stolen property, and one with drunk and disorderly conduct. One of the women is charged with spousal harassment. The other, daughter of slain developer Anthony Armstrong, faces a charge of murder in the first degree."

"Oh, dear," I said, clutching Luanne's arm.

"We don't have to watch."

"I'm afraid we do."

Jessica stepped back as a uniformed officer with a German shepherd swept past her. "Please bear with us. We were allowed in the courthouse only after we swore to stay out of the way as the investigation intensifies. It's hard to know exactly what happened earlier in this very hallway where I'm standing. An employee of the county clerk's office, who spoke to us only with a promise of anonymity, said that approximately an hour ago the prisoners arrived in a van and were brought up here in shackles, as is the custom. They were seated on the bench behind me. Shortly thereafter, Daphne Armstrong complained of stomach cramps and was allowed to use the restroom. A matron was waiting outside when the fire alarm went off, as did the sprinklers in the ceiling. All of the employees in the building attempted an orderly evacuation, but the main staircase has been roped off while the rails are being refinished. Several people claimed they smelled smoke coming from the ventilation ducts. Personnel from the fire department arrived in a matter of minutes, causing a traffic jam on the secondary staircase. Two lawyers were trapped in an elevator between floors and pushed that red button we've all looked at more than once." She gave us a pinched scowl meant to remind us that we'd best not indulge our curiosity. "In the ensuing confusion, Daphne Armstrong slipped away. Police are searching not only the building but also nearby parking lots, businesses, and residential neighborhoods. She was last seen wearing rubber sandals and an orange jumpsuit with the initials F.P.D. on the back. She is eighteen years of age, approximately five foot seven, one hundred and ten pounds, and has long brown hair. The police are asking for your cooperation." Jessica looked as though she had more breathtaking events to describe, but a cold and uncaring producer in the news studio cut her off for an update on a junior high science teacher who currently was being presented with a plaque at a Chamber of Commerce luncheon across town.

"I guess Peter didn't call to invite me on a picnic," I said.

Luanne turned off the TV. "You didn't have anything to do with this, did you?"

"Jorgeson saw me come out of Adrienne's house less than forty-five minutes ago. I spoke with Miss Parchester, and then with Randy and Jillian. There is no way I could have been inside the courthouse when all hell broke loose."

"Someone was."

"Well, obviously all sorts of people were, including clerks, judges, bailiffs, lawyers, police officers, and civilians renewing car tags. Monty Python's Flying Circus could have been rehearsing on the third floor. The Farberville Green Party could have been rescuing lichens in the basement. I most definitely was not there. Not even Peter can accuse me of having anything to do with this."

"Then you believe it was just one of those crazy coincidences? Daphne becomes ill and is in the restroom at the very moment the fire alarm goes off? Wake up, Claire. This is Farberville, not Hollywood."

"Point well taken," I said as I went into the front room to make sure Skyler had not been disturbed by my sputters. "Someone must have given Daphne precise instructions. She's not a model of self-motivation or ingenuity. I find it hard to see her mother behind this, though. And Joey didn't bother to ask how she was. Why would he risk violating probation?"

"Especially when he has the charming Bocaraton and bliss in the Pot O' Gold," Luanne said with a wry smile. "There is a certain justice in this universe, you know. He may end up plucking chickens for years to come. Three toddlers in diapers, two in-laws with beer bellies, and one yellow Trans Am on concrete blocks next to the trailer."

I refused to hum a few bars. "We are short a player. This was definitely planned, and Daphne was told what to do. But by whom? Not by Adrienne and Chantilly. Not by Miss Parchester. Not by you or me, or Skyler, who's too short to grab the fire alarm gizmo. Caron and Inez are worried about keeping Skyler away from Daphne, not creating a situation in which she could reclaim him. There has to be another player."

Luanne shrugged. "From what you've told me, Daphne is sadly lacking in friends and supporters. When Joey was sent to jail, she didn't have a single person to turn to. She was sleeping in an alley when—"

My blood turned to the consistency of chilled tomato aspic (which, for the record, was on the menu tomorrow at noon at the Armstrong villa). "Please don't even consider it, Luanne. Slap me if I so much as attempt to say the name aloud. Call Peter and tell him that I take full responsibility for everything that happened at the courthouse. So what if I find myself in shackles on the bench outside Judge Nott's courtroom next week?"

"Sooner or later you're going to have to say it, Claire. This approach-avoidance routine won't work. It won't help Daphne, Skyler, Caron, or yours truly, for that matter. Take a deep breath and say it."

My lips felt numb, as though I'd spent the morning at a dentist's office. "We could both be wrong," I mumbled. "Sheila might have sobered up."

"Say it," commanded Luanne.

"Oh, all right."

"I'm waiting."

"Daphne does have a friend, although he's more likely to be diving in a Dumpster than changing into tights and a cape in a telephone booth."

"Say it," she repeated.

My voice was very flat as I forced myself to comply. "Arnie Riggles."

CHAPTER TEN

For those who have the good fortune to have never encountered Arnold Riggles, congratulations are in order. He is of indiscriminate age, although anywhere between thirty-five and fifty would be a reasonable estimate. Personal hygiene is not among his hobbies. He is not evil, per se, but merely amoral in a rather generous way. Arnie would steal the shirt off his mother's back, but only to pass it along to someone in greater need. He would dance on his grandmother's grave to cheer up a funeral party, and then make off with the hearse. Because of reasons far too complicated to explain, he is convinced I am a senator.

For the record, I am not.

"Well, it makes sense," Luanne said, handing me a cup of coffee. "He rescued Daphne off the streets, provided her with food and shelter, and was present when she gave birth. As reluctant as we are to credit him with admirable qualities, he's not a total jackass."

"He's loyal when it suits him. There's no proof he's behind this petty jailbreak, though. We don't know where Sally Fromberger was this morning at ten o'clock, do we?"

"I think we can assume she wasn't setting off the fire alarm at the courthouse," she countered dryly.

"Or whisking Daphne away for a veggie burger and a cup of herbal tea, for that matter. Where can the girl be? It's not that easy to blend in when you're wearing a monogrammed orange jumpsuit. Her mother's house is only three blocks from the courthouse, but she must have realized that's the first place the police would go." I went to the window and looked at pedestrians ambling down the hill. "My duplex is at least a mile away from the courthouse. She doesn't have a chance of making it there without being spotted by some conscientious citizen with a cell phone. Even if she knows where Joey is—and I can't see how she could—she has no way to get there."

"So we're back to Arnie."

"Arnie does not own a getaway car."

Luanne poked me in the back. "But he could have stolen one."

"I suppose so," I said with a sigh. "The only thing we can hope is that Daphne is somewhere in Farberville. I think you'd better keep Skyler for the time being. I don't know what I'd do if she came into the Book Depot and attempted to take him away. She's his mother, admittedly, but she's a fugitive who's been charged with murder. She has to be frantic."

"Skyler and I are getting along very nicely. What are you going to do, besides dodge Peter?"

"Look for Arnie, I guess. I'll go by the stadium and make sure he's no longer renting corporate skyboxes to the homeless. He wouldn't have been stupid enough to drop her off at a shelter. You know, Luanne, I can almost feel his presence. It's as if greenish-yellow globules of oil are beginning to spatter on the sidewalks. The air's tainted with the redolence of rotting fish. The collective psyche of Farberville is askance. Jessica's doubting herself, wondering if she should go back to college and get a degree in astrophysics. Adrienne is thinking about canceling her hair appointment, and Chantilly's vacuuming the living room rug. The Reverend Simpleton's on his way to the Dew Drop Inn in hopes of meeting a really hot waitress. Sheila is plotting her new career as a motivational speaker."

"Have you considered therapy?"

"At the moment, I'd prefer a lobotomy. I'm going to the stadium, and after that . . . I don't know. If Arnie stole a car, he and Daphne could be anywhere. The police will have a better chance of finding them than I will. I'd better leave before a meter maid calls the police department to let Lieutenant Peter Rosen know that my car's parked out front. For some silly reason, he thinks I'm withholding information."

"You could rat out Joey," said Luanne.

"But only as a bargaining tool," I said virtuously. I crouched over the basket to stroke Skyler's cheek, promised Luanne to report back, and went out to my car. Caron and Inez would be released from Farberville High School in a matter of hours (if the former was not in restraints in the school nurse's office). Both would be hysterical when they learned Daphne might be in a position to snatch Skyler away from his temporary sanctuary. If they didn't already know. Caron has assured me on numerous occasions that she is The Only Person at the high school without a cell phone—except for Inez, of course, and a few dorky freshmen.

I drove to the stadium and slowed down as I looked at the tier with doors leading to the skyboxes. Remodeling and renovations were underway; workmen swarmed the balcony, toting lumber, tools, rolls of carpet, and bathroom fixtures. Arnie was no longer a landlord, at least for the time being. It was likely that evidence of illicit occupancy had resulted in a better security system, as well as a physical exorcism of lingering contamination. The president of the college could never pass the port to a generous alumnus who might leave the skybox with fleas and lice.

But I had no idea where else to look for Arnie—and, by extension, Daphne. If he had indeed stolen a car, which was possible if his persistent lack of sobriety had not precluded it, he could be anywhere in the city, or even the county. I did not think Daphne could have been persuaded to abandon Skyler and allow herself to be driven into the sunset, or as far as she and Arnie could go before they ran out of gas. If he was even involved.

Sheila was the only person who might have heard from Daphne. Hoping the police had already departed, I drove up Thurber Street and turned the corner. Willow Street appeared charmingly benign. Gray-haired residents were walking dogs. A few college students were sitting on a porch, sharing a quart bottle of beer. Three young mothers were pushing strollers as they chatted. I was about to pull over in front of Sheila's house when I saw the nondescript white car and its two nondescript white occupants. If I so much as slowed down, my license plate would be verified with DMV in a matter of seconds, and Lieutenant Rosen would have me handcuffed and hauled to the PD in a matter of minutes.

I decided to go home and phone her. As I turned into the alley behind my duplex, I noticed a cab parked just beyond the garage. Farberville has a small, unreliable cab service. Big cities have gypsy cabs; here we have cabs driven by gypsies (or so council members claim when the moon is full). If the downstairs tenant had called, the driver would be waiting at the front curb. None of the Kappa Theta Etas in the sorority house next door would be caught dead in such a bourgeois mode of transportation.

I parked in my allotted half of the garage and went upstairs. I was somewhat surprised to find the back door unlocked, but I knew Caron might have made herself a sandwich and left without bothering to lock the door— or closing the refrigerator door, for that matter. The shower might still be dribbling. Ill-tempered remarks might be written in lipstick on the bathroom mirror. I set down my purse and picked up the telephone directory to find Sheila's number. I was not prepared to find a guest in my living room, his filthy shoes on the coffee table, bread crumbs and beer cans scattered on the floor.

"Yo, Senator. How's tricks?"

"How did you get in here, Arnie?" I demanded.

"Well, it's like this," he said, pausing to scratch his head, "I found this little screwdriver that you can poke in the lock. It doesn't work with deadbolts, but with that cheap thing you've got, it took me less than five seconds. You ought to get yourself one, Senator. You could be using the president pro temp's private bathroom while he's presiding on the floor. Say, what's your take on this WTO business?"

I took a deep breath. "Allow me to rephrase the question. What in blazes are you doing here? Does this have anything to do with Daphne Armstrong?"

"Happens that it does, 'though I'll always think of her as Wal-Mart. When I found her out behind the pool hall, her belly was swollen but her arms and legs were skinny as match-sticks. The first time she tried to eat, she threw up. I had to put her on clear liquids for twenty-four hours so her stomach could readjust to solid food."

"Let's save our maudlin memories for another time. I now know how you got in here, but not why."

He pulled a grimy handkerchief from his pocket and blew his nose. "Even though she didn't name the baby after me, I still think of him as my godson, Arnie Junior. Maybe when he grows up I'll take him to a football game and point out the skybox where he was born. I can tell him all about how it was a dark and stormy night, or at least late afternoon, when—"

"See the telephone, Arnie? That's what I'm going to use to call the police if you don't answer my questions. This does qualify as breaking and entering, doesn't it? And the cab downstairs might result in a charge of grand theft auto. We're not talking the county jail here. It's going to be a long, hot summer weeding turnip fields at the state prison. Guards on horses, chiggers and ticks, bad food, no CNN."

"You must be a real tiger when debating tax relief on the Senate floor. What's your position on these new proposals to modify Social Security? Are IRAs going to be safe what with all the flux on the stock market?"

I crossed my arms and glared down at him. "I'm trying to decide if I should call the police or whack you with the directory and push you down the stairs. Shall we debate that, Arnie?"

He gave me a wounded look. "Don't get all testy. It so happened I was watching the news the other night when Daphne was arrested. I couldn't imagine someone so puny shooting anybody, much less her father. I've been sort of keeping an eye on things ever since. You know what's been most puzzling, Senator?"

I had a very good idea, but merely said, "Why don't you tell me?"

"That snooty reporter never mentioned the baby, and that's something she would have jumped on like a hairy ol' tarantula. No mention of him in the newspapers. It's like no one's even heard of him, much less noticed he's gone missing. So I asked myself, I said, 'Arnie, who's the most likely to know where the little fellow is?' Believe it or not, you were the first to come to mind."

"What about that black woman who offered to drive Daphne and the baby to a shelter?" I said, aware I sounded defensive. "She could be living in a little apartment down the hill from the stadium and operating a day-care center to pay the rent."

"She left town the next day, and I'd know if she was back on account of owing her a small sum of money. What's more, before you got here, I looked through your garbage and found soiled diapers and empty cans of formula. That stirred the flames of suspicion in the very soul of Arnie Riggles." He belched loudly enough to be heard across the campus. "You got any more beer?"

"Skyler is not here."

"Yeah, I know. Your daughter, by the way, has more dirty dishes under her bed than your standard diner has soaking in the sink. How 'bout a shot of scotch? A little hospitality might keep me from calling that lieutenant of yours and telling him what I know."

"Arnie," I said through teeth clenched so hard I could barely spit out the words, "we are not going to play this game. Let's up the ante. This morning you were responsible for helping Daphne escape. That lieutenant of mine, as you call him, will be very perturbed. He takes aiding and abetting even more seriously than he does grand theft auto. You might end up learning how to make license plates in Sing-Sing."

He went into the kitchen and opened a cabinet. "I may have had something to do with that, but my only motive was to reunite a mother with her baby."

"What precisely did you do?"

"This guy I know, Billy Beowulf, got into a spot of trouble the other night and ended up at the jail. Knowing from personal experience that everybody in custody would be brought to the courthouse this morning to be arraigned before the weekend, I visited Billy yesterday and gave him a note to slip to Daphne while they were on the bus." He returned with the bottle of scotch, flopped back onto the couch, and took a swig. "The note told her to fake stomach cramps and demand to go into the restroom, where she'd find sweatpants and a jacket. I guess she figured out the rest of it on her own. Now as to the identity of the person who set off the fire alarm, I can't say for sure. Could have been most anybody in the courthouse. People were coming and going like there was a Christmas sale inside."

"Were you waiting outside in the cab?"

"I only borrowed it an hour ago. There it was outside the Tickled Pink Club, just begging to take a li'l spin."

I sat down on the far side of the room, where his body odor was less oppressive. "So you don't know what Daphne did after she escaped? You have no idea where she is? She'd save herself a lot of grief if she turned herself in, Arnie."

"You, Daphne, and me might all be looking at some grief. We could be sing-singing three-part harmony in the future."

I narrowed my eyes. "Have you spoken to her in the last three days?"

"I don't recall." He finished the scotch and wiped his mouth on the back of his hand. "Guess I'd better be going. Don't you back off on campaign reform, Senator. All this soft money is corrupting the electoral process."

"Where is Daphne?"

"All I know is she ain't calling a cab. If you could spare twenty bucks, I'd be inclined to go back out to the Tickled Pink Club and save Wanita from losing her job. She's got three little boys, and her husband was last seen getting on a bus to Biloxi. I solemnly swear I'll give Wanita the money so she can say she had a fare. You can come along if you want, just so you'll know Arnie Riggles is a man of his word."

"You are a man of many words, but they all have four letters." I went into the kitchen and opened my wallet, but all the cash was gone. "I'll tell you what, Arnie," I said as I blocked his exit, "why don't you give me back all but twenty dollars and I'll forget about this. Don't make me start thinking of inhumane things to do with cooking utensils. The meat thermometer comes to mind."

He shoved a wad of bills (mostly ones, mind you) into my hand, winked, and went out the back door. I picked up the beer cans, what crumbs I could, and the empty bottle, and dumped it all in the trash. Then, after washing my hands with scouring powder, I called Luanne.

"A development," I said, then told her about Arnie. "I think he knows where Daphne is, but I doubt I could have gotten it out of him with tongs and a pancake turner. He admitted he planned her escape. He must have been waiting for her when she left the courthouse. Then again, he might have been telling the truth about the cab.

When he's been drinking more than usual, he slips up sometimes."

"So Daphne covered the jumpsuit with civilian clothes before she took off. Could she have made it to her mother's house?"

"No more than fifteen minutes before the police did, and they would have searched the house thoroughly. Now they've got it staked out. I'll call Sheila, but I doubt she's any more coherent on the phone than she is in person."

Luanne assured me that she and Skyler were plotting a lovely afternoon at the mall. I hung up, gulped down two aspirins, and steeled myself to call Sheila. No one answered, but I'd been told she walked to a grocery store and liquor store as her needs dictated. Perhaps the undercover officers had offered her a lift—or more interestingly, opted to follow her at a discreet distance. Which would leave the house without scrutiny.

Miss Parchester's house was only a few backyards away. Her dogs had been temporarily relocated to the countryside. There were other dogs, of course, and retired residents who might be planting their gardens and pruning their petunias. But it was possible I could park at the library and find a way to Sheila's house without being seen from the street. Even if Daphne was not there, I could look around for the albums Joey had mentioned, or any other indication of what they had believed would make them rich.

I changed into a more serviceable outfit of jeans and a T-shirt and drove to the library. Patrons were coming and going, and children were playing on the lawn in front of the brick building. I would have sat on a bench and appreciated the idyllic scene had I not been intent on committing a felony.

There was a neglected alley behind the houses on Willow Street, and I had little problem approaching the back of Sheila's house. Most of the yards had fences. Garages faced onto the alley. A few dogs barked, as expected, and an elderly woman came out onto her porch to stare at me. I waved and smiled, and she reciprocated, although she seemed to be intent on memorizing my features.

"Looking for my cat," I called in a neighborly fashion.

"I do not care for cats in my yard. I am hoping that the purple martins will nest here this year."

"I'm sure they will." I ducked my face and hurried on. Two more backyards and I was looking at a rusty chain-link fence covered with some sort of vine that had yet to begin to bloom. A car was parked in the garage, indicating that Sheila was on foot, sound asleep inside the house, or merely too caught up in a neurotic fantasy to bother to answer the phone. I glanced both ways, assessed the potential handholds, and managed to scramble over the fence and fall onto a pile of soggy leaves. When nothing much happened, I stood up and hurried to the back porch. Still no voices ordering me to stop, no sounds of weapons being cocked, no barking of ferocious dogs about to be loosed on my person.

The door was locked. For a second, I wished I'd taken away Arnie's handy-dandy screwdriver, then gave the knob a good shake. It obliged me.

"Sheila?" I called as I stepped into a kitchen of sorts. The sink was filled with dishes, and the linoleum on the floor was brown with grime. The refrigerator was significantly older than I was. Cereal was scattered on the counter. Two empty milk cartons, wadded paper napkins, and a half-melted stick of butter cluttered the surface of a breakfast table. The herbs in pots on the windowsill above the sink were yellow, most likely brittle. I could understand why Sheila limited her forays into the kitchen to pouring vodka.

I continued into the living room, prepared to find her snoring on the sofa or passed out on the floor. Still calling her name, I went upstairs and quickly searched the two bedrooms and antiquated bathroom. All were as unappealing as the kitchen but unoccupied as well. I came back downstairs, went to the window, and eased back the curtain. The nondescript car was no longer parked across the street. I had no idea what I would say if she were to come through the front door; it would be hard to sell my runaway cat story, even to someone as harebrained as she. Cats are seldom accused of picking locks, even those in mystery fiction with the ability to tapdance on keyboards to provide clues to their witless caregivers.

There were several photo albums piled sloppily on the coffee table. I considered the idea of snatching them up and exiting through the back door, but I was aware that Sheila might be too emotionally fragile to deal with their disappearance. Life was surely perplexing for her at the moment, with her ex-husband murdered, her daughter arrested, and her alimony checks imperiled.

I sat down on the sofa and opened the top album. Sheila, dressed in an ankle-length white dress, with daisies in her hair. Anthony, less bulky, perhaps less tense. In that I'd never met the man, it was hard to tell. An asymmetrical wedding cake that Sheila must have made herself. Guests in embroidered shirts. A band composed of three drummers and a ponytailed guitar player. Jugs of wine. A retro wedding, I thought, shaking my head.

I flipped though pages with photographs of runny-nosed children and glazed adults. Depictions of Daphne in a receiving blanket, and later in a bathing suit in a wading pool. Anthony, washing a car. Sheila, mugging at the camera. Daphne, in an Easter dress and straw hat. Anthony and Sheila on the deck of a cabin. Daphne, in a tutu, her hair pinned up and her smile taut.

There was nothing in the album that suggested cash on demand. I set it aside and opened another, which seemed to focus on Anthony's successes in civic affairs and his propensity for posing with heavy machinery. Cutting a ribbon at an apartment complex. Standing in front of a fountain. Shaking hands with what I supposed was the mayor or a councilman. Accepting a golf trophy. Standing on a pier beside a large fish. Sheila was rarely at his side.

I wasn't sure how far away the grocery store or liquor store might be, but I figured the clock was ticking. I picked up a third album and opened it. The photographs were much older, and after a bit of squinting, I determined that they were of Sheila's family. Most of the people in the earliest black-and-white compositions were rigid and expressionless. Their clothes were durable, no doubt, but uninspired. A ramshackle barn in the distance looked as though a heavy rain might send it sliding down the hillside, taking a mule and several chickens with it. A few pages later, I found a wedding picture, the groom in an olive drab uniform, the bride in a knee-length beige dress with a lace jacket. When Sheila began to appear, first as an impish child and then as a teenager, the backgrounds were filled with station wagons and barbecue grills. Her parents had achieved middle-class nirvana in the form of three bedrooms, one-and-a-half baths, and a tiny patio.

But where, I asked myself, was anything that suggested there was a buried treasure in the backyard, so to speak? No one was holding up a prototype of an electric lightbulb or a printing press. The mule had not gone on to win the Kentucky Derby. The barbecue grills would not set any records at an antiques appraisal show on PBS. Relatives, friends, memories. Valuable to those who cared, but hardly marketable.

I let myself out the back door, conscientiously locking it behind me, and walked down the alley.

"Find your cat?" the elderly woman shouted.

"No luck," I answered with appropriate despondency. "He must have run off with a Siamese that lives next door."

"Foreigners. Can't trust them."

"No kidding," I said. "The next thing you know, they'll be giving out the Nobel Peace Prize in Sweden." When I arrived in the library parking lot, I checked the time. I still had an hour before Caron and Inez would be thrust back into the complexity. Skyler was at the mall with Luanne, Adrienne was having her hair done, Peter was threatening his underlings with double shifts if they didn't find Daphne, Arnie was spending my twenty dollars at some sleazy bar, Miss Parchester was settling her account with Howie, Sheila was staggering home from shopping, Jessica was powdering her nose in preparation for the next late-breaking story, the weatherman was eyeing the low front coming our way, and Finnigan Baybergen was annoying a large class of undergraduates who wanted nothing more than a passing grade and an opportunity to nap. Busy, busy people.

I had an hour of free time.

And, it occurred to me as I walked up the steps to the library, I might be able to use it wisely. I stopped at the reference desk and asked a young woman how I might find newspaper stories from a year ago.

She peered at me almost suspiciously. "On-line, of course. The archives go back forty-three years thus far."

"I don't know how to find the archives," I whispered, as one was taught to do in such sacred institutions.

She pulled off her glasses. "Please wait while I find Marian."

"The lady librarian?"

"She will not find that amusing. Just sit down at that desk and try not to touch anything until we return."

I did as ordered. The computer in front of me appeared to be no more alien than the one in my office that I used infrequently, to my accountant's chagrin. I did not doubt, however, that with an imprudent touch I could erase the entire inventory of the library, and possibly that of the Library of Congress as well. I tend to overestimate my as yet undefined supernatural powers, but one never knows.

Marian proved to be a woman of my age. She was not horrified at my ignorance, and carefully led me through a series of commands until I was looking at the archives of the local newspaper.

"Do you have a particular date, or do we need to search by subject?"

"Subject," I said. "The Oakland Heights condominium development."

She stopped smiling. "I suppose you're wanting to find articles about the fire last year. A terrible thing it was. My niece's former roommate was living there. The poor girl miscarried the day after. But let me find it for you." She typed rapidly, then stopped as an article appeared on the screen. "Just click on that button to see related articles. When you're done, click on this."

I settled back to read about the fire. No one had been killed, and the damage had been limited to three units. One of them had belonged to Finnigan's sister, Kendra Baybergen, who'd collapsed behind the building. In an adjoining unit, a retired couple had barely escaped, both suffering second-degree burns. The husband had also fractured his shoulder in a fall. The third unit had involved a couple in their twenties; the wife had been transported to intensive care. Marian's niece's roommate.

The subsequent investigation had determined the fire to be an accident. The ground had shifted, rupturing gas lines. Sparks set off fires in the utility rooms. The smoke detectors had performed according to specifications. Ultimately, Mother Nature received the blame. Anthony Armstrong had issued a statement to that effect, adding that he was saddened by the event and offering his sympathy to those who had been harmed. Alternative housing would be provided at no cost until the structural damage was repaired and the interiors cleaned and repainted.

Residents in other units had nothing to contribute except anecdotes of gathering in horrified huddles and doing what they could to provide first aid until the paramedics arrived. Randy and Jillian Scarpo had not been among those who were interviewed.

I logged off, nodded at the young woman at the reference desk, and left the tranquil confines of the library, where harmony and clarity came from the quintessence of the Dewey decimal system. If only I could classify individuals as neatly.

I drove up Willow Street, noting that the inconspicuous

car was once more parked across the street from Sheila Armstrong's house, indicating that she was home. She could have had a phone call from Daphne and arranged to meet her somewhere between the Absolut and the Popov, but she'd left the store alone (and not necessarily empty-handed).

When I got to the Book Depot, I unlocked the door, removed the Closed sign, and tried to think where Daphne might have taken refuge. Not at her mother's house, and certainly not at the faux villa, where she would be greeted as warmly as a pimple on Adrienne's nose. The skyboxes were no longer a haven. Arnie was likely to be at the Tickled Pink Club, although I doubted the cabdriver had seen more than a glimpse of my twenty-dollar bill.

When the bell above the door jangled, I looked up, hoping to see a customer but expecting to see Caron and Inez. Three strikes, and it looked as though I might be out.

"Peter," I said with a flimsy attempt at a smile. "Luanne told me earlier that you were looking for me. As you can see, here I am."

He stopped in front of the counter. "Where is Daphne Armstrong?"

"I have no idea. I saw on the news that she managed to escape from the courthouse this morning. I solemnly swear I had nothing whatsoever to do with it. Jorgeson can testify on my behalf. After that, I went to find out if Miss Parchester was doing well. She's spent four nights in the tree, and at her age—"

"Don't play games with me, Claire. I want to know where she is."

"She's on a platform in an oak tree. I thought you knew that, Peter."

He failed to appreciate my wit. "Daphne Armstrong."

I frowned. "I just told you that I have no idea. You're welcome to search the office. Watch out for brown recluse spiders if you crawl behind the boiler. Their bites can be nasty."

"So can mine," he said. "The chief has been bawling me out for the last hour. I'm liable to be back in a patrol car if we don't find her. Think how the police department looks right now. That reporter, the one with the hair and—"

"Jessica Princeton?"

"Yes, that one. She damn near tackled me on the courthouse steps, and if a camera hadn't been in my face, I don't know what I would have done. You may see me foaming at the mouth on the six o'clock news." He took a deep breath. "Please tell me where Daphne is. We're not saying publicly that she's armed and dangerous, but we don't know for sure because we haven't found the weapon. Do you happen to have it in the drawer beneath the cash register?"

"Don't be ridiculous," I said. "Did you check the wooded area between the Armstrongs' house and Oakland Heights? She probably threw it as hard as she could, but she doesn't look like she has an abundance of muscles."

"A dozen men swept the area three times with metal detectors and found only a few rusty beer cans, coins, and spent shotgun shells. Daphne had the weapon in her possession when she drove away. She may have tossed it out the car window, or she may have hidden it before she was arrested. For all we know, she may be planning to commit suicide."

"She wouldn't do that," I began, then stopped. She'd sounded concerned about Skyler, but also resigned to losing him after she'd been arrested, and, at least in her mind, convicted and sent to prison. Could she have been thinking about suicide when she'd chosen to follow the directions on Arnie's note—or even four days ago, when she'd left Skyler on my front porch?

"Why not?" demanded Peter.

I was not pleased to be back in the middle of the mine-field, where a single misstep was potential disaster. "Because she said she didn't kill her father. I believed her."

"Why would she confess to a stranger? You did tell me you didn't know her, didn't you?"

Left foot, right foot. "I didn't know who she was until I saw her being escorted into the police station."

"And you haven't seen her since your little interview yesterday?"

"No, I have not."

He looked at me for a moment. "And you don't know anything about what happened at the courthouse?"

"I knew nothing whatsoever until I saw it on KFAR at noon," I said virtuously. "Has her mother heard from her?"

"If she has, she won't admit it. The only thing she will admit is that she's been channeling Nostradamus and he warned her that the revamped Volkswagen Beetle will lead to global destruction. Jorgeson is nervous, since that's what his wife drives."

I was casting about for a retort when Caron skidded into the store, almost colliding with the rack of cookbooks.

"Mother! Did you hear about—" she started, then gurgled to a halt as she saw Peter.

"Is something wrong at the high school?" he asked.

Inez popped up from behind the yellow study guides.

"No, Lieutenant Rosen. Well, a toilet in the girls' restroom on the second floor got stopped up and made a horrible stench. The vice principal says that—"

Peter held up his hand to avoid hearing the details. "That hardly seems a crisis, Inez. Caron must be thinking of something else."

Caron's eyes grew so round that I could easily imagine her pleading her innocence in a court of law. "What happened was that somebody took a gallon container of that slimy processed cheese sauce from the cafeteria and rigged it in Rhonda Maguire's locker so that when she opened it, it spilled all over her. She started screeching so loudly that Mrs. McLair told her class to evacuate. The cheese sauce was all over the floor and as slippery as ice. A dozen kids, including Rhonda, had to be hosed down." She paused for maximum effect. "It was just awful, Mother."

"Oh, dear," I murmured. "Has the culprit been identified?"

"Not yet. Maybe Peter should go take fingerprints. Rhonda's locker is just outside the library."

"And you can take fingerprints in the restroom, too," added Inez.

Peter muttered something under his breath, then said, "Claire, you have to promise to notify me if the person we were discussing attempts to contact you. Can I trust you?"

"Have I ever lied to you?" I replied sweetly.

CHAPTER ELEVEN

Peter gave me a skeptical look, then left. As soon as the door closed, Caron and Inez advanced on me like salivating wolves, or at least drooling puppies.

"Did you hear about Daphne Armstrong?" said Caron. She vanished behind the fiction rack, then reemerged with the stage presence of a diva prepared to sing a heart-wrenching aria, clutch her throat, and crumple to the floor for a piteous and lengthy demise. "She staged a getaway this morning in the courthouse. Two guards were shot, and one's in critical condition. She started a fire, then set off the alarm and came racing out—"

"No, she didn't," I said flatly.

"But that's what Kerry told us," Inez said. "And Aly heard that three clerks from the tax collector's office were taken hostage, and nobody's seen them since eleven o'clock. They could be dead by now, their bodies in the woods somewhere."

I reminded myself that only a few hours earlier I'd been begging to hear gossip at the fitness center. I told them the gospel according to Saint Jessica, then added, "No shots were fired and no one was hurt. The three clerks are likely to be in the restaurant up the street from the courthouse, drinking tequila shots. Any trace of smoke probably came from custodians too lazy to go outside for a mid-morning cigarette break. Daphne did leave the courthouse, but there's no suggestion she was armed."

Caron stared at me in much the same way Peter had minutes earlier. "So where is she?"

I should have been flattered that everyone seemed to believe I was masterminding the melodrama, but I was neither. "I don't know. If I did, I'd track her down and persuade her to turn herself in. She's making the situation worse."

Inez's lips began to tremble. "Where's Skyler? She didn't—"

"No, she didn't. Luanne took him to the mall to window-shop for summer booties. She'll call me when they get back."

"What if Daphne comes here, or to the apartment later?" asked Caron. "I won't let you hand him over. He's not a library book, for pity's sake! She can't just check him in and out when it suits her."

I caught her hand. "I agree, dear. Luanne won't object to keeping him until we know what's going to happen to Daphne."

"What will happen to her, Ms. Malloy?" Inez said solemnly.

"It's hard to say. There are some inconsistencies in her story, but I'm not sure what to make of them. Other potential witnesses are less than candid. One would think the long arm of the law could get to the truth."

Caron smirked. "Is that why Peter was huffing at you? He knows that you know stuff you're not telling him?"

"You have cheese sauce in your hair."

"Eew!" she howled as she darted toward the bathroom in the office.

Inez began to snicker, but prudently. "My grandmother had all these ducks and geese on her farm. When the pond froze, they'd go blithely marching onto the ice, then start flipping on their"—she glanced at me—"tail feathers. It was funny, but not as funny as today. I don't think Rhonda's going to be ordering nachos at Taco Bell anytime soon."

"Should I expect a call from the vice principal?"

"Well, Rhonda's pretty sure, but no one saw Caron messing around near her locker. Waylan made some wisecracks later, acting like he was responsible. He wasn't any happier than Caron about the rumors, since he has a girlfriend who looks like Xena. Luckily, we've got the weekend before Rhonda can launch her next ambush."

Caron came out of the office. "Why don't you tell us what you're not telling Peter? We could help, you know. I'm kind of starting to like having Skyler around, even if it's not for long. He's, like, the only baby brother I'll ever have."

"Me, too," said Inez, her lenses fogging up. "When I was born, my father calculated the cost of college tuition and had a vasectomy."

I looked at them, wishing I could see them as children, or even the egomaniacal postpubescents they'd been only two years ago. "Let me lock the store, then we'll go home, make a pot of tea, and I will tell you everything I know. You may be able to make more sense of it than Luanne and I have thus far."

"That shouldn't be too hard," Caron said.

• • •

Miss Marple had never been burdened with sixteen-year-old girls, unless they'd been adenoidal maids who brought in tea trays, but only after straightening their aprons and caps. Caron and Inez poured themselves sodas, then flopped down on the sofa and eyed me like raptors, one more disconcerting than the other. The One Who Spoke In Capital Letters, naturally.

During the next hour, hushing them when they tried to interrupt every third sentence, I related it all—from my previous and inevitably exasperating encounters with Arnie; the specifics of Skyler's birth; and my conversations with Daphne, Sheila, Adrienne, Chantilly, Joey, and Finnigan Baybergen. I told them about Randy and Jill Scarpo. I even went so far as to repeat the exchange with Arnie only a short while earlier. Both of them moved from the sofa to chairs on the far side of the room.

"You delivered a baby?" said Caron. "Weren't you grossed out?"

"I didn't have time to think about it. Even the most ordinary people, like the three of us, can and will rise to the occasion when the situation demands it. Afterwards, if it's all gone wrong, we may lie awake at night, wondering if we should have done something differently. In this case, I had no regrets."

Inez stared, either appalled or awed; in that she often tended to look like one or the other, it was hard to know. "And you didn't tell anybody?"

"I wasn't ready to share it. I told Luanne a couple of days ago, and now I've told the two of you. I was waiting for the right time."

Caron went into the kitchen, slammed a few cabinet doors, then came back into the living room. "So the stork didn't deliver Skyler, but now we've got him—so it must be the right time, Mother. This whole thing is such a mess. It's like one of those comedies by Shakespeare where half the cast are twins, the girls pretend to be boys, and everyone is infatuated. They're impossible to make sense of without a study guide."

Inez shook her head. "It's more like one of the tragedies where everybody goes blind or dies in the end."

"We haven't quite come to that," I said. "It's possible that Daphne did shoot her father. She couldn't have felt much love for him after he kicked her out of the house."

"She wouldn't have given up hope, even with Adrienne muddying things up. Maybe she just went back to talk to him when she thought he was alone," Caron said, sipping pensively on her soda.

"She said she didn't think anyone was home," Inez corrected her, and at her own peril, added, "She went there to get something."

"Like a suitcase of counterfeit money? Did her mother just happen to remember the printing press in the basement? Are there clotheslines bedecked with damp hundred-dollar bills?"

Inez did her best to stick out her chin, but the effect was marginal. "She could have tried to blackmail him because he had a collection of porn movies hidden in his office. Some of them, the ones with minors, aren't protected by the First Amendment. We studied that in my government class last week."

"The cops didn't notice a stack of videos? Give me a break!"

"The cops are going to stop to watch movies? You give *me* a break!"

I cut them off before they went off on a tangent, which they often did without any discernible provocation. "What's really important is to figure out where

Daphne is right now. She's only two years older than you, and although she's had some experiences I hope you'll never have, she's naive. Where could she be?"

"In a shed in the alley behind Thurber Street," said Caron without hesitation. "She stayed there before."

Inez fluttered her hand as though she were seated in the front row of her government class, where I was sure she always sat. "In the garage behind her mother's house. You didn't search there, Ms. Malloy. She knows her mother never drives the car. She could have been hiding in the backseat when you climbed over the fence. Now she's in the house."

"Those are both feasible theories," I said. "Why don't you two take the car and check both of them out?"

"Then you're sure she doesn't have a gun?" said Caron.

I sank into the upholstery. "I'm not sure of anything except where our next meal is coming from, and that's from a box of macaroni and cheese. I'd go with you, but I think I'd better be here in case Daphne shows up looking for Skyler. She's never seen either of you. Knock on Sheila's door and pretend you're taking orders for Girl Scout cookies, recruiting for a sect, or rallying support for a demonstration tomorrow on Thurber Street to save the noble oaks of Oakland Heights."

Inez looked less than confident. "My parents are going to be so mad if I get shot. They have tickets for a performance at the college tomorrow afternoon, something about three oboes, a piccolo, and a mime. I'm supposed to go."

Caron stood up. "Wouldn't you rather be killed in the line of duty?"

"I guess so," she said.

I described Daphne as best I could, then said, "If you

find her, persuade her to come back here. I can't promise her that I won't call the police, but I will listen to her story and do everything I can to help her."

"What if she demands to know where Skyler is?" asked Caron. "Do we lie about that and tell her he's here?"

"No, don't lie," I said. "You can, however, fudge. Tell her that if she cooperates, she'll have the opportunity to see Skyler."

"Will she?"

I looked up at Caron. "Yes, she will. You seem to have a low opinion of me these days."

Inez mumbled something and fled to the bathroom, leaving Caron in the middle of the room. She sat down on the sofa and stared at the floor. "I'm sorry, Mother. I have a low opinion of myself these days."

"Even after you took out Rhonda Maguire with such an admirable coup de grâce? You must have been chortling all afternoon."

"I would have been if I hadn't heard about Daphne. All I could think about was Skyler and what was going to happen to him." She glanced up with a rueful look. "A first for me, worrying about somebody else. I worry about you and Peter, but mostly because I don't know what it'll mean for me. Same thing with how the Book Depot is doing, profit-wise, so I can shop at the mall and go out for pizza with everybody. If I'll know what to major in when I go to college. If Louis Wilderberry will ever notice me, which isn't going to happen before the advent of the next millennium."

"If your father loved you?" I said carefully.

"Well, that, too. Did he ever wish he could have put me in a basket and left me on the steps of a church? Did he even want me to be born?"

"Of course, he did," I said as I hugged her. "He was just ill-equipped to deal with fatherhood. Academia can be a narcotic as powerful as heroin. Your father wasn't at the top of the hierarchy by any means, but there were plenty of warm bodies below him. When he walked into a lecture room, conversation stopped. All of his opinions were jotted down in notebooks in case they might require regurgitation on a test. Coeds in short skirts showed up during office hours to beg for a few minutes of his precious time." I paused for a moment. "He lost his perspective. That doesn't mean he didn't love you, just that his priorities got screwed up."

"Did you know about his affairs?"

"I was suspicious," I said. "I didn't know what to do about it, though, and I wasn't making enough money from my assistantship to pay the rent. Getting a full-time job would have meant getting a full-time baby-sitter. I just looked the other way when he claimed he had to stay late for a meeting or attend a poetry reading at a café."

"Weren't you terribly angry?" she whispered.

"Yes, at times. Picking you up at the day-care center, bathing you, shoveling strained peas down your throat, reading and singing to you—all that was more meaningful to me."

"You can't sing."

"I can, too," I protested. "Want to hear the Motown version of 'Rockabye Blues'?"

"In E-flat? I don't think so." She stood up again. "Inez and I will go poke around for Daphne. She may just be panhandling on Thurber Street."

"Watch for rubber sandals."

"You'd better watch out for Peter, Mother."

"Let's hope that will be limited to the six o'clock

news," I said. After she and Inez left, I went into the kitchen to pour myself some scotch, then realized the empty bottle was in the garbage. Just as well, I thought, as I settled for orange juice and a plate of crackers and cheese.

An hour later, Luanne called to say that she and Skyler had enjoyed their outing at the merchandising mecca of Farberville. I gave her an update, then asked if she would keep Skyler until Daphne was taken back into custody by the police or swooped up by Caron and Inez. Arnie might have offered odds, but it seemed like a toss-up to me. In either case, it wouldn't be circumspect for me to have Skyler in the apartment.

"Sure," she said. "We'll slap together baloney sandwiches and watch old movies."

"Don't let him watch anything too violent."

"Strictly Doris Day and Rock Hudson," she assured me before promising to call in the morning.

I was too distracted to do more than nibble a cracker as I paced within the limited confines of the apartment. Daphne most certainly had not had a gun in her possession when she fled from the courthouse—but she'd had one when she drove away from Oakland Heights. She could have tossed it out the car window, as Peter had suggested, or she could have stashed it somewhere, as he'd also suggested.

When my legs began to protest, I sat down and dialed Sheila Armstrong's number.

"Hello?" she answered, her voice slurred.

"This is Claire. Have you heard from Daphne today?"

"I've already told you a dozen times today that I haven't. Why do you insist on badgering me like this?"

I wasn't sure who she thought I was. "I'd really like to talk to her."

"I'm not granting interviews unless I get paid. Put your best offer on the table, whoever you are."

"And then you'll tell me where she is?"

"I gotta go. There are some girls at the door, probably selling magazines. Like I need magazines, ferchrissake!" she snapped, then hung up.

I resumed pacing, and had done several hundred laps around the sofa when the telephone rang. Praying that Caron and Inez had not been arrested, I answered with a subdued, "Hello?"

"Claire? Is this you?" said a breathless voice.

"Yes, it is. Who's this?"

"Adrienne, silly. I wasn't sure about your last name, so I've been trying all kinds of possibilities. There are a shocking number of vulgar people in this town. I was even accused of being a telemarketer, if you can imagine. Do I sound like someone selling long-distance plans? I was so absolutely offended."

"Why are you calling me?" I asked, perplexed.

"I'm not exactly calling you. I was wondering if Chantilly might be there."

I was glad I hadn't had so much as a drop of scotch. "Why would Chantilly be here, Adrienne?"

"I was just hoping," she said as she began to sniffle. "She borrowed my car more than three hours ago to pick up a few items at the drugstore. She hasn't come back, and I'm beginning to worry. You did hear about Daphne, didn't you?"

"I heard about her, but what does that have to do with Chantilly?"

"Don't sound angry with me, Claire. All these relatives of Anthony's have been coming by all afternoon. If I'd known about his family, I would have thought twice about marrying him. They all look so, I don't know, diseased. They kept insisting on squeezing my hand and kissing me until I thought I was going to throw up. Then this hideous man who's supposedly an uncle cornered me in the dining room and had the audacity to put his hand on my . . ." She gulped several times. "Anyway, it was all I could do not to slap his greasy face. I've only been widowed for three days, and I deserve respect. You must have gone through this kind of thing."

"Not exactly," I said. "So why do you think Chantilly might be here?"

"Because I can't think of anywhere else she might be. She met a few of my friends at the fitness center, but I don't think she'd remember them. You were such a big help this morning."

"She might be on her way to Atlanta."

"She wouldn't do that to me. Well, she would, but not without telling me. We're very close. Just before she left, I told her how much I appreciated her staying until after the funeral. Both of us almost cried."

I could not envision either of them risking mascara madness. "What does this have to do with Daphne? She hasn't shown up at your house, has she?"

"Of course not. She knows perfectly well that the first thing I'd do is call the police. I'm convinced she came here to steal money. When she went into the office, dear, sweet Anthony was there, immersed as usual in paperwork. He came around his desk to reason with her, and she shot him. I'm not saying that she intended to do it. The gun might have gone off by accident. But it doesn't matter, does it? Anthony's at the mortuary. He wanted to have more children, you know, especially a son to carry on the business. There's a room upstairs that would have been perfect for a nursery, once we'd ripped down those posters. Only last week I called the decorator to bring out some wallpaper and fabric samples. I told her I wanted a nontraditional effect, earth tones but with a bit of whimsy."

"I'd be surprised if Chantilly remembers my last name, and I still don't see why Daphne's causing you concern."

"Some policemen came by to warn me that Daphne had escaped and might have a gun. They still don't know where she is. In the meantime, I'm out here all by myself. I can't believe Chantilly is doing this to me. She knows perfectly well that I'm on edge. There's no one within shouting distance except for that peculiar person in the tree, and I can't see her coming to my rescue if Daphne shows up, waving a gun and making accusations. Maybe I should call the police to report Chantilly as a missing person."

"Three hours isn't the same as three days. She left voluntarily, and she may be doing nothing more than shopping at the mall for a scarf to wear tomorrow. The police won't even take your report for forty-eight hours."

"Forty-eight hours?" Adrienne said, hitting a note that eluded many sopranos. "That means she won't be here for the funeral! I cannot face all these people without support. You are coming, aren't you, Claire? I don't know what I'll do if you say no. Yes, I do—I'll call the whole thing off and check into a hotel under a false name. Then Sunday I'll book a flight to Palm Springs and spend two weeks at a spa."

I felt as if I were trying to reason with the pigeons that pooped on the portico in front of the bookstore. "You have lots of friends, Adrienne. Cling to Mary Margaret and let her fend off the lecherous uncle."

"Mary Margaret would just die if I asked her to do that. She had hysterics when we saw a groundhog on the sixteenth fairway last month. By the time she told the story in the bar, she was sure it was a bear cub and she'd heard the mother bear in the woods. Last week her husband had to come home from the office because she found a spider in the bidet. You have to do this for me, Claire, or wait in front of the church and tell everybody to go home."

"I was planning to come at ten o'clock to oversee the preparations. I won't go to the funeral, but I suppose I can stay for the luncheon."

"Thank you so much! You're the best friend I have. When things have settled down, you must let me take you to lunch to show my gratitude."

"We'll see about that later," I said, imagining myself eating a salad of field greens and arugula. Our conversation was likely to be limited to the weather, as long as we focused on its impact on her hair.

"I don't guess you could come out now and stay with me until Chantilly gets back? I realize the house is within the city limits, but it feels like it's in some remote forest. Daphne could be hiding out there, watching the house and waiting for a chance to sneak inside. I'm already a nervous wreck, and it's not even dark yet. We can heat up some of those casseroles people have been bringing and have a picnic in the living room. There's all kinds of wine in the cellar. Oh, do come, Claire! It'll be fun."

I started to tell her it was impossible because I didn't have a car, but I didn't want to pretend that was my sole impediment and have her insist on picking me up in Anthony's car. "I can't do it tonight. Chantilly's likely to show up any minute with bags from the mall. If you're worried about Daphne, lock the doors."

"What if she still has a key?"

"If you hear her come inside, lock yourself in your bedroom and call 911."

"We don't have to eat the casseroles. There are at least half a dozen cakes and pies in the refrigerator, and Anthony stashed away all kinds of gourmet ice cream in the back of the freezer where he thought I wouldn't find it. The doctor was constantly on his case about his cholesterol, and I did everything I could to control his diet. He always stayed up later than I did, and I'd hear him easing open the freezer door like a naughty little boy. I didn't want to be a nag, though, so I never said anything to him. He never criticized me about spending so much time at the fitness center, and he didn't mind that we went out to dinner every night, since I can't cook anything more complicated than toast. That was why our marriage was so happy."

"Good-bye, Adrienne. I'll be at your house when you get back from the cemetery."

"Oh, all right," she said sulkily. "I don't know what time that will be. Reverend Simpleton has refused to fast-forward through even one tiny prayer or homily. Everybody better bring an umbrella."

"Tomorrow, then," I said, and hung up.

Caron and Inez came slinking back an hour later, annoyed at their lack of success. We were all thinking of Skyler as I fixed macaroni and cheese, adorned it with slightly brown lettuce, and suggested we watch the local news.

"So we can hear what?" said Caron.

"We don't know what's been happening," I said. "Daphne might have been found and taken back into custody."

"Yeah, if they implanted a chip with a homing device. We looked everywhere, Mother. Inez even went inside the pool hall on Thurber Street. I would have gone with her, but I had to double-park outside in case we needed to retreat."

"I did not enjoy it," said Inez. "It had a nasty smell, and all of the patrons had excessive body hair and tattoos. Several of them are probably featured on those 'most wanted' shows. If they're not, they should be."

Caron curled her lip at the macaroni and cheese. "What's your mother cooking?" she asked Inez.

"This layered thing with lentils and leeks."

"Leeks or leaches?"

"Leeks. They're like—"

"I know what leeks are," Caron said scathingly. "Let's go to the pizza place and see if Rhonda dares show her face. Do you have any money?"

"I'll give you some money," I said, relieved that she was willing to be seen in public after a very difficult week. "If Rhonda's there, you'd better not turn your back on her."

"She's more likely to be rigging a bomb in Waylan's pickup truck. He told a couple of guys on the football team that she'd been hitting on him and begged him to take her to the dance at the end of the semester. Come on, Inez. We'll get a large pepperoni with leeks."

I handed over a reasonable amount of cash and turned on the news as they thudded down the back stairs. Jessica was in the studio, indicative that there were no late-breaking stories to be shared with her faithful viewers.

"Good evening, and thanks for turning to KFAR, your hometown news station. As many of you know, there was chaos at the courthouse today, when Daphne Armstrong escaped from custody while awaiting arraignment." She related the earlier events, then added, "The authorities have acknowledged that they are still searching for the fugitive, who is thought to have changed into inconspicuous clothing and may be armed. No one from the police department agreed to be interviewed on the air, and repeated calls from KFAR have not been returned. Our sources tell us that tomorrow the county prosecutor will hold a press conference shortly after Anthony Armstrong's funeral. Daphne Armstrong's mother is in seclusion at her home on Willow Street."

"What about the widow of Anthony Armstrong?" asked Jessica's coanchor, pretending they weren't reading off the same TelePrompTer. "Has she issued a statement?"

Jessica's eyes glinted for a nanosecond. "Adrienne Arm-strong has said through the family lawyer that she is deeply distressed by everything that has taken place in the last three days, and prays that Daphne will turn herself in before anyone else is harmed. Although she declined to speak to the media, she has been cooperating with the authorities."

"And she has no theories about where Daphne might have taken refuge?"

"How would I know!" Jessica growled, then regained control of herself and smiled, albeit sternly. "Moving along, Miss Emily Parchester has now maintained her vigil in the oak tree at Oakland Heights, Phase Two, for five days, despite inclement weather earlier in the week and the possibility of thunderstorms tomorrow. The spokesman for the Farberville Green Party, Assistant Professor Finnigan Baybergen, declined to speak on camera but issued a statement that although his group sympathized with Anthony Armstrong's family, the party would not back away from its moral commitment to the local environment."

Their focus drifted on to other stories. I switched off

the TV, glumly ate as much of the congealed macaroni and cheese as I could stomach, then tried to sort through what I knew. It took very little time. At some point I heard footsteps downstairs, but they were followed only by the sound of the tenant going into his or her apartment. My novel did not appeal. Network TV was tedious, and my accountant had forbade me from paying for additional channels. Next door, the Kappa Theta Etas squealed, as was their custom, then subsided. I flinched as a branch scraped against the side of the house, and again when a car slowed down on the street. I realized I was quite as paranoid as Adrienne Armstrong, and her pretext was stronger than mine.

When the telephone rang, I lunged for the receiver as though expecting the governor to grant a last-minute reprieve. "Yes?" I gasped.

"Are you okay?" demanded Caron. "You sound like there are rabid monkeys beating at the window."

"No, I'm fine," I said as I untangled my feet and sat up. "The monkeys gave up half an hour ago."

"You are so bizarre, Mother. I just called to say that Inez and I are going to sleep over at Luanne's tonight. We're going to watch movies."

"Luanne is more than capable of looking after Skyler. She has two children who both started out as babies."

"I know that. We just think we ought to be there in case something happens. At the press conference, Luanne was pushing the stroller. Daphne could have shopped at Secondhand Rose, or at least seen Luanne through the window."

"That's a little bit far-fetched, isn't it?"

"It may be, but it's what Inez and I want to do, and Luanne was agreeable. You don't need the car, do you?"

"No, I'm not planning to go anywhere," I said. "However, I want you to be home tomorrow morning at nine o'clock. I promised Adrienne I'd go out there at ten to flap my hands at the caterer, who'll probably respond in kind with a butcher knife. If we don't have adequate lemons and limes, I'll have to go to the grocery store. Randy's wife doesn't appear to actually go anywhere, but she seems to feel strongly that their car should be parked in front of their condo."

"Whatever," said Caron. "Nine o'clock."

I wished her a pleasurable evening, then hung up. The phone rang almost immediately. I picked it up, expecting Caron to argue that she didn't need to be home before nine-thirty.

"Claire!"

This time I recognized Adrienne's voice. "Is something wrong?" I said.

"Chantilly's not back and I'm really scared. I turned on all the outside lights and set the security system so that no one can so much as touch a doorknob without the alarm blaring. I've tried to sit down and read a magazine, but I keep hearing noises. I think I should call the police and demand that they send someone to patrol the grounds."

I wondered if Caron and Inez could be diverted to baby-sit for someone older than Skyler. The casseroles wouldn't appeal, but all the desserts might.

"No, Adrienne," I said patiently. "You're inside with the doors locked and the security system on. Why don't you have a bowl of ice cream and watch TV? Chantilly will be back before long."

"I don't see how I can go to sleep until she's here. That means tomorrow my eyes will be red and my face all puffy like a raw biscuit. The media are going to be crawling all over this, from the church to the cemetery, and then out in front when guests arrive. I'll be a laughingstock on the news tomorrow night. That horrid reporter will be gloating during every second of the film clip."

"Then go to bed so you'll be presentable."

Adrienne must have realized the futility of trying to talk me into a pajama party. "I know I'm being silly. I'll just go upstairs and take a bath and give myself a facial. Chantilly has a prescription for sleeping pills somewhere in her bathroom or on the dresser."

In that she was entirely too self-centered to commit suicide and therefore miss her Tae Bo classes and the opportunity to be recruited for Junior League, I wished her a peaceful night.

Then, wishing myself the same, I went to bed.

CHAPTER TWELVE

I was drinking coffee and reading the newspaper when Caron came home the next morning. "Did you have a good time?" I asked.

"Yeah, everything was fine, but Luanne must have the most uncomfortable sofa bed on the planet. If prisoners of war were forced to sleep on it, they'd spill their guts after eight hours." She went into the kitchen and returned with a glass of milk. "She said she was happy to keep Skyler until she heard from you. You didn't hear from Daphne, did you?"

"No," I said. "Do you have a black or navy skirt?"

"So I can audition to be in an orchestra? I hate to remind you, Mother, but I flunked out of the rhythm band in kindergarten, and was the only kid in the fifth grade who never learned to play 'Greensleeves' on a recorder. It was very traumatic."

"So you can accompany me to the preluncheon frenzy at Adrienne Armstrong's house. The caterer will have a staff of ten or twelve. Jacque, as he calls himself, won't even notice that he didn't hire you. If need be, I'll pass you off as the bartender's apprentice."

"Do I get tips?"

"You might. What's more important is that you'll have the chance to poke around inside and see if you can figure out what Daphne was looking for. The guests won't start arriving until shortly after noon. If you dress like everyone else, you'll be faceless."

"That is, like, so appealing," Caron said. "Can I also aspire to be nameless, aimless, and listless?"

"Adrienne's afraid that Daphne is hiding in the woods around the house, waiting for an opportunity to sneak inside. She could be right. The staff will all be bustling about, and I'm not sure I can disappear for more than a minute or two. I'll draw you a layout of the second floor."

Caron sat down and crossed her arms. "And if Daphne actually is there, with a gun, frothing at the mouth, I'll rate a bartender at my funeral? Better still, how about three oboes, a piccolo, and a mime? Rhonda will be so envious she'll commit suicide just so her parents can hire the Rockettes."

"Take a shower, dear. We need to leave in forty-five minutes."

Which we did, with some grumbling from the passenger's side of the car.

Having never attended a catered wake, I wasn't sure that there wouldn't be a tip jar on the bar. For all I knew, protocol would demand a string quartet seated at a discreet distance, diverting us from our grief with Bach and Vivaldi. Military jets might fly over in formation to offer a salute. It was just as well I wasn't rich, since I would have flubbed it at every turn.

Jacque and his forces had already descended with the subtlety of a high school drill team. Several vans were parked haphazardly on the road and in the driveway. Minions, dressed as I'd predicted, hustled back and forth, toting covered trays and roasting pans. No violins, violas, and cellos were in evidence, but the possibility could not be dismissed—unless, of course, the current vogue was bugles and bagpipes.

Caron stared. "And I'm supposed to say, 'Excuse me while I run down to the basement to search for clues'?"

"Try to blend in. If Jacque notices, tell him that you're with the bartender."

"I'm going to have to get a new role model, Mother—one who won't oblige me to learn how to make martinis for mourners. Doesn't this seem just a Little Bit Ludicrous?"

"No more so than filling Rhonda Maguire's locker with cheese sauce," I said. "Now go inside and pretend you're a staffer. When you have the chance, wander away from the action."

"Upstairs, downstairs, and in my lady's chamber?"

"Don't forget the attic," I said, then sent her into the fray.

Randy Scarpo came walking out of the woods beyond the driveway, dressed in the standard outfit. "I thought I'd better start the prep work," he said cheerfully. "Slice lemons and limes, stick toothpicks through olives, that sort of stuff."

"You've done this before?"

"At the country club before I took the job at the fitness center. The pay's about the same, and now I can work out four or five times a week."

"Did you encounter Anthony Armstrong at the country club?"

"Oh, yeah," he said, grimacing. "He and his pals had their own reserved table in a corner where they played poker when it was too cold or rainy for golf. It used to take me half an hour to clean up after they left. If I was lucky, someone left a couple of dollars as a tip."

"What did their wives think about it?"

"Some of them bitched about the cigar smoke and the noise, but there wasn't anything I could do about it. Adrienne was one of the few who thought it was funny. She used to say they reminded her of rowdy children playing 'Go Fish and Chips.' If that's all, Ms. Malloy . . ."

"Is Jillian coming for the luncheon?"

"No, she's taking Connor to the park—even though, according to her, he's likely to be kidnapped by men in black ski masks and held for ransom. She has a vivid imagination for someone so dull."

I felt an irrational need to defend Jillian despite her flagrant dislike of yours truly or, as far as I could tell, anyone else except Connor. "I read the article about the fire last year. That must have alarmed both of you."

Randy smirked. "She didn't even know what was going on until the fire trucks and paramedics arrived. It wasn't like we were in any danger, but she acted as though we were in the path of a lava flow from Pompeii. She wanted to pack suitcases and move to a motel—in another state."

"I'm a mother," I said, "and I know how the maternal instinct kicks in when the cubs are threatened. Did you try to talk to her?"

"Yes, and in words of one syllable. I'd better start setting up the bar."

I refrained from tripping him and followed him into the house. He continued out to the backyard, but I dutifully went into the kitchen. A man who looked more like a burly carnival roustabout than a master of haute cuisine was bellowing at a girl who was slouched over a cutting board. Carrot fragments were scattered on the counter.

"I said thin! These are chunks! Disgusting chunks! Throw them in the garbage and start again, but this time pay attention. Otherwise, I'll demonstrate for you, using your thumbs!" He glared until she nodded, then looked at me. "I was told no guests would arrive until noon. You'll have to find some other place to stand. I suggest the middle of the nearest highway."

I considered bristling but decided it was below me. "I'm Claire Malloy. At Adrienne Armstrong's request, I spoke to you on the phone yesterday. I promised her I'd come here this morning in case any problems arise."

"I am Jacque Chambrun, not a short-order cook at a diner. Three weeks ago I catered a banquet for five hundred corporate executives and their spouses. Next week I'm doing a wedding dinner for three hundred. If I have a problem, I see to it myself. At this moment, you are a problem, since you're blocking the door. Are you able to escort yourself out of the kitchen, or should I help you?"

"*Pardonez-moi?* Oh, sorry, you're not French, are you?" I winked at him, then left before he could attack me with a chunky carrot stick. I went on to the backyard, where Caron and several other staffers were spreading tablecloths on round tables. Randy was behind a make-shift bar, transferring maraschino cherries from a jar to a glass. The grass was clipped, the flower beds beginning to show promise. The clouds rolling in, however, were promising something entirely different.

Caron gave me a piteous look, but I ignored her and returned inside. My presence was not needed outside, and clearly was not welcome in the kitchen. I dodged a

couple of boys with cartons of china, considered the possibilities, and finally decided to do a more careful search
upstairs. I'd looked around Daphne's bedroom, but I'd
done nothing more than peek at the master suite or any
of the other bedrooms. Or the attic, if indeed there was
one. It seemed inordinately gothic to go there with a
storm approaching, replete with flashes of lightning to
illuminate the horribly mutilated lunatic crouched behind
the chimney.

Mary Shelley, please meet your party at the gate.

As I reached the bottom of the staircase, I noticed the
door to Anthony's office was ajar. I'd closed it the day
before, so it was obvious that someone else had been
there since then. Which was interesting. I smiled brightly
as a girl came through the front door with a suitably
stunted floral arrangement, waited until she continued on
her way, then moved quietly toward the office.

I wasn't really expecting to find anyone inside as I
opened the door, and therefore gurgled unattractively as
I gaped at Finnigan Baybergen, who was seated behind
the desk.

"This is really most fascinating," he murmured.

I stepped inside and closed the door. "Yes, it is. Feel
free to elaborate."

"I was speaking of the abstract," he said as he held
up a thick pad of pages. "I found it in the bottom drawer
of the filing cabinet in the closet."

"Adrienne made it very clear yesterday that you're
not welcome in her home. I doubt she's changed her
mind since then."

"Which is why I waited until I was sure she would
be at the funeral. I didn't expect to see you here, though.
I find it difficult to understand your role in this, Ms.
Malloy. You claim to be an ally of Miss Parchester, yet

you seem to be spending a lot of time in this house."

"So do you."

"Only because it's important that I confirm the existence of particular information that Armstrong was privy to. His wife does not seem inclined to allow me access to his files, and she'll have me arrested if I'm here when she returns. Why don't you run along to your little bookstore? I'll put everything back where I found it and be careful to close the door when I leave. It will be for the best if you don't mention I was here."

"I'm not one of your freshman botany students, Baybergen," I said. "What's the document you're reading?"

"As I said, the abstract."

"The abstract of what?" I said, thinking of slides from an art appreciation class that I'd taken to avoid modern dance. I am a woman of many talents, but fluttering is not among them.

"Oakland Heights, of course. You do understand what an abstract is, don't you?" My blank look answered his question, and he continued as if he were lecturing the hapless on the distinction between liverwort and moss (which I am sure is a very sublime distinction, indeed). "It traces the ownership of a parcel of land back to its original grant from the government, in this case in 1854 by President Franklin Pierce. The parcel stayed in one family until shortly after the Civil War, when one must think the sons who might have inherited the homestead did not return. After that, the parcel changed hands quite a few times, sometimes for cash and other times as part of an estate, but in 1937 came into the possession of a family named"—he flipped through the pages—"Zorelli. Luther Zorelli inherited it from his father, Riccardo, in 1969. When Luther died in 1991, the parcel was passed on to his daughter, Sheila Armstrong, nee Zorelli. She immediately sold it to Armstrong Development, Inc. for one dollar and other valuable consideration. Three years ago she signed a quit claim deed, which terminated any lingering issue of dower rights."

"Sheila." I sat down on the leather chair and tried to process what he'd said. "It must have included this area, too. I saw some old family photos with a farmhouse and a barn."

"Forty acres," said Baybergen wistfully, as if imagining his own little house on the prairie. "In these days of vast corporate farms, it doesn't sound impressive, but it must have been adequate for Riccardo and his wife. Bear in mind that in 1937 this land was well out in the country. They wouldn't have been burdened with utility bills."

"I'll have to agree it's fascinating, but it doesn't explain why you sneaked into the house and put yourself in danger of being arrested once again for trespassing. Couldn't you have found all this at the courthouse?"

He rocked back in the chair and gave me a supercilious smile. "What makes you think I didn't?"

"Because you're here."

"You have a point. Mr. Constantine and I did no more than a brief search of the deed books to determine the most recent owners of the property. What I find fascinating is the link all the way back to the pre–Civil War era. It's hard to imagine why settlers would have come here. There's no convenient access to a navigable river or—"

"What is it that you're hoping to find?" I said. "There's nothing in the abstract that you couldn't have found in an extended search, and President Pierce is not going to revoke the grant."

"Unfortunately, he is not," Finnigan conceded. "I believe that somewhere in these files is a geological map that specifies the demarcation of the fault line, which will prove that Armstrong knew of the potential risk when he constructed Oakland Heights. It may be too late for the bastard to face criminal charges of reckless endangerment, but his estate will be subject to a civil lawsuit. We'll see how many more condos Armstrong Development can construct after they pay a judgment of several million dollars. Juries can be generous to victims of callous disregard."

"But you haven't found the map?"

He shook his head. "I'd hoped it might be tucked in the abstract along with the survey maps, but it was not."

"Did you mention this to the police or the prosecutor?"

"Ms. Malloy, I don't think you could pass the midterm exam in my freshman botany class, much less the final. The chief of police played both golf and poker with Armstrong several times a month, and the prosecutor owns ten percent of the Phase Two limited partnership. If the authorities find the map, I imagine there will be a little bonfire behind the clubhouse, followed by a round of drinks in the bar."

I found myself wondering how much Peter knew about the glaring conflicts of interest. Had he been instructed to charge Daphne on his boss's orders, despite the dubious evidence of two eyewitnesses who'd been drinking margaritas for a couple of hours? Was convicting her the most expedient way to keep the development on schedule?

"Why are you so certain this map still exists?" I asked him. "Wouldn't Armstrong have destroyed it a long time ago?"

"One of my sources said he did not, that he glanced

at it, then dismissed it and put it away with other non-essential paperwork concerning Oakland Heights. The planning commission doesn't require a geological survey, so why worry them?"

"And this source would be Sheila Armstrong, nee Zorelli?"

Finnigan replaced the abstract in a filing cabinet in the closet behind him. "I'm afraid I can't answer that, Ms. Malloy. As much as I've enjoyed our conversation, I think I'd better leave before the hostess arrives home."

I moved in front of the door. "Did the police question you about your whereabouts on the night of Armstrong's murder?"

"As in my alibi? Dear, deluded woman, do you honestly think I crept into the house and shot the man because he wouldn't hand over a map?"

"Did you?" I said bluntly.

"If I had, I most assuredly wouldn't admit it, would I? The police did inquire. I was home all night, and on the Internet until well after two in the morning, networking with environmental and civil liberties groups to find a way to thwart Armstrong's no-trespassing dictum. One of the officers confirmed that I was downloading documents at the time of the murder."

"Unless someone else was using your computer."

"All things are possible."

After he left, I approached the filing cabinet in the closet. I'd noticed it the day before, but I doubted I would have examined it even if the telephone hadn't rung in the kitchen. The clock on the desk indicated I had most of an hour before flowers were tossed onto the coffin and the gentlemen (in this case, limo drivers) started their engines.

The drawer in which Baybergen had replaced the

Oakland Heights abstract contained several others of the same ilk. Most of them had notes stapled on the covers specifying names of apartment and condo complexes. Another drawer contained ledgers and thick files of bank statements. My accountant might have been able to find damning evidence, but I had neither the time nor the inclination to muddle through the various corporate records to determine Anthony's bottom line.

The top drawer proved to be much more intriguing. I took out a file that pertained to the divorce, and sat down. A restraining order threatened Sheila with contempt if she came within a hundred yards of his house, office, or person. An audit seemed to imply that Anthony himself had almost no assets, and that various partnerships and corporations paid for the maintenance of the house, cars, country club membership, health insurance, and annual vacations to Baja and Bimini. I wondered if he'd played poker with the chancery judge who'd deemed him a veritable pauper when the issue of alimony arose. The remaining documents were dry: a copy of the divorce decree, a copy of the quit claim deed Baybergen had mentioned, a delineation of child visitation, and so forth.

I set the file aside and moved on. The next was marked with Adrienne's name. Anthony had chosen his trophy bride with a certain amount of circumspection, having obtained a copy of a transcript of her grades (middling), a printout of her prior traffic violations (numerous), and a background check done by a private detective. This was more entertaining than fiction, I decided as I read the first page. Adrienne had been born in Memphis, and according to my calculations, was indeed twenty-five years old. Her parents had died while she was in grade school, and she and her younger sister (burdened at birth with the boring moniker of Carla Anne) lived with relatives until she enrolled at Farber College seven years ago. Adrienne had been popular with her high school peers, but less so with the faculty, who remembered her only as an uninspired student. She'd been arrested twice for possession of alcohol, once for attempting to forge a prescription for a narcotic drug, and once for shoplifting from a department store. Her driver's license had been suspended for three months for driving while intoxicated.

Sadly typical, I thought as I turned to the next page. It proved to be a prenuptial agreement drawn up three years previously by a local law firm. I glanced at the clock. If Adrienne had rushed the Reverend Simpleton through any part of the ritual, she and her guests might appear soon. Even though I could see the driveway from where I was sitting, I got up and opened a window in case I became so engrossed in what I was reading that I failed to pay attention. The catering vans had been moved in order to provide more parking. As I looked, the KFAR van rolled up and stopped. Jessica did not emerge, but I was confident she would provide live footage on the six o'clock news that would rival the annual Oscar red carpet fanfare.

I realized I'd better sprint through the files if I didn't want to be found with the equivalent of a smoking gun on the desk. The prenuptial agreement was padded with legal jargon, but it seemed to state that Adrienne would receive a piddly $50,000 if the marriage ended in divorce before its tenth-year anniversary, and a maximum of $100,000 after that. No alimony, although in the event of the birth of a baby that DNA testing confirmed to be Anthony's, child support would be negotiated by the court. She would retain all gifts given to her during the duration, as well as her share of Oakland Heights Phase Two.

Attached was a bare-bones synopsis of the last will and testament of Anthony Armstrong, also written three years ago by the same legal firm. In the event of his death—I must admit at that moment I shivered, realizing I was reading the will as his coffin was being lowered—Sheila Zorelli Armstrong was to receive $25,000. A set of antique golf clubs was to go to one friend, $50,000 to the Disciples Christian Academy, $10,000 to an organization that gave the ACLU cause to purchase aspirin in bulk, $10,000 to a housekeeper whom I had yet to see, and a few minor bequests to civic clubs that subtly managed to exclude minorities and women. The remainder of the estate, which I sensed was not minimal, was to be divided between Daphne Armstrong and Adrienne Durmond Armstrong. Two rather chilling conditions were attached: Adrienne would inherit nothing if it could be proved that she had had an affair during the course of the marriage, and Daphne's share was to remain in an impenetrable trust until she turned thirty or proved to the satisfaction of the executor that she was of pious and exemplary moral character.

If Anthony Armstrong had been on the carpet (and already dead, mind you), I might have struggled with the temptation to slap him with the will. If there'd been a marker handy, I would have written "pious and exemplary" on his forehead. All capital letters.

I rubbed my temples until my outrage—and that is exactly what it was—began to lessen. Had he been sitting behind the desk when he ordered Daphne to have an abortion in order to protect his reputation? Had he sneered when he reviewed the private detective's report of Adrienne's pitiful teenaged indiscretions? Had he and his lawyer chuckled as they filed the restraining order to prevent Sheila from setting foot on her grandparents' farm? And how pleased he must have been when he enrolled Daphne in the Disciples Christian Academy, where she was buffered from anyone who might have darker skin or an accent—or a contrary opinion.

And what could he have thought when he saw the geological map that indicated the earthquake fault? Nothing worthy of the celebrated San Andreas Fault, obviously, but conceivably dangerous. Anthony Armstrong had not so much as hesitated. He'd tossed aside the pesky documentation and built Phase One. The fire was peripheral damage, but not reason enough to delay Phase Two. After all, despite a miscarriage, a broken bone or two, and significant lung damage, housing was still in demand. The very idea of preserving hundred-year-old oak trees must have bewildered him. Trees? What next— spotted owls and albino cave newts?

I stood up, feeling unclean from even minimal contact with his petty domain. He hadn't been evil, but he had been hurtful. I felt as though I should don a white hat and ride out to save his daughter, grandson, ex-wife, and current wife, but I lacked a trusty steed—and a loyal sidekick, since my only candidate was baby-sitting.

As it was, I thumbed through several other folders and was beginning to think that a carrot stick might be welcome when I heard a gunshot. I say this, but there are sounds—and there are sounds. Nothing appeared to be happening in the driveway; no staffers collapsing, no television reporter clutching her helmet of hair and tumbling to the ground, no deer staggering out of the woods to take up valuable parking space.

I crammed the files back into the cabinet, closed the closet door, and went into the foyer. Laden trays were flowing smoothly from the kitchen to the buffet tables in the backyard. No eyebrows were raised, no eyes widened. Business as usual.

I was beginning to doubt myself when Caron clutched my shoulder.

"Mother," she whispered, peering over her shoulder, "I saw Daphne."

"You saw her where?"

"In back. I was putting out silverware when I saw someone crouched behind the azaleas. I didn't know what to do, so I just kept following instructions while I tried to watch this person. I wasn't positive it wasn't a dog or a cow or something silly, but then I saw this girl who fits your description. Somebody yelled at her and she took off, running toward the front of the house."

"Did she have a gun?"

"I didn't think to tackle her and inquire," said Caron.

"I thought I heard a shot."

"Lucky you. All I've heard is the proper placement of salad forks and the need to fold napkins with hospital corners. Does this make sense, Mother? Are really tiny sick people going to show up and tuck themselves into napkins? Promise me that you'll never be this banal."

"So Daphne ran across the driveway and into the woods? How long ago?"

"A few minutes ago, maybe five or ten. I didn't want to get everybody else all agitated, so I waited until I could sneak inside and find you."

"Keep folding napkins," I said, then went out the front door and past the KFAR van. A path to Oakland Heights had been mentioned several times, and indeed there was one. I wasn't precisely jogging, since I find it an abomination, but I was moving briskly as I pushed through tangles and progressed downhill.

I stopped abruptly when I realized I was under the platform of Miss Parchester's contested oak tree. No bleeding bodies were splayed nearby. Squirrels were regarding me. Luckily, Howie was not.

"Miss Parchester," I called softly.

"Why, Claire," she said, appearing overhead to look down at me, "you do seem to visit often. As I said, I am not in need of anything at the moment, but—"

"I heard a gunshot."

"Oh, dear, how distressing for you."

"Miss Parchester, I was told that Daphne Armstrong came running this way—and I most certainly heard a gunshot not more than ten minutes ago. You must have heard something."

"I suppose I must have."

I took a deep breath and exhaled slowly, resisting a sudden impulse to claw my way up the tree to her perch. "Would you please elaborate?"

"Daphne did come by here a few minutes ago. What you heard, however, might have been a backfire from a car. Hunting is limited to autumn and winter, and would never be allowed within the city limits in any season."

"Can you describe the vehicle?"

"I do not have a view of the entirety of the parking lot."

And I wouldn't have been amazed if the theme music of *Twilight Zone* had begun to waft from the woods. Out from behind the construction shed would come Rod Serling, as opposed to Howie the Wonder Dogsbody.

"Daphne's up there, isn't she?" I said.

"Up here?"

"Yes, Miss Parchester."

Her face disappeared. I sat down and listened to a whispery conversation, not at all sure what I was going to do if the rope ladder came tumbling down. Did Daphne have a gun? Was she holding Miss Parchester hostage? Was I less astute than an acorn to be forcing the issue? What I needed, I thought, was Caron, who, at her advanced age of sixteen, had one hundred percent of the answers. Multiple choice or true-false, the answer was always there somewhere.

"Claire," Miss Parchester trilled, "it is possible that Daphne may be here. She would like to reaffirm that she did not shoot her father."

"Where's the gun?"

"The gun is not in Daphne's possession."

"The police aren't so sure. At this moment, the word's out that she may be armed and dangerous. She needs to turn herself in." I looked up at the bottom of the platform. "I promise she can spend a few minutes with Skyler before we go to the police department."

After an interlude during which more whispering ensued, Miss Parchester said, "It's much more complicated than you realize, Claire. You are doing the best you can, but you are not cognizant of the complexities of the situation. If Daphne were to turn herself in, the court would do nothing more than assign an incompetent neophyte to her case, who might make a few halfhearted objections and then nap throughout the trial. Daphne has good reason to doubt she will receive justice. Papa was painfully aware of the fragility of the system."

It was all I could do not to clutch my own throat and throttle myself. "Miss Parchester, Daphne has been charged with her father's murder. She was seen running out of the house, and she admitted to me that she had a gun in her hand. If she didn't shoot her father, then someone else did." I upped my volume. "She can hunker up there as long as she wants. Eventually, though, the ecology issue will be resolved and the platform will be dismantled. Odds are that KFAR will provide live coverage. Maybe Daphne doesn't care about Skyler. I can always call social services and hope they'll find him reasonably clean foster homes for the next eighteen years."

The ladder dropped, and Daphne followed in a clumsy sprawl. "You won't let them take Skyler, will you?" she said between gasps. She was wearing civilian clothing, but traces of orange were visible beneath her ankle cuffs.

"He can't stay in a basket. You've put me in a truly precarious position. I'd feel more confident if I were out on the limb with Miss Parchester."

"But Skyler's just a baby."

"And so are you, but you need to clamp down on your lower lip and start acting like an adult, as well as a parent. You obviously weren't ready for either role, but that doesn't alter the reality."

"They'll put me in prison."

"They might if we don't get to the bottom of this. Has a lawyer been assigned to help you?"

"Yeah, this lame guy. He thinks we can cut a bargain and I'll only go to prison for six years. Do you realize how much of Skyler's life I'll miss? First steps, walking and talking, birthday parties, riding a bicycle, catching a fish, throwing a ball? This so-called lawyer wants me to plead guilty, Ms. Malloy."

"You have to tell me what happened," I said.

"I already did. I was upstairs when I heard a gunshot."

"I need to hear the truth, Daphne. You weren't upstairs picking up an extra pair of pajamas. You were looking for something."

Miss Parchester peered down at us. "Howie might

return at any moment. I do not think it wise for him to find the two of you."

"Does he have a gun?" I asked.

"Yes, he became very edgy when Daphne extricated herself from custody. I'm not at all convinced he knows how to employ it, and thus far he's created more havoc with his cell phone. Miss Whitbred and Louis Ferncliff were arrested yet again this morning. Those three unsavory men who were here the other night returned, too, but when Howie threatened to call the police, they left. Perhaps the backfire was from their pickup truck."

I looked at the confusion of trees, scrub pines, and thorny undergrowth that only Finnigan Baybergen could love. "Where's Howie now?"

"I don't know," she said. "He was very nervous, and has been prowling about all morning. He kept hearing car doors slamming and voices, although I gather most of it has been coming from the direction of the Armstrong house. I tried to tell him that, but he is quite sure the Green Party is plotting an offensive. Howie watches entirely too many movies."

"I'd better get out of here," said Daphne. "I want to see Skyler, Ms. Malloy, but I don't want to go to prison."

I grabbed her arm. "Do you have the gun?"

"No, I swear I don't. Just promise me you'll take care of Skyler until I can figure this out."

"Until you can find the geological map? What if your mother is wrong and the map no longer exists?"

Daphne gaped at me. "How do you know about that?"

"I'm a bona fide snoop. Did you and your mother think that if you had possession of the map, you could blackmail your father? That's why you went to the house on Tuesday, isn't it?"

"Maybe," she said sullenly.

"And why you were in your father's office?"

"I already told you I was upstairs. My mother said he kept some old files in the guest bedroom closet. You have to believe me when I say I didn't know he was home. I came in through the conservatory. I figured I'd better search upstairs first, so that if they came back, I could look in his office after they'd gone to bed."

"And then you heard the gunshots?"

"Claire," said Miss Parchester, "you are not permitted to badger the witness. Daphne has explained her presence in the house."

"Yes, Your Honor," I said, then turned back to Daphne. "Where have you been staying since yesterday morning?"

"So you can tell the cops?"

"So they can take you back into custody before anyone else gets hurt, including you. Did Arnie find a place for you to stay?"

"Arnie?" she said with the wide-eyed gaze of a porcelain doll.

"I know that he helped you escape yesterday. He's admitted to the note, the clothes, and a lift from the courthouse. Where did he take you?"

"He didn't take me anywhere. I went down to the basement and out the door."

Miss Parchester cleared her throat. "I truly think you should be leaving. I don't know what's gotten into Howie, but he's usually very diligent. You both are likely to find yourselves in police custody should he return."

"Let me take you to see Skyler," I said to Daphne.

"And then turn me in? I know you're trying to help, Ms. Malloy, but I have to take care of myself first. If I can just find Joey, I'll ask him to look after Skyler."

I wanted to shake some sense into her, but settled for a sigh. "How do you think you're going to take care of yourself, Daphne? You're broke, homeless, and have the questionable distinction of meriting an APB. The police will distribute flyers with your mug shot to all the establishments in Farberville, as well as to a certain bar in Waverly. You haven't found this map that you and your mother are hoping will provide fodder for blackmail—which, by the way, happens to be a felony. Adrienne may well laugh and tell you to give the map to whomever you wish, including Finnigan Baybergen. She'll be living in the Cayman Islands off the proceeds of your father's estate long before the lawsuit reaches the court. Your share will be jeopardized, but you won't see a penny of it for another twelve years, anyway."

"I won't?" she said.

"Did you think you would if you killed him?"

"I didn't kill him, Ms. Malloy. As soon as I got there, I went upstairs. Why won't you believe me?"

"I wish I could, at least for Skyler's sake." A thought as unpleasant as the gathering storm clouds crossed my mind. "Are you protecting your mother? Do you think she went to the house to find this map?"

Daphne jumped to her feet. "No, she didn't! I don't trust you, Ms. Malloy. Maybe I'll be in touch in a few days."

She ran down the slope to the parking lot of Phase One. A car started seconds later and drove away.

"Goodness," said Miss Parchester.

"Gracious," I added.

CHAPTER THIRTEEN

"Miss Parchester," I said plaintively, "you have to tell me what you know."

"If you don't mind, my dear, I'd like to listen to the radio. News from the BBC comes on at noon, and although I don't always understand the issues, I am an Anglophile. One of these days I aspire to take a bus tour of Kent and Cornwall. Oh, just imagine the cream teas, the gardens, the cathedrals, the pubs, the vicars . . . I become misty just thinking of it all."

Only one word penetrated my mind. "Noon?"

"That is what I said. I've put on the kettle so I can have a cup of tea while I curl up with the members of Parliament. Such an elegant group, if a bit rowdy."

The rope ladder had been retrieved while I'd talked, albeit unsuccessfully, with Daphne. I did not want to encounter Howie and find myself handcuffed in the backseat of a police car, or being obliged to write a check for bail. And it was approaching noon, when Adrienne and her guests would arrive, recuperating from their sorrow and ready for marinated *coeurs d'artichaut,* as I was sure Jacque called them after he'd spilled them out of jars and splashed on a little olive oil and garlic.

"I'll be back," I called to Miss Parchester.

"So will Howie."

I muttered an expletive as I stood up, brushed off my derriere, and hurried up the path to the Armstrong house. Surely Adrienne would be swaddled by her close friends by now, or clinging to her lawyer's arm as she stumbled to the buffet table. I no longer had a reason to search the house. The geological map was more likely to be at Anthony's business office than on a dresser in Chantilly's room or the master suite. Or in Finnigan Baybergen's pocket. Or long sent blowing in the wind. A treasure map it was not, but only a squiggly hodgepodge of lines that might have indicated the presence of a fault line that might have caused a fire.

If all was running smoothly, I could clutch Adrienne's hand and offer condolences, then spirit Caron away before she became too enamored of spending time in the company of the rich and pretentious. I much preferred her as she was, a rare combination of childishness and artfulness well beyond her years. She had an impressive repertoire; boring was not part of it.

A limousine drove up as I arrived at the edge of the road. I pasted on a properly sympathetic smile as Adrienne stepped out. I was somewhat surprised when Lieutenant Peter Rosen followed her. She wore a modest black dress; he wore a dark suit and muted navy tie.

Ken and Barbie, returning from Barbie's Dream Cemetery.

"Bless you, my dear friend Claire," said Adrienne. "Is everything set for the luncheon? There was just an absolute crush of people at the funeral, and I have no idea how many of them will be coming."

I forced myself to join them. "Oh, yes. Jacque is

adamant that he has it under control. The tables in the backyard are set with linens and silverware. Randy arrived two hours ago to prepare the bar."

"And Chantilly? Is she here?"

Ignoring Peter, whose eyes were flickering in a somewhat ominous fashion, I said, "No, I assumed she was with you. I didn't go upstairs, but I will now."

"She didn't come back last night," said Adrienne, her eyes filling with tears. "I don't understand how she could do this to me. She must know how much I needed her at the funeral. If it hadn't been for Peter, I would have totally lost it and humiliated myself in front of all those hundreds of people."

I was trying to come up with a suitable response when the back door of the KFAR van opened and a cameraman appeared, accompanied by a man balancing a boom mike, and the omnipresent Jessica Princeton, dressed in an appropriately conservative outfit and ready to wrench a display of raw emotions from the widow.

"Mrs. Armstrong," she began, "I'm Jessica Princeton from KFAR. As I'm sure you know, your stepdaughter escaped from police custody yesterday. Were you worried that she might show up at the funeral this morning?"

"No, but Lieutenant Rosen offered to escort me just in case."

Jessica turned on Peter. "Then you are concerned for Mrs. Armstrong's safety?"

"We are concerned about every citizen's safety," he said tightly.

"Have you made any progress in locating Daphne Armstrong?"

Peter glanced at me, and then said, "No, we haven't, but we are continuing to investigate possible locales and interview those who might have knowledge of her current whereabouts. Anyone with information should call the police department immediately."

Jessica raised her eyebrows, although not far enough to tempt a wrinkle. "Is she still considered armed and dangerous?"

"No comment."

"Mrs. Armstrong, do you have any reason to fear that Daphne may attempt to cause you harm? You are, after all, a key witness."

"I am also a widow who has just now come from the cemetery. I'm sure you and your viewers will understand if I decline to make further statements. Please address any other questions to my lawyer." She slid her hand beneath Peter's arm. "Lieutenant Rosen, will you be so kind as to help me inside? I'm a little unsteady on my feet."

"Yes, of course," he said, then looked at the reporter. "Uniformed officers will be arriving at any moment to provide security. You and your crew need to vacate the premises or risk being cited as a public nuisance. Do I make myself clear?"

"Are you familiar with the concept of freedom of the press?" she countered.

"Would you like to film a documentary from inside the cellblock at the Farberville Police Department?"

My lips may have quivered as Jessica reeled around and gestured to her crew to follow her to the van, but I maintained my composure and trailed Adrienne and Peter into the house. Once inside, I scurried upstairs, tapped on Chantilly's door, and when I received no response, went into the room.

Some of the clothes might have been shifted from this chair to that, but they hadn't been stuffed in suitcases to be transported home to Atlanta via airplane or

Adrienne's Jaguar. The array of makeup on the vanity in the bathroom defied description, and there were at least two dozen bottles of shampoo, conditioners, and other esoteric hair products on a shelf by the shower. After some hesitation, I opened the closet door, looked under the bed, and quickly searched all the other upstairs rooms without finding anything more telling than a used condom under Daphne's bed and a titillating array of sex aids in the back of a cabinet in the master bathroom.

It was likely that Chantilly was still in Farberville, possibly shacked up with some muscular college boy she'd met the previous afternoon. But she wouldn't have blown off Anthony's funeral, I decided. Adrienne was stressed, if not stricken with grief. Chantilly wouldn't have left without explanation, and she'd had nearly twenty-four hours to resurface. Or sober up, or return impulse purchases at the mall, or whatever.

There was definitely something rotten in the mini-state of Oakland Heights. I went downstairs and out to the backyard, steeling myself to yank Peter away from the poor little widow. He could be persuaded to send a bulletin to officers on patrol to watch for Adrienne's car, even though Farberville had more apartment complexes and motels-by-the-hour than it ever would migratory hawks. Chantilly would not be pleased should she be found in a scurrilous situation, but I really didn't care.

The postfuneral party had arrived, and there did seem to be more than a hundred people buzzing about the buffet and bar, sipping wine and cocktails, and chatting at the tables with centerpieces of exemplary height. Caron was behind the bar with Randy, her lower lip extended and her face flushed. Jacque's army moved deferentially among the guests, retrieving platters to be replenished, discreetly gathering abandoned plates and glasses, resetting tables, their eyes glazed and their smiles carved like those on moldy jack-o'-lanterns. I wondered if Jacque kept them in cold storage until he needed them.

I spotted two of the women I'd seen at the fitness center, and the lawyer who'd been at Anthony's side during the press conference. Farberville's esteemed mayor was present, slapping backs and shaking hands as if at a political rally. Other faces were vaguely familiar, perhaps from feature stories in the newspaper about community luminaries who read books once a year at elementary schools and sponsored golf tournaments to benefit the victims of disabling diseases.

Not my crowd.

It seemed impossible to find Peter without shrieking his name or firing a nonexistent weapon. I was about to go inside and call Jorgeson when Adrienne grasped my arm and dragged me aside.

"You have to do something!" she whispered so urgently that I felt the need to dry my ear with the nearest napkin. "This is so awful!"

"It seems to be going nicely," I said, trying not to wince as her fingernails dug into my arm. Bruises, if not scabs, were inevitable.

"She's here."

I stared at her. "Daphne? Where is she?"

"Not Daphne. Jacque told one of the waiters to tell me that Sheila's in the kitchen, making herself a sandwich. How on earth could she have found the nerve to show up at a time like this? Why is she doing this to me? What if Jacque storms out? I won't be able to show my face at the club ever again!" She gulped down what appeared to be a martini (sans olive, which was lucky, since I'd never learned the Heimlich maneuver). "This is going to be a total disaster, and it'll be her fault. Promise me you'll make her leave, Claire. I'll buy you whatever you want—a new car, a trip to Tahiti, a decent wardrobe, anything!"

I extricated her fingernails from my flesh. "I'll see what's going on in the kitchen, Adrienne. Pull yourself together and go talk to Mary Margaret or one of those relatives you mentioned. I can probably convince Sheila to leave without causing a commotion."

"A commotion? Do you think she'll barge out here and start ranting? I am really, really having a bad day. I hope you appreciate that."

I had not the slightest idea what I thought Sheila might do, but I gave Adrienne a reassuring smile and said, "Deal with your guests."

I gave her a gentle shove in the direction of the bar, then went inside and into the kitchen. Sheila was indeed slathering pâté on a slice of bread, seemingly oblivious to Jacque's livid glare. For the occasion, she'd chosen a black taffeta gown seen more often at formal affairs frequented by those who spend daylight hours in coffins. And the cowboy boots. And a tattered mantilla.

It was not a fashion statement that would speak to the crowd in the backyard.

She glanced back at me as I approached. "My goodness, you do get around. I'm not surprised to find you here, though. This house must be overrun with vermin."

I took her sandwich, put it on a plate, and growled, "Follow me."

When we were in the dining room, I handed her the sandwich and told her to sit down.

"But I don't have anything to drink."

"Don't move," I warned her, then went outside and elbowed my way to the bar. "A double vodka straight up," I said to Randy. Caron gave me a quizzical look, but I could only shrug in response. I took the glass, loaded a plate with hors d'oeuvres from the buffet, and hurried back to the dining room.

Sheila was greedily eating the sandwich. I set the glass and plate within her reach, and sat down across from her.

"Why did you come today?" I asked her.

She swallowed what was in her mouth and took a gulp of vodka. "I may not have been fond of Anthony these last three years, but I was married to him for almost twenty years. Those people outside used to be my friends. They came to my parties and I to theirs. I just thought I'd stop by so we could share our remembrances of Anthony and the good old days." She adjusted the mantilla. "Do you find this overly dramatic?"

"How did you get here? Did you drive yourself?"

"Heavens, no. My car hasn't run in years. I'd get rid of it, but several cats have had their litters in it. It's as though I'm providing a homeless shelter for our little feline friends."

"Then how did you get here?"

"Why don't you be a good little exterminator and fetch me another drink? Anthony refused to give me enough money for expensive vodka, so I might as well enjoy this while I can. Better yet, bring a bottle and I'll take it with me to the cemetery. Anthony might roll over a few times while I sit on his grave and tell him what I'm drinking."

She was stuffing mushrooms and asparagus spears down the front of her dress as I went into the kitchen. "Is there a liquor supply in here?" I demanded.

Rumbling like a pressure cooker, Jacque pointed at a cabinet below the shelves of cookbooks. I grabbed a bottle of vodka and returned once again to the dining room.

"I'll let you have this after you answer my questions," I said with all the compassion of a prison matron. "First, how did you get here?"

"Do you think I saddled up a mule and rode out here? I called a cab, of course."

"A cab?"

"The driver was half an hour late, and very peculiar. He claims to manage the local office of a United States senator. When I pointed out the absurdity of him driving a cab, he said he was keeping his finger on the pulse of his boss's constituency. I made it very clear that he was not going to put his finger on my pulse or anything else of mine. I think I shall write a letter of complaint to the cab company."

She reached for the bottle, but I shook my head and said, "I'm not finished. Did you come here in hopes of finding the geological map?"

"I've never heard of that kind of map, and if I had one, I wouldn't have the foggiest idea what to do with it."

"Oh, yes, you would. Finnigan Baybergen told me all about it. In fact, I discovered him in Anthony's office this morning, searching through the filing cabinet."

Her face turned pale. "You did? But he wasn't supposed to do that. He came to my house a few days ago—I don't remember when—and said he was researching the history of the property. I told him all about how my grandfather moved his family here from Sicily and bought the land to start a vineyard. When the soil wasn't right, he had to settle for vegetables and some chickens. My parents weren't interested in farming, so they rented the property over the years. Then it came into my possession, and I sold it to that son of a bitch. The house that my grandparents built was in this exact spot. When I was a child, I used to come out here all the time and play in the woods or climb around in the barn. When I was six or seven, I fell out of the loft and broke my arm. I still have a scar."

"What about the purported fault line?"

"Oh, that," she said, laughing. "There were stories from other families who lived out here about dishes tumbling off shelves and pictures crashing to the floor. My grandmother swore the farmhouse was haunted, so my father went to the geology department at the college and they gave him a map. She never forgave him."

"What happened to this map?"

"My father folded it up and stuck it in the abstract, and it was still there when it came to me. When I found it, I told Anthony all the silly stories about poltergeists and disgruntled ghosts with an aversion to carnival glass. In his contemptuous way, he thought it was all very amusing, as though my grandparents had been nothing more than superstitious peasants." She picked up her empty glass and studied it. "I wanted to punish him."

"By blackmailing him?"

"Well, yes," she said as she reached for the bottle. I passed it to her and waited. Once she'd filled her glass, she continued more cheerfully. "He had a major financial investment in Phase One, and enough acreage to eventually have condos all the way down the hillside—as long as the information about the fault was not made public. I mean, who'd want to buy a unit that might catch on fire or slide over the bluff? And of course there might be pesky little lawsuits from tenants who'd already suffered damages. I used to sit back and imagine his expression when I told him what it would cost to keep me quiet." She drained the glass and refilled it. "But now, alas, he's not here and poor Adrienne's financial future is in danger. What a shame."

I retrieved the bottle. "And Daphne's. She stands to inherit half the estate."

"You've been reading the will, haven't you?"

I nodded. "What's to keep Baybergen from going public?"

"Why would he do that? He told me he was writing a book about the history of the county. He brought me a bottle of vodka, a box of chocolates, and a little fern to put on the windowsill in my kitchen. So few people come to visit these days."

I felt a flicker of sympathy for her, but not enough to ignite even the smallest fire. "So you told Daphne about the map, and she came here to find it. Did you tell her where to look for it?"

"He stored boxes all over the house," she said. "I didn't tell her to shoot him, but I don't blame her."

"And you believe that she did?"

"From what I've been told, I suppose I do. Anthony was once a good-natured man with a semblance of a sense of humor. He and I used to go on picnics, fly kites, rescue kittens, make love in the morning and again that evening. But something happened to him as he began to make money. We joined the country club so he could make deals in the locker room. His taste in music changed. He shopped with me to make sure I was buying clothes that were competitive. An interesting concept, don't you think?" She stopped for a long moment. "I knew it was a matter of time before I was replaced, and I have to admit I did not handle it well. Odd, being condemned as an anachronism at thirty-nine."

This unexpected turn in the conversation was making

me uncomfortable, to put it mildly. "But why did you abandon Daphne?"

"Early retirement. I'd like to leave now."

"How will you get home?"

"My driver is waiting at the road. If you'll give me the bottle, I won't make a scene, as entertaining as it might be."

"One last question," I said, keeping the bottle out of her reach. "Do you have any idea where Daphne is staying at the present? Tell me the truth, Sheila, or I'm going to water the plants."

She struggled to her feet and tucked an errant asparagus spear back in place. "I have not seen or heard from her since the day after Anthony was killed and the police found her at my house. I haven't the slightest clue where she may be."

"You're not worried about her or Skyler?"

"Oops, you're out of questions. Now, if you'll be so kind as to hand me the bottle, I'll be on my way."

I did as she'd demanded, then guided her to the front porch and asked an officer to help her navigate the driveway to the cab awaiting her. A carriage it was not, and most certainly not chauffeured by Prince Charming, who'd seemingly forgotten to return it to its rightful operator. Arnie would always be a frog (or a loathsome toad), no matter how many kisses he coaxed out of misbegotten princesses.

As I headed for the backyard to once again try to find Peter, Jacque burst out of the kitchen. Although he was not waving a cleaver, I suspected it was an oversight on his part.

"Are you through barging into my kitchen like a drunk at a pool party?" he demanded. "I have tried very hard not to lose my temper, but this is too much. Food presentation is an art. I must have space to express myself."

"The space you have is between your ears," I said. "Those people out in the backyard may be impressed by your displays of temperament, but I am not. Why don't you *mettez un haricot vert où le soleil ne brille jamais*?"

"That was dirty, wasn't it?"

"Oh, yes," I said, then went outside to find Peter.

He was hovering at the fringe of what was becoming a festive occasion despite the darkening sky and flashes of lightning in the distance. I gave Adrienne a quick nod to let her know that she and her friends would not be interrupted by such pesky intrusions as an ex-wife or a homicidal stepdaughter, then joined him.

"Is there anything you'd care to share?" he said.

"Such as *un haricot vert* or *un coeur d'artichaut*? If you'll wait here, I'll fight my way to the buffet table and come back with a plateful. We can find a quiet spot and nibble ourselves crazy. How much do you think this costs? Two, three thousand dollars? Jacque's probably charging a dollar apiece for the crab puffs."

"Would you please stop this?"

"Yes," I said as I sat down on a brick wall bordering a flower bed. "It's all too complicated. There are things I have to tell you, things I want to tell you, and things I can't tell you. Can you understand that?"

"Do I have a choice?"

"If you start threatening me—no, you don't."

Peter managed a smile, although I could see it required effort. "So let's start with the things you have to tell me."

He was no longer smiling after I'd told him about Chantilly's disappearance. "She was with Adrienne when they saw Daphne run out of the house," I added, "but I'm starting to think she might have seen someone else. It seems logical that Adrienne hurried inside to make sure that Anthony was all right, which he most surely wasn't. Chantilly probably parked the car, combed her hair, touched up her lipstick, and took their gym bags out of the backseat."

"That's not what she told us, but I agree that she wouldn't have voluntarily disappeared like this. I'll put Jorgeson on it, even though it's his day off and he promised to stain the deck. What else do you feel compelled to tell me?"

"I saw Daphne about forty-five minutes ago," I said in a very small voice.

"You what?"

"Don't bluster, please. People are staring at us, and I'm hoping to be invited to the fashion show at the country club next week. I could end up as the president of the Junior League if Adrienne proposes me. She is my best friend, you know."

Peter was perilously close to spontaneous combustion. "Where did you see Daphne? Here?"

"Caron thought she did, but she's never met Daphne. After the gunshot, I went down—"

"The gunshot?"

I held up my palms. "Miss Parchester assured me that it was a backfire from a pickup truck, so I may have been mistaken."

"I should have you arrested right this minute."

"If you try it," I said, offended, "I shall swoon. You'll need four officers to carry me off, and an equal number to restrain Caron, who is giving us a very beady stare as we speak. What's more, when I recover, I won't remember anything. After years of psychoanalysis, I may be able to recall a few details. Your move, Sherlock."

"You have many attributes which I dearly love," he said. "You are warm, witty, passionate when it suits you, quasi-fluent in French, well-read—"

"Quasi-fluent? Hey, buster, *la plume de ma tante est sur le table. Sur le pont d'Avignon. Crepes suzette. Haricot vert!*"

For some reason, he sighed. "Let's backtrack to Daphne, the gunshot, and Miss Parchester. Forty-five minutes ago, you said?"

"Roughly. I was searching Anthony's office when I—"

"You were what?"

"Am I not allowed to finish a sentence?"

"By all means, please continue."

"I shall," I said, "but before I do, you need to take out that tiddlywink of a cell phone and call Jorgeson. Chantilly would not have just vanished like this. Adrienne can give you the information about her car."

I pondered the pansies until he returned. "About Daphne," I began cautiously. "She seems to have become friendly with Miss Parchester. She was on the platform when I went down there earlier, but she ran off and drove away. It's very curious that she has access to a vehicle. It's certainly not Joey's, since she can't drive a—"

"Joey's?" he said.

In that I'd concluded Joey had nothing to do with the current events, I decided to sell him down the river and hope he wouldn't mention Skyler. "Her boyfriend. He's out at some dumpy trailer park, shacked up with your worst nightmare. He swore he hasn't seen her since the day before Anthony was killed."

Peter was beyond displeased. "So you tracked down

the boyfriend and questioned him? Did it occur to you to share this with us?"

"No, not really." I yanked up an unsightly weed and tossed it over my shoulder. "It only took me a few hours, and I lack the pervasive resources of the Farberville Police Department. Deductive reasoning, a few questions here and there, and then—voilà! It's merely a matter of ingenuity, Lieutenant Rosen."

"And interfering with an investigation."

"When did I interfere?" I said. "Are you accusing me of tackling an officer as he sprinted for the trailer?"

Peter was clearly not appreciating my wit. "Where is Daphne staying?"

"I don't know. Based on what Sheila said a few minutes ago, I don't think she's—"

"A few minutes ago?"

"This habitual interrupting is beginning to annoy me. Why don't you find Adrienne and allow her to paw all over you? She had a very good reason to wish for her husband's demise. She's at least a few million dollars richer than she was a week ago."

Peter caught my wrist before I could stand up and stalk away like a proper Regency debutante. "How do you know that?"

"I read the will, or at least a summation of it. After a few bequests, she and Daphne split the estate. I don't really know how much money is at stake, but I should think a lot, considering all the real estate and developments. Daphne won't inherit if she's found guilty, of course, so Adrienne may well end up with everything."

"She has an alibi," he said. "She and her sister were at the fitness center until ten o'clock, and then annoyed the holy hell out of the employees at some Mexican restaurant until midnight. When they drove up, they both saw Daphne come running out of the house with a gun in her hand—and Daphne admitted as much."

"Everybody could have been lying," I said loftily.

"And everybody could grow up to be president," Peter said in a remarkably unfriendly voice. He took out a notebook and a pen. "Give me the details about Joey."

I did so, although I omitted any mention of Cannelletti's garage, the biker bar, or Bocaraton. "I truly have no idea where Daphne's staying," I added.

"Does Miss Parchester?"

"I would think so, but I wish you luck trying to convince her to tell you."

Thunder rumbled as Peter stared at me. "Have you told me everything?"

"I've told you quite a lot, haven't I?" I said with a few flutters of my eyelashes, which has driven him to impetuous lust on occasion. I hadn't mentioned Finnigan Baybergen's expectations of a crippling lawsuit if he found the map, or Sheila's vision of blackmail should she find it first, but I doubted either of them had been in Anthony Armstrong's office the night of the murder. Well, unless either of them had been there, or a posse of Green Party members, or a disgruntled condo owner such as Jillian Scarpo. Or the ghost of Riccardo Zorelli. Or Daphne. Or Sheila, while Arnie let the meter run outside.

"I'm sorry if I've upset you," said Peter, feigning contrition. "I suppose I'll have to see what Miss Parchester is willing to tell us about Daphne, although I don't suppose she'll be much help. Would you like me to have an officer drive you and Caron home?"

"No, that's not necessary," I said. "I came here in my car."

"I had it towed half an hour ago. Are you sure you don't need a ride?"

"You did what?" I said loudly enough to garner some nervous glances from the guests. "You had my car towed? How could you?"

"Just impeding your investigation, ma'am. We do what we can." He gave me a smile, then stood up and left me fuming on the wall.

If looks could kill, I thought tritely, he might survive—but he'd certainly have scorch marks all over his back and his curly hair would be singed, if not smoldering.

CHAPTER FOURTEEN

I waited until Caron finished splashing white wine in a glass, then quietly said, "We're leaving in a few minutes."

"Suits me," she said. "I'm getting tired of all these old goats leering at me and asking me how old I am like they're thinking about taking me to the prom. Their wives, in contrast, only stop talking to each other long enough to demand a drink. I could be covered in scales for all they'd notice."

Randy gave her a wry smile. "One of the women at the country club called me Roger for two years. Then again, I overheard all kinds of lurid stories about botched plastic surgery, affairs, pending bankruptcies, hot checks, and shoplifting. I could write a helluva exposé if I thought anybody cared about these people."

"You and Adrienne were friends, weren't you?" I said.

"Yeah, for a while. She felt like she was out of her league when she first married Armstrong. She's a lot younger than most of them, and she didn't know how to play golf or bridge. I guess that's why she started spending so much time at the fitness center."

"And helped you get a job there?"

"She just told me about the opening."

I told Caron I'd be back shortly, and went into the house. I opted to use a telephone in the living room, since Jacque might have chanced upon a French-English dictionary and deciphered enough of what I'd said to determine I had not wished him a pleasant afternoon.

"Luanne," I said when she answered the phone. "I've got a problem."

"That's one way to put it. I was thinking more along the lines of a catastrophe."

"He just did it to annoy me, which it did." I hesitated for a few seconds. "How do you know about this?"

"Because I was here, dammit! I tried to call you, but some bizarre man disavowed any knowledge of you. I'm very close to ripping out my hair, Claire, and it's already started to fall out of its own accord. Would you please stop making all these cryptic remarks and tell me what to do?"

"About what?" I said, bewildered.

"Skyler, of course. What else would I be talking about? How soon can you get here?"

"Is he okay?"

"What is wrong with you?" Luanne said, her voice shrill enough to shatter the antique crystal pendants in her display case. "Skyler's been kidnapped! Should I call the police? Is Peter there? I just don't know what to do!"

I felt as though I'd been slapped. "He was what? Kidnapped by whom?"

"How should I know? Just get here—okay?"

"You'll have to come pick us up. We'll be out at the

end of the driveway in five minutes. Don't run into any pickup trucks on the way."

Despite her sputters, I hung up and made my way back to the bar. Rather than proffer any explanations (because I didn't have any), I grabbed Caron's wrist and hauled her through the house and out to the sidewalk. The two uniformed officers stared at us as we headed toward the road.

"What is wrong with you?" Caron demanded as she disengaged my hand and cradled her wrist as if I'd destroyed her hopes at Wimbledon.

I repeated as best I could the conversation I'd had with Luanne, then said, "She's hysterical, and I'm close to lining up right behind her."

"But who could have done this?"

We reached the road. The KFAR van was long gone, as was the cab. I sat down on the gravel shoulder. "I don't know. You did see Daphne earlier, and I tried to talk to her, but she bolted. Her mother crashed the luncheon and left half an hour ago. There's no way Skyler's father could have known where . . ."

"This guy named Joey who's living in a trailer park?"

I flapped my hand at her while I tried to think. "We went out there in Luanne's car. He didn't strike me as a promising candidate for international accolades in biochemistry, but he could have written down the license plate number and come up with her name and address. We never implied we had custody of Skyler, though."

Caron sat down beside me. "Is there any possibility Daphne got in touch with him? If she went to that biker bar, she could have found out everything you did. She went out there and persuaded him to grab Skyler."

"Why would he risk it?"

"How should I know?" said Caron, her face puckering. "Because deep inside he's overwhelmed with guilt for abandoning them. Because Daphne told him she was going to be rich."

"Not if she's convicted."

"Maybe he doesn't know that. She'll arrange to meet him, collect Skyler, and promise to send him a check. Not everyone is cognizant of the finer details of inheritance law, Mother."

I got to my feet. "There's Luanne. Don't start yelling at her, please. She's as upset as we are, if not more so. We'll find out what happened and then decide what we ought to do."

Luanne pulled up as if she were driving a getaway car. I got in the front seat and Caron flung herself in back as we squealed away, à la Bonnie and Clyde.

"Slow down," I said as I battled the recalcitrant seatbelt. It seemed prudent to buckle it.

"I think I should be at the store," she said, passing a van on a hill. "What if someone just borrowed Skyler and is overcome with remorse—or wants to demand a ransom? We have to be there to answer the phone. Did you tell Peter? Shouldn't the police be doing something?"

"Either slow down or pull over and let me drive," I said.

"Good idea," chimed in a thin voice from the backseat.

Luanne eased up, although her fingers still gripped the steering wheel so tightly the plastic was in danger of deforming from the pressure. "Don't you want to know what happened?"

"Well, yes," I said. "Why don't you tell us?"

"Skyler and I went out for a stroll after his morning nap. Sally Fromberger was lurking in the parking lot across from the Book Depot, but I saw her before she saw me and I took a detour. We went past the Azalea Inn, over the railroad bridge, and back past the bicycle shop and the new sushi restaurant across from the—"

"This is not the time for a travelogue," I said.

"I know." She took several gulps of air. "I guess I'm trying to stall. When we got back, I parked Skyler behind the counter and went into the back room to warm up a bottle of formula. No one could see him from the street. I came out three or four minutes later and he was gone, as was the diaper bag."

"Someone must have been watching," I said. "He or she saw you return from your stroll and then loitered in front of the store until you went to the back room. The door was unlocked, wasn't it?"

She nodded. "I even flipped over the sign in the window so customers would know I was open."

Caron draped herself over the seat. "Would you have recognized Daphne if she was standing across the street?"

"It's Saturday afternoon," said Luanne. "Even with the threat of rain, there are lots of pedestrians out and about. I might have recognized Daphne had I been watching for her, but the only time I've seen her was on a very short news clip, less than half a minute. I was thinking more about a fresh diaper and a warm bottle of formula."

"Let's go back to your store," I said.

"Where's your car?"

Caron poked my shoulder. "I'd like to know, too. Did you give Daphne the key or something screwy like that?"

"No, I did not." I told her and Luanne everything that had happened since our arrival at the Armstrong villa.

"I heard Daphne drive away from Oakland Heights, and my car was parked near the catering vans when I returned. As much as I'd like to discuss various forms of retaliation against Peter, we need to figure out where Skyler is."

Luanne began to snuffle. "I never should have left him alone, not even for a minute. All I had to do was take him in the back room with me."

"And I should have stayed with you," said Caron. "Inez wanted to, too, but she was afraid her parents would get annoyed if she didn't go to that totally twisted concert."

"No," I said, "what we should have done was call social services that first evening. Now let's think where Skyler might be and do something about it."

Luanne parked behind Secondhand Rose and we hurried inside, each of us no doubt envisioning Skyler asleep in his stroller behind the counter. He was not. "Okay," I said, "I find it hard to believe Joey would be involved. He showed little interest in Daphne and none whatsoever in Skyler. Bocaraton did not strike me as a thwarted madonna. He couldn't have thought Adrienne or Sheila would pay a ransom."

"I agree." Luanne went to the front of the store and stared through the window. "Someone must have been in the vacant lot over there and saw me come back with the stroller. All this person had to do was wait until I went into the back room, sneak inside, get the stroller and the diaper bag, and then take off. There's a maze of side streets and alleys around here."

"But who?" Caron demanded.

I mentally crossed Joey's name off my list. "Probably not Sheila, either. She wouldn't have any reason to think Skyler was here—and she wasn't doing much thinking when I last saw her. And she has no particular motive."

"Which leaves us with Daphne," said Luanne. "She saw me pushing the stroller at the press conference. She lived on the streets for several months, so she might have recognized me. When I receive clothes that aren't vintage, I take them to the shelter. Maybe someone there told her who I was."

I sank down on a steamer trunk. "Let's work on that assumption. For starters, she has access to a vehicle. It's not Joey's, and it's not Sheila's. Whose is it?"

"Arnie's cab?" suggested Caron.

I considered it. "I don't think so. She was driving something four nights ago, when her father was killed. Randy Scarpo saw her drive away."

"Him?" Caron said with a derisive laugh. "He's a weasel."

"Why do you say that?" I asked her. "Did he attempt to get too cozy over the cocktail napkins?"

"I am most definitely Not His Type. He was fawning all over the rich women, practically licking their hands when he made them drinks. What's worse, just when we got really busy, he told me he had to take a break and went into the house. Am I supposed to know how to make a manhattan and a vodka collins? I'm in high school, for pity's sake!"

"Let's go back to Daphne. She's been driving somebody's car since Tuesday evening. If she had any friends, she wouldn't have lived on the streets."

"That's what's so awful." Caron wrapped her arms around her shoulders. "Her father dumped her, her mother dumped her, and Joey dumped her. I don't know what I'd do if I didn't have a single person to turn to."

Luanne looked at me. "She does have one other friend besides Arnie."

"Yes, she does," I acknowledged unhappily. "And this friend has a house and a car, neither of which she's used since Monday."

"Who are you talking about?" said Caron. "Surely not Miss Parchester . . ."

I stood up and held out my hand. "Luanne, I need to borrow your car. You call the police department and convince them to give you Peter's cell phone number, then call him and tell him where I'm going. Caron, you need to stay here."

"While you storm Miss Parchester's house by yourself?" she said. "I don't think so."

Luanne snatched up her purse. "I'm going with you."

It seemed I lacked the leadership skills to command a battalion, or even a platoon of two. "Someone has to stay here and try to get through to Peter," I said, sensing the futility even as I spoke.

"Then you stay here," said Caron. "Daphne's never seen me. I'll just knock on the door and say I'm Miss Parchester's niece. If I have to, I can cry so she'll let me inside. At least that way we can make sure Skyler's okay, and I can stay until the police arrive."

"Or until she gets suspicious and shoots you," I said.

"I don't much want her to shoot you, which she's more likely to do."

"No one is going to shoot anyone," Luanne said firmly. "As for calling Peter, that may be premature. Daphne and Skyler could be driving across the Missouri state line as we speak."

I shook my head. "She may have a car, but she doesn't have any money."

"Unless she stole some Tuesday night when she was prowling upstairs at her father's house," said Caron. "I agree with Luanne that we shouldn't call the police until we see if Daphne's really at Miss Parchester's house. Besides, she's not pissed at us. She'll know we took good care of Skyler."

"All right," I said, "we'll go to Miss Parchester's house and peek in a window. If Daphne's there, we have to call the police. We are not going to face charges of aiding and abetting a fugitive."

We went outside and climbed into Luanne's car, this time more decorously. Once we neared Willow Street, I told Luanne to park at the library in case the nondescript officers were still keeping Sheila's house under surveillance. We hurried up the alley, then stopped to catch our breath and assess Miss Parchester's backyard. Luckily, her basset hounds were on vacation in the country, and therefore unavailable to alert every other homeowner along the alley of the proximity of burglars.

"We need to stay behind the forsythias until we get to the porch," I said.

Caron ignored me and continued on to the garage. "The car's here," she called, "and the hood's warm. We know Miss Parchester hasn't been driving it."

"Then let's get out of here and call the police," I said.

"Don't be ridiculous." Caron went through the garage and into the yard. "Stay out of sight. You look like a couple of freshmen planning to toilet paper the trees." Before I could respond, she walked up the steps to the back door and knocked. "Hello? Is anybody home?"

"Oh, my god," said Luanne as she pulled me down. "How did Daphne seem earlier?"

"Very tense," I muttered, struggling to free myself from Luanne's grip on the back of my shirt. "Miss Parchester doesn't seem to think Daphne has a gun, but she could be wrong, you know."

Caron knocked again, then cupped her hands and

peered through the glass pane. "Aunt Emily? It's your niece from Boise. Remember how you invited me to stay for a week and help you plant your vegetable garden? When you didn't meet me at the bus station, I had to walk. I was on the bus for more than twenty-two hours, and I sure would like to use your bathroom."

"Your child is a master of improvisation," said Luanne. "She may have a career in it."

"I just hope she lives to have a career in something." I was going to add more when the door opened and Luanne jerked me into a honeysuckle vine.

"Miss Parchester's not here," said Daphne.

"Drat." Caron began to squirm rather convincingly. "Do you know when she'll get back? I'm so tired and grubby and hungry that I could just stretch out here on the porch and cry."

Daphne stepped back. "You can come in for a minute, but you'll have to find somewhere else to stay."

"Thanks so much," Caron said as she disappeared into the house.

I finally managed to free myself. "Go to the library and call the police."

"Shall I mention that there's a potential hostage inside?"

I leaned against the fence and rubbed my face. "I solemnly swear I'm going to send that girl to band camp every summer until she's twenty-one."

"You're making no sense whatsoever."

"And this situation is?" I let my head fall back into the vine. "What do you suggest we do—just sit here and wait until a garbage truck rolls over us on Monday morning?"

"All we can do is wait," said Luanne. She flicked dried leaves off her jeans and sat down next to me.

"Caron knows we'll call the police if she stays in there too long."

"How long is that?" I said, nearly whimpering.

"We have to trust her."

I tried to smile. "Did I tell you about the cheese sauce?"

Luanne and I had run out of diversionary topics and were reduced to listening to spouses bickering in nearby yards when the back door opened. I rolled over to my knees and peeked through the vine.

"Thanks again," Caron said as she came out to the porch. "It's kind of you to house-sit for Aunt Emily while she's protesting. She's always been one to sacrifice her personal comfort for a just cause."

Once the back door was closed, she came back through the garage to the alley and stared at us with a disapproving frown. "You both look as if you've been wrestling with a leaf blower. I hope you'll tidy yourselves before we get to the library. Mrs. McLair lives just up the street and insists on telling us how she spends every Saturday afternoon at the library doing genealogy research. I would be so humiliated if she saw you like this. She might wonder just how long ago my ancestors came down from the trees and learned to use tools—like combs, for instance."

"Is Skyler in there?" Luanne asked before I could react in a manner unequivocally discouraged by Dr. Spock.

"No," she said. "I looked in all the rooms, and there's not so much as a diaper or a bootie. I don't think Daphne had anything to do with abducting him."

"What did you two talk about?" I said as we walked toward the library.

"School, mostly. She hated that place her father sent

her, and she may have hated her stepmother even more. According to her, the first thing Adrienne did after she moved in was to fire the housekeeper, who'd been there fifteen years. A cleaning service came in once a week, and the rest of the time Daphne had to keep the house in impeccable shape so her parents could entertain on the weekends. And clean up afterwards, on top of that."

"What did Cinderella's father have to say about it?" asked Luanne.

"That it wouldn't hurt her to develop a work ethic. Her allowance was ten dollars a week, and she had to take her lunch to school every day because she couldn't afford the cafeteria."

I put my arm around her shoulder. "You do realize I have to call the police, don't you? Peter's going to do a lot more than have my car towed if he ever finds out I knew where Daphne was and didn't tell him."

"Yeah, I know, and it's probably for her own good. She's pretty jittery. The whole time I was there she kept prowling around the living room, pulling back the drapes to look at the street, and scratching herself like she has poison ivy. Tell Peter that she needs to go to the psych ward, not the jail. When she went into the bathroom, I looked in the refrigerator. It's emptier than ours, which is saying a lot. I guess Miss Parchester cleaned it out in preparation for a prolonged protest. We're talking mustard, mayonnaise, a stick of margarine, and a bottle of vitamins."

I stopped her. "Do you think she has a gun?"

"I don't know. She didn't say or do anything remotely threatening."

"And she bought this niece-from-Boise business?" asked Luanne, who'd been trailing us with uncharacteristic silence.

"She just wanted to talk to someone who wasn't accusing her of anything. We agreed that dissecting frogs was disgusting and that cheerleaders will never rule the world—after graduation, anyway. I was going to tell her about Rhonda's locker, but I was afraid I might inadvertently allude to Skyler. She acted like she wanted me to hang around, but I figured the two of you would lose what little you have left of your moldy, middle-aged brain cells if you had to wait much longer." She looked at me. "And I didn't like lying to her. I tried not to once I got inside, but I had to stick with the Boise nonsense. Now I'm going to betray what little faith she has left. Why did all this have to happen?"

I wanted to tell her that it was all Daphne's father's fault, but I wasn't at all sure she'd resolved her problems with her own father. "It just escalated until it was out of control, dear. I'll stress the need for an immediate psych evaluation. At least she can have some decent meals and a chance to rest."

"What about Skyler?"

"I wish I knew," I admitted.

Luanne nudged us back into motion. "We agreed that Joey and Sheila wouldn't have taken him. Is it possible Arnie might have?"

"I don't see how," I said. "He's never even met you, and he has no reason to think Skyler would be anywhere except in my possession—and he approves of that."

"What if Daphne begged him to retrieve Skyler so she could run away?"

"It's hard to predict how he'd respond, but he most certainly wouldn't have been sniffing around outside Secondhand Rose. Besides, he supposedly drove Sheila to the cemetery for a private sacrament involving expensive vodka."

Caron sighed. "Could Chantilly have something to do with this? I mean, she's disappeared, and now so has Skyler."

"I can't find any logical connection," I said. "Neither Adrienne nor Chantilly displayed the slightest solicitude for Daphne or Skyler. Babies are not welcome at social events unless high-priced clowns and ponies are involved."

"Then where's Chantilly?" asked Caron, who was keeping a not-so-subtle lookout for Mrs. McLair as we went across the library parking lot.

I shrugged. "I'm going to use a pay phone inside the library to try to get in touch with Peter." I left them sitting on a bench and went into the lobby. I fed the appropriate coins into the phone and dialed the number of the police station, which I happened to know all too well. "Lieutenant Rosen, please," I said when my call was answered.

"He's out of the office. If you tell me what this is about, I'll connect you with someone who can assist you."

To tell her what this was about would require a couple of hundred manuscript pages of a convoluted mystery novel. "I really need to speak to Lieutenant Rosen. Can you give me his cell phone number?"

"I'm not allowed to do that, ma'am. If you tell me what this is—".

"What about Sergeant Jorgeson?"

"He hasn't been in today."

"Can you share his home telephone number?" I asked without optimism.

"I'm not allowed to do that, ma'am. Are you in danger?"

Only of having my derriere towed to jail. "Okay, contact Lieutenant Rosen right now and tell him that Claire called and has information concerning Daphne's whereabouts. He has three minutes to call me back." I gave her the number on the pay phone, hung up, and sat down on a stool. Patrons were coming and going, their arms laden with books. I'd met Mrs. McLair at the fall open house, but I wasn't sure we'd recognize each other. For Caron's sake, I hoped not, since my blouse had lost a button and my knees were caked with dirt.

The pay phone rang less than a minute later. I grabbed the receiver, but before I could say anything, Peter said, "This had better not be a hoax, Claire. What's more, if you've known all along where Daphne's been since yesterday morning, you're in big trouble. Once the chief is done with you, he'll throw your scraps to the prosecuting attorney and assign me to lunchroom duty at the police academy."

"Are you finished?" I said politely.

"Where is she?"

"At Miss Parchester's house, and close to snapping. Have one of those pimply adolescent officers put on jeans and a sweatshirt, and ease her out. She needs a full psychiatric evaluation. Caron doesn't think she has the gun."

"Caron dropped by for cookies and tea?"

"Mustard and mayonnaise, anyway. There is one other little problem."

"Yes?" he growled.

"Well, Skyler's been kidnapped. We thought Daphne might have him, but she doesn't. I don't see how Arnie could have—"

"Skyler?" he growled much more loudly. "Who's Skyler?"

"Daphne's son. He's a month old, with a little dab of black hair and rough patches on his cheeks. A well-behaved baby, usually contented. Daphne left him in a basket on my porch the day before her father was killed." I paused to nod at a white-haired man using a cane as he came past me. "It was all perfectly legal, Peter. Daphne wrote a note that gave me permission to look after him for a few days. It just got stickier, and now he's been kidnapped."

"Daphne has a baby? She didn't say anything to us."

"She wouldn't have, would she? You and your thugs were browbeating her and trying to trick her into confessing to a crime she didn't commit."

Peter was very quiet. In the background, I could hear lively chatter and the faint sound of music that could hardly be described as doleful. I waited patiently, although I knew Luanne and Caron were apt to be gnawing their knuckles on the bench outside.

"My thugs and I did not browbeat her," he said at last. "So you've had this baby since Monday night?"

"He arrived on the porch in a basket."

"You didn't think to tell me?"

"Of course I considered it, but I thought Skyler would be better off with me than in the clutches of the system. Caron and Inez have been amusing him, and Luanne had just taken him for a stroll before someone snatched him."

"Where are you calling from?" Peter asked in an ominous tone.

"Not from a car phone, obviously," I said. "I don't even know where my car is, thanks to you. Having my car towed was rude, and most likely illegal. As soon as I can afford a lawyer, I may decide to sue. All I was doing was helping Adrienne host a luncheon out on the lawn so that her dear friends could express their sympathy and share their grief with the widow. Do give her my love."

I hung up and went outside. Caron and Luanne were throwing acorns at the squirrels scampering across the grass, but in such a desultory fashion that I doubted any missiles had found their targets. "I told Peter about Daphne—and about Skyler," I told them. "I suppose all we can do is go back to Secondhand Rose and hope someone calls."

"But who?" said Caron.

"I don't have a clue," I admitted. "I thought we were aware of all the players in this ghastly game, but it seems as though we're not."

Luanne hauled Caron to her feet and steered her toward the car. "Who are we leaving off the list? Do you think Jessica was having an affair with Anthony? That Chantilly was worried that her biological clock was ticking away at the advanced age of twentysomething? That Mr. Cannelletti was so enraged on Daphne's behalf that he shot her father out of righteous indignation? Joey, the sorry excuse for a sperm bank? Jacque, who wants to expand his stainless steel kitchen? Who is it?"

"Well, Adrienne," I said as I got in the car, "except Daphne said that the car drove up well after she heard the shot. Adrienne and Chantilly were at the fitness center until ten, then at the restaurant until midnight. They left together, and came home together."

"What a perfect alibi," cooed Luanne. "Iron-clad, and so convenient."

Caron grabbed my shoulder. "They must have done it, Mother. You have to tell Peter."

"He's got a lot on his plate at the moment," I said. "We're all likely to be hauled off to a shabby room replete with rubber truncheons and thumbscrews. Besides, I don't see how Adrienne and Chantilly could have done it." I paused as I thought. "But they do have a perfect alibi, don't they?"

"So do I," Caron said as she sat back, "but that won't get me a hall pass. I think the weasel did it."

"Shot Anthony or kidnapped Skyler?" Luanne asked.

"Both," she said with postpubescent conviction. "He shot Anthony because he didn't want to have all the construction chaos, and he kidnapped Skyler because . . . I don't know. Maybe his wife wants another child and he doesn't want to pay the hospital charges for the delivery room."

I turned around to stare at her. "Do you honestly think Randy did all this?"

"Well, he probably didn't kidnap Skyler, but he could have shot Daphne's father."

"Because?"

"He and Adrienne are having an affair, Mother. I can't believe you didn't notice. It took me all of five seconds. Even Rhonda Maguire could have figured it out, and she's got processed cheese sauce for brains."

"And you do remember what you said about the prenuptial contract," said Luanne as she pulled into the alley behind her shop. "Adrienne would have been sent away with a pittance if Anthony found out about the affair. There's her motive."

"It doesn't explain her alibi, though," I said. "Daphne heard the gunshot before Adrienne and Chantilly drove up."

Caron gave me a long-suffering look as we got out of the car. "Weren't you listening, Mother? Randy did it. Adrienne knew that Anthony would be home alone, and she made sure her butt was covered. Chantilly must have realized how she'd been used and threatened to go to the police. She's probably buried in Phase Seventeen of Oakland Heights."

"Then Randy's wife would have been in on it. According to his statement, he was at his condo at midnight, jiggling their baby."

"Did anyone ask her when he got home?" said Caron.

I replayed my previous encounters with Jillian. "She may well have suspected he was having an affair, but she'd be more likely to go at him with a cleaver than lie for him. If he shot Anthony, he would have had to dash out the door minutes before Daphne came downstairs and sprint to his condo. Miss Parchester's been keeping secrets, but she wouldn't have lied to protect him."

Luanne unlocked the back door and ushered us inside. "You don't know what secrets Miss Parchester's been keeping. She doesn't necessarily know where Daphne's been staying or that her car was putting on mileage. I'll bet the farm that she keeps a house key under a flowerpot or on the top of the doorsill. The car key was on a cute little corkboard by the back door. Daphne knew Miss Parchester's whereabouts, but that doesn't mean the reverse is true."

Rain had finally begun to splatter on the sidewalks of Thurber Street—and elsewhere, I assumed. Adrienne's guests had been allowed several hours to booze and graze, and it was likely that Jacque had run low on crab puffs by now. Not that I cared, frankly.

"I don't know what to do about Skyler," I said, sitting down on the stool behind the counter. "We should be doing something, but I just don't know what it is. Maybe we ought to call all the churches and have someone check the doorsteps."

"People don't kidnap babies to drop them off at churches," Caron said in an odd voice.

I glanced at her. "No, I don't suppose they do."

"I'm going to make coffee," said Luanne. "Would you rather have a soda, Caron? I've got a couple of diet colas and a bottle of designer water."

"No thanks," she muttered. "There's no reason all three of us should sit around and wait for Peter to have us arrested. If I'm going to make the evening news, I'd prefer to be wearing something a tad more acceptable so that Rhonda and Louis won't be sniggering. That's not to imply I think they watch the news, or anything else that doesn't include music videos with full frontal nudity. I'll be at home if you need me."

I was so surprised that I could only gape as she went out to Thurber Street and headed in the direction of our apartment.

"What was that about?" Luanne said, as bemused as I.

I shook my head. "I don't know."

CHAPTER FIFTEEN

Luanne began to pace. "You know something? I don't care who shot Anthony Armstrong! I know I should, and I know I should be worried about Daphne and her fragile self-esteem, and about Sheila and her drinking problem, but I'm not. Maybe Adrienne and Chantilly schemed to murder Anthony. I just don't care! You trusted me with Skyler, and I blew it. I couldn't protect him for twenty-four hours."

"Only one of us is allowed to have a meltdown at any one time," I said.

"Then it's most assuredly my turn—but I am not having a meltdown, dammit! I am merely pointing out my egregious lapse of responsibility. I lost a child once before. Everybody said it wasn't my fault, but I knew it was. This time, I should have—"

"You lost a child?"

"A miscarriage in the seventh month," she said as she circled the rack of evening dresses and disappeared. "I was shopping for sheets for the crib, and this maniac came screaming into the store and literally ran over me. I didn't need more sheets; I was just shopping. That's what Stepford wives do while their husbands are slaving away in their air-conditioned offices or playing racquetball in their exclusive clubs. I lost the baby in a department store while security guards wrung their hands and clerks tucked towels under me. It was over before the paramedics arrived."

I hugged her so tightly that neither of us could get a breath. "You never told me."

"Because I didn't want your sympathy. It happened a long time ago. I got over it. I had two children, both happy and healthy, if not skewed by their indulgent upbringing and sizable trust funds. It pains them to call me on major holidays. They send flowers on my birthday and on Mother's Day. I'm a little too eccentric to be welcomed at the clan gatherings on Nantucket every spring. After all, I gave up everything and ventured into uncharted territory to run a used-clothing store for would-be beauty queens of both sexes."

"Luanne," I began, then broke off as I tried to find the words.

She pulled herself free. "This is precisely why I didn't tell you, Claire. You seem to think you're supposed to supply the platitudes, the verbal aloe vera, the—I don't know—maternal mantra. There is nothing you can say that will erase that memory. Nothing."

"What do you want me to do?"

"Don't get gooey. We have to find Skyler."

I fought back responses that might well have been deemed "gooey." "Yes, we have to find Skyler. Is it possible some sorority girl wandered in and . . ."

"Were you drinking wine coolers all afternoon?"

I realized I had not only stayed away from the bar but also from the buffet table. "I haven't had anything since nine o'clock," I admitted. "Not even bread and water."

Luanne went into the back room and reappeared with half a sandwich of dubious heritage. "Eat this before you keel over. Caron seems to believe Adrienne was sleeping with Randy. What do you think?"

"What is it?"

"Tuna salad and cucumber slices. When did you get so picky?"

"Since I read an article about salmonella," I said as I took a bite. "Very tasty."

"So what difference does it truly make if Adrienne and Randy are an item? Anthony was twenty years older, and a hard-nosed bastard. He was long past his sexual prime, while she's approaching hers. Maybe they had an agreement."

I thought for a moment. "They did, and it was delineated in the will. If it can be proved that Adrienne had an affair during the marriage, she can't inherit."

"And Chantilly found out?"

"She might have overheard something. If Caron could pick up on it after an hour, then how subtle could they have been?"

Luanne sat down on the steamer trunk. "Which means that Chantilly is buried in the backyard, along with the Jaguar? We're talking one big pit. Is Adrienne all that athletic?"

"No," I said, "and I can't imagine Adrienne killing her sister."

"Or her husband?"

"I wish I could, but neither she nor Chantilly seems that cold-blooded—or able to sustain a fabrication. They're shallow and annoying, but they're . . ." I paused for a moment. "They're the reason I don't go to class reunions."

"Adrienne and Chantilly?"

"You know what I mean. Didn't you go to school with them? Blond, perky, and promiscuous?"

"One of these nights we'll buy a gallon of wine and I'll tell you about boarding school life in New England, as well as summer camps that stressed dressage, elocution, and anorexia."

"As long as it's cheap," I said. "In the meantime, we need to figure out what to do. The first thing is to retrieve my car, which is impounded somewhere in this fair city."

"We do need to leave," said Luanne as she stood up. "Peter's likely to have us arrested at any moment, and—"

Two uniformed officers came into the shop, neither old enough to have graduated from junior high school. The more mature of the two, possibly fifteen, said, "Claire Malloy? Luanne Bradshaw? Lieutenant Rosen wants to talk to you."

"They just went down to the vegetarian café, not more than five minutes ago," I said glibly. "Three doors down, on the opposite side of the street. They're blond, perky, and, I'm sorry to say, promiscuous. Be very careful."

"And you are?"

"Customers," said Luanne. "Don't you just love these old-fashioned clothes? Beads and bangles, glitter and glitz. They make me want to shimmy all night." She began to offer a rather impressive demonstration of talents heretofore unseen.

The officers were alarmed enough to back out the door. I would have followed them had Luanne not grabbed my wrist and dragged me out the back door.

"Now what?" she said as we got into her car.

"Just drive."

"To Miss Parchester's house? To Sheila's? To Oakland Heights? I can hardly wait to see myself on *America's Most Wanted*. The only photograph they can dig up will be from my yearbook. I was voted the most likely to die of leprosy in a penal colony off the coast of South America."

"You're kidding."

"We played lacrosse, field hockey, and hardball in Connecticut. So where are we going?"

"Well, not Miss Parchester's house, since Peter is likely to be there. Sheila's no doubt having a fine time at the cemetery despite the rain, with Arnie to keep her company. We could go to the Tickled Pink Club and commiserate with Wanita, but she's probably beyond that. My apartment seems risky. Maybe we should go to the mall and try on designer jeans and tank tops."

"Or Adrienne's?" said Luanne as we went up Thurber Street. "If nothing else, we should be able to overindulge on leftovers. I love leftovers."

"Let's check on Miss Parchester first, and then, yes, we're going to have to talk to Adrienne."

Ten minutes later, Luanne parked as close as she could to the revered oak tree. Howie must have taken shelter from the rain, probably in the construction shed. Miss Parchester had rigged a tarp to form a tent of sorts, although I suspected she was not warm and dry. If I'd been blessed with extraordinary powers, I would have transported Finnigan Baybergen to the platform and Miss Parchester to somewhere more agreeable, such as Miss Scarlet's ballroom or Professor Plum's billiards room.

"Are you okay?" I called as we approached the platform.

"I am a bit damp," Miss Parchester said. "It's to be expected."

"Why don't you come down and let us take you home? You can return later if you insist."

"I wish I could," she said, peering down at us. "I have to admit I'm getting chilly, and even my thermal undergarments are damp. I left the lid off the brownies, and now they're sodden."

"You can go home," I said. "No one will know."

"But I would have to live with my capitulation to blatant commercialization. I vowed when I came here that I would not waver in my dedication to the cause of environmental sanity. Yes, I am cold and wet, and quite likely coming down with a bronchial malady. I will not, however, slink away like an abused animal."

Luanne looked as though she was ready to climb the tree and forcibly remove its occupant. I planted a hand on her shoulder and said, "Miss Parchester, I've met a couple who live here. Would you consider briefly leaving your post to toss your socks in their clothes dryer and have a cup of tea?"

"For just a few minutes?" quavered Miss Parchester. "No one would have to know?"

"Absolutely not. As soon as the rain lets up, you can climb right back up and cook acorn fritters for supper."

"If they're home," Luanne said under her breath.

"Jillian will be," I said. "I doubt that Connor's ever seen a raindrop, much less experienced one. Whether or not she'll let us in the condo is another issue."

The ladder came tumbling down, and Miss Parchester followed with impressive dexterity. "Howie went home," she said apologetically, as if he should have been present to arrest us. "I suppose he did, anyway. I haven't seen him since late this morning, when he went off to investigate noises. He did mention earlier this week that the shed doesn't provide adequate shelter when it rains. Neither does my tarp, I'm sorry to say. Papa would be disappointed with me."

"No, he wouldn't." I took her arm and led her toward the row of condos. "You've survived on the platform for five days, despite Anthony Armstrong's attempt to force you down. You deserve a respite."

I could almost hear Luanne shaking her head as we stopped at Randy and Jillian Scarpo's door. I knocked, then stepped back so that I was in view of whoever might peer from behind the living room drapes. Miss Parchester was trembling, and I realized I was supporting most of her weight. I was about to resort to pounding when the door opened.

"I know you," Jillian said to me, sounding as though she'd seen my picture on an FBI flyer at the post office.

"Yes, and you saw Miss Parchester on the nightly news. She's very close to collapsing. May we please come inside?"

Jillian waved us inside, then took Miss Parchester's hand and led her to a sofa. "You poor thing, you're soaked to the skin. Let me get you a quilt, and then I'll fix you something hot to drink. Would you like coffee?"

"Tea would be nice," Miss Parchester murmured. "I must admit I am not feeling robust."

"And some soup?" Jillian said as she settled Miss Parchester on a sofa and tucked a pillow behind her. "Canned, I'm afraid. I wish I had something homemade, but I don't go to the grocery store very often."

"I believe I could enjoy a cup of soup. It's very kind of you to do this, dear girl." Her head sank back and she closed her eyes. "I'll just rest, if you don't mind."

Jillian went into another room and returned with a crocheted afghan. After spreading it across Miss Parchester's legs, she whispered, "I'll heat some soup."

Luanne offered to stay with Miss Parchester. I accompanied Jillian into the kitchen, which was probably more sterile than that of the local hospital. "Thank you for letting us inside," I said. "Would you mind if I used your telephone?"

She took a teakettle from a cabinet and began to fill it with water. "Go ahead. It's in Randy's office, back that way."

The makeshift office had been designed to serve as a storage room. A small desk and two bookcases allowed very little floor space. Stacks of papers waited to be graded before the end of the semester. The computer appeared to be state-of-the-art, the gnawed pencils less so. I found a telephone directory in a desk drawer, looked up Finnigan Baybergen's home number, and dialed it.

I was relieved when he answered. "This is Claire Malloy," I said, "the woman with the little bookstore. Miss Parchester is very close to developing pneumonia, but will insist on returning to the platform when the rain stops. I want you to come out here, collect her wet clothing and her sleeping bag, and take them to a Laundromat to thoroughly dry them. Also, see what supplies she has and restock whatever she needs."

"Where are you calling from?"

"A condo in Phase One. If you're worried about being arrested, don't bother. Howie has disappeared for the time being. Or am I asking too much of you, Professor Baybergen? Should I call Mr. Constantine or Eliza Peterson? Are any members of the Green Party devoted enough to the environment to actually go out in the rain?"

"I'll take care of it," he said without enthusiasm. "Do you have any suggestions where I might find this thing you referred to as a Laundromat?"

"Were you born with a graduate degree and transported from the nursery to your ivy tower? Consider this a field trip, Baybergen. Maybe you'll find a new species of mildew behind the machines."

I hung up and dialed the number of my duplex. "Caron," I began when she answered, "I'm sorry to ask you this, but you need to go back to Secondhand Rose in case someone calls about Skyler. Luanne and I had to leave rather hastily."

"Where are you?"

"I don't think I'd better tell you. Peter may show up there, and I don't want you to have to lie to him. Inez should be home by now. Why don't you have her meet you?"

"Inez isn't home. I called a few minutes ago, and according to her mother, she didn't go to the concert. She told her mother Luanne wanted her to work at the shop all afternoon."

"That's odd," I said. "Do you think she went to the cemetery in hopes she might spot Daphne?"

Caron paused. "She might have, I guess, but that was hours ago and she wouldn't still be lurking under a bush, watching Sheila and Arnie get sloshed. Then again, she was acting pretty weird last night, even for herself. She insisted on sitting in a chair until dawn in case Daphne tried to sneak in and snatch Skyler. I must have pointed out a dozen times that the doors and windows were locked."

"It seems her anxiety was justified."

"Yeah, I guess so."

"Do you suspect she has Skyler?" I asked carefully. "Is that why you decided so abruptly to go home—in case she was there?"

"Maybe. She's not here, though, and she's not at home. She can't be pushing the stroller around in this rain. I thought when the phone rang . . ."

"I'm sure she's found someplace where she and Skyler are protected. Any ideas? Could she have taken him to one of your friends' houses?"

"Like their parents wouldn't notice she has a baby with her? I don't think so, Mother. She didn't know where you and I were going, since you didn't even tell me until I got home this morning. I can't see her coming here, or even to the Book Depot. And before you say she couldn't get into the bookstore, she knows where you stash the key in case of an emergency. You're lucky Arnie doesn't, since otherwise you'd be peddling pretzels from a cart."

I squeezed my temples as the teakettle began to whistle. "You have to think, Caron," I said. "She can't have gone very far. She might have tried to bluff her way into the women's shelter, but it's a good three miles away. There's a homeless shelter near the old post office. Would she have thought of that?"

"How should I know what she might have been thinking, beyond this paranoia of hers that Daphne could somehow scale the wall of Luanne's building and slither through a crack like a spider? She deserves a bed next to Daphne's in the psych ward."

"Calm down," I managed to say. "Go down to the Book Depot to make sure she's not there, then go back home in case she does call. Tell her she's not in trouble—

unless Peter finds her first. I'll call you at the store in ten minutes."

"It's raining."

"It is most definitely doing that, but if you remember, my car is behind a fence topped with concertina wire and will remain there until I write what I am sure will be a hefty check. Take an umbrella."

I hung up and replaced the directory in its rightful drawer. After a very brief moment of debating the morality of pawing through other people's possessions, I began to systematically search all the drawers.

The packet of photographs was at the back of a drawer filled with old class notebooks and papers on erudite mathematical topics such as differential equations and irrational numbers. I felt like an irrational number myself as I gaped at depictions of Adrienne in very explicit poses. Exercise machines at the fitness center provided inspiration, as well as the sauna and whirlpool. And if I had any doubt as to the identity of the photographer, Randy himself had found some interesting things to do with the equipment.

I shoved the packet back where I'd found it and slammed the drawer shut. Randy had, or was still having, an affair with Adrienne. Caron had noticed, and perhaps I should have as well. This certainly gave Adrienne a more than compelling motive to kill her husband—but not an opportunity, unless Chantilly and Daphne were accomplices. And Randy had been at home.

I returned to the living room. Miss Parchester was now stretched on the length of the sofa, snoring in a genteel fashion. Luanne and Jillian were not to be seen, but I wasn't flabbergasted, since there was something in the ether that was causing people to vanish from view like droplets of water on a hot skillet: *ping, sizzle, poof.*

I kept an eye on Miss Parchester until they appeared in the tiny dining room.

"We went up to see Connor," said Luanne. "He's napping."

"Would you like to see him?" Jillian asked me.

"Maybe later. On the night that Anthony Armstrong was killed, Randy told the police that he was up late with Connor. Do you remember that?"

"I had a terrible headache. Connor had fussed and whined all day, then threw up all over me after I fed him supper. I got him settled down about ten, but then he started crying again. I just couldn't deal with it, so I called Randy at the fitness center and told him that if he didn't come home within half an hour, I was going to pack a suitcase and leave him to deal with Connor on his own for a few days." She looked down. "He was really angry, but he did come back."

"So he was here at ten-thirty or so?"

She nodded. "We had an argument. The neighbors on both sides can probably confirm it. What's this about?"

"I can't quite explain. Will you please watch for a car being driven by a man with a clipped beard? I need to make another phone call. Luanne, why don't you come with me?"

I propelled her into the office and closed the door. "There is something so wrong with all this, but I can't figure out what it is. Ponder the dust bunnies in the corners while I call Caron."

"Caron?"

"We think Inez took Skyler." I dialed the number of the bookstore, but no one answered, naturally, confirming my *ping, sizzle, poof* theory that would never merit a seminar in Randy Scarpo's exalted course of studies. When numbers were irrational, they were in some way rational. Human behavior did not correspond as neatly.

"We were hoping she'd be at the bookstore, but she must have gone somewhere else," I said to Luanne.

"Why would Inez take Skyler anywhere?"

"Because she didn't think you were properly obsessed with the possibility that Daphne might come looking for him."

Luanne leaned against the edge of the desk, unmindful of the stack of papers she sent sliding across the desk. "Last night Inez was . . . well, weird."

"Caron used the same word. Today, Inez begged out of the concert, and her mother has no idea where she is. Now it seems as though Caron has thought of something."

"Wouldn't she have called you before she left for this unknown destination?"

"If I'd told her the number, she might have. I need you to stay here and watch for Finnigan Baybergen, who agreed to take Miss Parchester's things to a Laundromat and toss them in a dryer. Don't allow her to go back up in the tree until he's done that much."

"While you do what?"

"Go talk to Adrienne, I suppose. Chantilly may have staggered in and gone to bed, or the police may have located her. Peter may still be there." I ran my fingers through my hair, wondering—yes, irrationally—if I smelled like a wet dog. "There's something so wrong with this whole thing. I would have said that Adrienne and Chantilly were behind the murder, but Daphne's their best alibi. Unless Jillian's lying, Randy couldn't have done it."

"Randy?"

"I found photographs of Adrienne in his desk. You don't even want to look at them. They were having an affair, and if Anthony had cause to be suspicious, Adrienne could kiss the villa, the country club, the Jaguar, and the fitness club good-bye and start reading the want ads."

"But he's dead," Luanne pointed out.

"Conveniently so. Alternate calls to my house and the Book Depot every five minutes while you're waiting for Finnigan."

"Do you want to take my car?"

"No," I said with a grimace. "You might be able to persuade Miss Parchester to allow you to take her home. What's more, if Peter's at the villa, he might take perverse pleasure in having your car towed, too."

I patted Jillian on the shoulder as I went through the living room and out into the rain. I considered rummaging through Luanne's car for an umbrella, then shrugged and walked up the path, mindful of the slick, sodden leaves.

The catering vans had gone, as had the plethora of expensive cars. The only car visible was a gray Mercedes parked in front of a garage that could easily accommodate his-and-hers SUVs, along with the Mercedes, the Jaguar, and Santa Claus's sleigh and eight tiny reindeer.

I recalled the photos I'd seen of Sheila's grandparents and their farm. She'd said the villa was situated where the farmhouse had been. The barn that had looked as if it might slide down the hill had been much farther away, across a reasonably level expanse that would have been a vineyard had nature cooperated. The garage occupied what had been, in the photos, a vegetable garden and chicken coop.

I tapped on the front door and then let myself in. "Adrienne?" I said cautiously. "It's Claire."

"I'm out here."

I went through the living room, then stopped as I reached the door to the conservatory. Adrienne had clearly decided to overindulge in not only the leftover hors d'oeuvres but also the remains of all the liquor that had not been consumed. The glass-topped table was a veritable thicket of bottles of gin, scotch, bourbon, vodka, wines of all hues, vermouth, dishes of olives and onions, and several name brands I did not recognize. Nor did I recognize what Adrienne was currently sipping from a glass in her hand, but I doubted she did, either.

"Fix yourself something," she said. "We'll drink a toast to Anthony."

I sat down on an ottoman. "Where did everybody go?"

"Well, the rain got rid of most of them. A few of the relatives had this grand theory that they could hang around, but I had Jacque run them off." She finished off the contents of her glass and refilled it from the nearest bottle. "Then he left, which made me very sad. I went to my husband's funeral today, after all. I should be sad. Anthony wasn't what you'd call exciting, but we had some good times. If you want, I can show you our honeymoon pictures. He put on this stupid little native outfit, then—"

"Did Chantilly come back?"

"You know, she didn't, and I'm starting to get very annoyed with her. I'm glad you're here, Claire. Make yourself a drink. If you want ice, you'll have to get some from the kitchen. Try the pantry."

Houston, we have a problem.

"In a minute," I said. "I'm a little surprised none of your friends insisted on staying with you."

"You're my only friend. I thought Chantilly was my best friend, as well as my sister, but I was so wrong.

She's hateful and I hope she never comes back. Want a mushroom stuffed with lobster? I love lobster. Anthony tried to convince me that I loved caviar, but it's way too salty and kind of pops in your mouth. I almost threw up the first time I tasted it."

"Would you like me to make some coffee?"

She laughed. "Why would I want coffee? I've got everything I need. I've got a house, expensive cars, a freezer filled with ice cream, a big-screen television, a personal trainer, and a fat inheritance. I may just buy some racehorses so I can sit in a box at the Kentucky Derby and sip mint juleps with senators." She squinted at the array on the table. "Now there's an idea, Claire. Why don't you mix up a pitcher of mint juleps?"

"Where's Randy?"

"Oh," she said, blinking. "I don't really know. I ordered him to put all the opened bottles of booze out here, then told him to send me a bill. I think he may have gotten a ride to the fitness center with Mary Margaret."

"I know about your affair."

"Don't be silly. Why would I have an affair with Mary Margaret? She's a real bitch, if you want to know the truth. She cheats at golf, for one thing, and—"

"With Randy."

"Oh, him," said Adrienne. "That doesn't count. Nobody else knows about it, and you have to promise you won't say anything. It just wasn't realistic for Anthony to expect me to forget about sex after we got married, was it? All he wanted to do was sit in his office every night and study blueprints. Even when he'd come upstairs, he acted like it was his duty so I'd be content to sit home and watch movies the rest of the time." She picked up the nearest bottle and sloshed its contents into her glass. "This is kinda fun, not knowing what you may find yourself drinking. What do you think this is?"

I looked at the label as she banged down the bottle. "Gin. Would you like some tonic to go with it?"

"What are you—a bartender?"

"No," I acknowledged. "I'm just a bookseller. The reality of your affair does matter, Adrienne. Are you aware of the conditions in Anthony's will?"

"Of course I am. Before we got married, he made me go with him to his lawyer's office and listen to every last boring detail of the prenuptial contract and his revised will. I thought I would fall asleep."

"You won't inherit if evidence of your affair is presented to the probate court."

"Nobody's going to do that. What's even better, little ol' Daphne can't inherit a penny since she killed him. I'm beginning to feel kindly toward her. Maybe I'll send a box of cookies to the prison once or twice a year just to prove I'm not such a wicked stepmother. I could even have Jacque bake a cake with a file inside it. He does a yummy chocolate mousse concoction with raspberry glaze."

I felt as if I were stalking a baby seal, even if Adrienne was far from wide-eyed innocence. "Did Chantilly find out about your affair?"

"How would she do that?" Adrienne crossed her arms and stared at me. "You're the only one, Claire."

"That's not true. Randy knows, and I suspect Chantilly does, too. Did one of them threaten to blackmail you?"

Her mouth tightened for a moment. "That is so tacky, Claire. I think you'd better leave, and you can just forget about having lunch one of these days."

"Where's Chantilly?"

"How should I know?" retorted Adrienne. "She took

off in my car and didn't have the decency to show up for the funeral. Lieutenant Whatsit assured me that his officers will find her. He's quite a catch, isn't he? When all this is over and done with, I may just give him a call. He gave me his home telephone number in case I need to get in touch with him. I'd like to get in touch with him, if you know what I mean."

Apparently I was once again her best friend and confidante. I watched as she finished off the gin and moved on to a bottle of tequila. "Why don't I put all this away and help you upstairs? You must be exhausted."

"I suppose I am. Let's have one more drink, and then I'll take a nap in the living room. It's a darn shame Chantilly can't join us. She should have kept her nose out of my business, Claire. She had a perfectly decent job in Atlanta. I mean, she couldn't afford the country club or anything like that, and her apartment was cramped, but that was no excuse for her to . . ."

I wanted to shake Adrienne out of her alcoholic stupor and force answers from her, but I realized she could turn truculent with only the most minor incitement. "I agree she had no excuse."

"Nope, none whatsoever." Adrienne selected a bottle of bourbon this time, and forgoing her glass, drained most of it. "It wasn't my fault. Maybe I should find Randy. Do you know where he is?"

"He left," I said gently. "Why don't you lie down on the sofa and take a nap? You've had a hard day, what with the funeral and the luncheon and all the well-wishers. You deserve to rest."

"I think maybe I do. I'll just close my eyes for a few minutes, then call Randy and tell him to keep his damn mouth shut."

"An excellent plan." I helped her to her feet and

steered her into the living room, wondering how many more babies I would encounter before I could stop singing "The Rockabye Blues" on a regular basis. "You'll feel better in a couple of hours."

"You are my best friend," she mumbled as her eyes closed.

CHAPTER SIXTEEN

As Adrienne's best friend (a temporary designation, clearly), I carried all the bottles into the kitchen and left them on the counter for Adrienne's best cleaning service to deal with. I had a good idea why she'd banished the housekeeper, who might have been an inconvenience on afternoons when Anthony was at a construction site and Randy's schedule allowed him to leave the campus.

I remained in the kitchen to call the condo. Luanne answered almost immediately. "Claire?"

"Yes," I said mildly, in that I was, above all other roles, a mild-mannered bookseller. "Have you spoken to Caron?"

"No, and I think I should do something. Miss Parchester is still snoozing, and Jillian's promised that she can stay here. Baybergen never showed up. I went to the platform and gathered up all her clothes, and then put them in the dryer downstairs. The sleeping bag's too sodden, but Jillian says she has one in her garage. Why aren't we trying to find Skyler?"

"Because we don't have a clue where to look for him. Caron must, though, and she's more likely to figure out where Inez might have taken him than the two of us could. What do you suggest we do—drive up and down Thurber Street, yodeling like displaced Alpine hikers?"

Luanne snuffled. "I just feel as though I should be doing something."

"So do I."

"What happened at the villa?"

I told her about Adrienne's engagement with enough alcohol to stock a bar on a Friday night. "She's asleep," I added, "but I'm really worried about Chantilly. Adrienne slipped up and used the past tense several times. I don't think she dug that pit you mentioned, but I have a bad feeling. Any suggestions?"

"You're not going to like it."

"I don't like anything that's happened since Miss Parchester climbed that damn tree five days ago."

"Call Peter. He needs to know that Chantilly's not just shacked up in a motel room."

I gazed wistfully at a bottle of scotch I could never afford to drink. "He's just a bit annoyed with me, Luanne. If I call him—"

"Call him. I'm going to leave Jillian in charge of Miss Parchester and swing by my shop, your bookstore, and your apartment. Caron is more than capable of not answering the phone if she doesn't think it's in her best interest at the moment. Her reasoning can be murky, as you well know."

I told her the number where I was, then sat back and nibbled carrot sticks until I found the nerve to call the police department. If I was lucky, the same dispatcher would give me the same runaround, and I could subsequently gloat in the knowledge I'd tried my best. Modestly, of course.

I was put through to Peter immediately. "Hey," I said,

"I was wondering if you located Daphne."

"Where are you?"

"With Adrienne. She's asleep at the moment. After everyone left, she decided to tidy up the surplus liquor by drinking it. Did you take Daphne into custody?"

"We delivered her to the hospital for a seventy-two-hour evaluation. The psychiatrist on call ordered sedation and rest. He doesn't think she has any major problems."

"So all you have to do is wait in the hallway until you can drag her back to jail? If someone sends her a cake with raspberry glaze, examine it carefully."

"I'm beginning to wonder if you need a vacation in a room with padded pastel walls. She claimed she never had a baby. There's no record at the hospital, no birth certificate on file. Who was the attending physician?"

"No one working the obstetrics wing," I said. "Have you located Chantilly?"

Peter let out a long-suffering sigh, which I'm sure he felt made him deserving of canonization, if not instantaneous sainthood. "Adrienne seems to think she just took off in the Jaguar. Chantilly hasn't committed a crime, since she was authorized to use the car. If it turns up in a used car lot in Amarillo, Adrienne may be able to press charges for theft."

"How mad are you?" I asked in a meek voice, hoping to soften him up before I asked for a favor. I strongly oppose the use of feminine wiles unless they provide some direct benefit. When I had time, I vowed to myself, I would go split wood and catch rattlesnakes barehanded. Afterwards, I would have blisters and festering wounds, but a clear conscience.

"On a scale of one to ten, I'd say I was hovering between eight and nine," Peter said. "You've reached a new personal best in evasiveness. Why do you insist on seeing me as an adversary? Don't you trust me?"

This was not the time to explore the question in painful detail. "I'm going to trust you now," I said. "Find a way to escape the vigilance of KFAR and come out here. I'm beginning to think I know where Chantilly is. The last thing we need is Jessica Princeton and a camera crew."

"Too graphic for the six o'clock news?"

"I don't know. Maybe."

"Then wait at the house. I'll be there as soon as I can get away from the captain, who's been apoplectic since yesterday morning and is on his third pot of coffee since noon today."

"Okay, I'll wait," I said, then hung up and went out to make sure Adrienne hadn't crawled off the sofa in search of a drink. She seemed peaceful, and unlike Miss Parchester, in no danger of pneumonia or anything else more threatening than a significant hangover, replete with the gastric aftereffects of too many stuffed mushrooms. The cleaning service might have its professional expertise challenged, but I wouldn't be around to watch.

I went upstairs and looked in Chantilly's bedroom. I could see no indication that anyone had moved so much as a pair of panty hose. Two sisters, one passed out on the sofa, the other—where?

As I went downstairs, I briefly toyed with the idea that Howie, who was also missing, might be involved, but it was beyond me to come up with anything that even verged on making sense. Women such as Chantilly did not dally with arrested adolescents such as Howie unless there was significant monetary compensation. He must have gone home, as Miss Parchester had suggested.

Chantilly was either long gone or not gone at all. I decided to investigate the latter premise while I waited for Peter. I took one of the umbrellas from a stand by the front door, but the rain had stopped and the clouds were dispersing. I avoided puddles as I made my way down the road in the direction of what I assumed would be the barn. This might have been construed as standard gothic heroine foolhardiness, but it was only late afternoon and I was hardly investigating the sounds of a chain saw in the cellar.

And I didn't have any idea of whether or not the barn had indeed ended up at the bottom of a gully, along with a mule or two and Mrs. Zorelli's jars of pickled okra and spiced peaches. I was feeling as intoxicated as Adrienne (well, not quite that much) as I savored the aroma of the aftermath of a spring storm. Sunlight sparkled on foliage beaded with raindrops. No one demanded that I produce a cast of characters and their whereabouts. No one pointed out the flaws in my hypotheses, as numerous as they were. The only sounds were of birds and insects reclaiming their domain after a tactical retreat. I found myself hoping the road would lead nowhere and I could just keep walking until all the issues were resolved.

I was almost expecting a bluebird to alight on my shoulder and break into an anthropomorphic song when I saw the barn. To my dismay, I realized there were tire tracks on either side of me.

"It's the truth, it's actual," I said under my breath as I pushed open the weathered door. The Jaguar was hard to miss, even in the dim light. My pulse began to quicken as I went inside. There was no body in the car, or visible smears of blood. I stopped for a moment to take deep breaths, and then, most tentatively, forced myself to stare into the dark reaches of the barn. The loft had collapsed, possibly decades previously, which I gratefully interpreted as an excuse not to have to crawl up a ladder into a sequestered community of spiders, rats, and bats.

I froze as I heard a thumping noise. "Is someone here?" I whispered.

"Whmp!"

It seemed I had elicited a response. I picked up a piece of a broken rake handle and moved cautiously toward the back of the barn, hoping that I could actually swing at someone if the situation demanded it.

"Whmp!"

"Calm down," I said. "I'm not very good at this. Give me a minute."

"Whmp!"

"I said I'm coming, for pity's sake." I edged around what I supposed was a defunct tractor and saw a figure seated on the floor, legs outstretched. The ash blond hair provided an eerie frame around her face. "Chantilly? What are you doing?"

"Whmp!"

I moved forward until I could see the duct tape across her mouth. More duct tape was wrapped around her ankles and wrists, and even more bound her to an upright beam. I knelt next to her and gingerly removed the tape from her mouth.

"That bitch!" she croaked. "Get me out of here."

I removed the rest of the tape and helped her to her feet. "Can you walk?"

"Yeah," she said, then began to wobble so violently that I had to steady her. "I'm okay. Do you have any water?"

"No, but maybe we can find a container of rainwater." I held on to her arm as we went out the barn door. She jerked free of my grasp and sank to her knees by a puddle to scoop up water with her hands. It was, I was sure, the first time she'd slurped liquefied mud, and most likely the last.

She finally sat back. "I thought I was going to die, which is exactly what that bitch intended. She just didn't have the nerve to do it outright."

"Adrienne?"

"Oh, yeah. When I find her, I'm going to carve her up like a turkey, but I'm going to do it slowly so she doesn't bleed to death too quickly. I'll start with her fingers and toes, then—" She broke off with a sob. "How could she do this to me? My own sister?"

I wiped the mud off her chin. "How did she get you to come here?"

"Whenever it was—yesterday afternoon—she told me that Anthony had a red Corvette convertible stored here that he'd meant to give to Daphne before she dared to disobey him. Adrienne said I might as well have it, so we drove over to have a look at it. She tricked me into going to the back of the barn and then smacked me with something. When I came to, I was taped up and she was gone. What time is it?"

"About five. You stay there while I see if the keys are in the car. We might as well drive back to the house." Where I would be an eyewitness to a very nasty scene, if not a gory homicide. "Maybe I ought to take you to the emergency room. You must be dangerously dehydrated."

"Looking like this? Don't be ridiculous. All I need is a Bloody Mary and a butcher knife. Afterwards, I'll take a shower and put on clean clothes, and you can take me anywhere you damn please."

Adrienne had left the keys in the ignition. I backed

out, waited while Chantilly got in on the passenger's
side, and then drove very slowly while I tried to decide
what to do. She was regaining her color, and although
she was small, I wasn't at all sure I could protect myself
if I attempted to continue past the house. She'd had
twenty-four hours to refine the details of her revenge.

"Why did Adrienne do this to you?" I asked.

"Because she's a greedy, hateful, conniving bitch."

"You tried to blackmail her, didn't you? You knew
the terms of the prenuptial contract and the will. Did you
demand half of her inheritance?"

"Nowhere near that much," Chantilly said sulkily. "I
pointed out nicely that she would inherit at least a million dollars, and it wouldn't hurt her to be generous. I
covered for her plenty of times when we were growing
up. I even took the rap for a drunken driving charge.
She showed the cop my license, and we look so much
alike that he bought it. Guess which one of us spent eight
hours in traffic school, then got grounded for a month?
I took her SATs so she could get into college." She
opened the glove compartment and found a box of tissues. "I am absolutely filthy, and I stink so bad I could
peel paint. She's going to pay for this."

I was still debating what to do as we came into view
of the house. The Mercedes was no longer parked in
front of the garage, which was both the good news and
the bad. The homicide—or, to be more precise, sorori-
cide—would have to wait, but it also seemed likely that
Adrienne had stumbled out to the car and driven away.
This would be one case of drunken driving for which no
one else could take the responsibility.

Even though the car was still moving, Chantilly
opened the door and stepped out. "Thanks for the ride,"
she said as if I'd dropped her off after a tennis date.

I parked, and was trotting after her when Peter drove up and got out of his car. "Oh, good," I said. "We have either a crisis or a disaster. Go arrest somebody."

"Would you care to be more specific?"

"Later. Now go inside and make sure Chantilly hasn't grabbed a butcher knife from a kitchen drawer. Approach her carefully; she's pumped with adrenaline and blind rage. A bad combination."

"I thought Chantilly was missing," he said.

"Not anymore, but Adrienne may be. She was here half an hour ago, but now the car is gone. Nobody else was inside the villa. Well, somebody could have been upstairs. I didn't do more than take a quick look." The sound of a gunshot from inside the house stopped me before I could add that I'd searched the Armstrong villa so many times I knew the color and placement of the soap dishes. "What do we do?"

He thrust his cell phone at me. "You are going to stay here, call the department, and tell them what's happening. I told the dispatcher where I was going, so she'll believe you. Ask for backup and Jorgeson, if she can track him down."

I almost dropped the phone as another gunshot echoed. "Why don't you stay here with me?"

"Get in my car and wait," Peter said. "Don't even think about going into the house."

Which is exactly what I did think about after I'd obediently made the call. During the terse conversation, I'd heard two more gunshots. No one appeared in the doorway or at a window. If the Mercedes had been present, I could have imagined Adrienne and Chantilly in a classic Western showdown, although both of them merited black hats. Chantilly had attempted to blackmail Adrienne, who'd attempted to murder her in retaliation.

Atypical family dynamics, to say the least.

I'd gotten out of the car and was inching toward the house when Jorgeson drove up. "What's going on?" he asked.

"Peter and I were standing here when we heard a gunshot. He went inside to investigate."

"While you stayed out here. I'm impressed, Ms. Malloy. Just who's in there beside the lieutenant?"

"Chantilly. I don't think Adrienne is, but I could be wrong."

"I can assure you that Mrs. Armstrong is not. Anybody else?"

I shook my head. "Shouldn't you be doing something, Jorgeson?"

"What I should be doing is staining the deck, which is what I was doing before I got the call to come out here. Do you ever take a day off, Ms. Malloy?"

"Are you planning to stand here and discuss extra-curricular activities?"

"We should all have interests. I'm giving serious consideration to putting in a lily pond near the deck. At the nursery, I saw a very clever waterfall pump that recirculates the water so that the algae doesn't build up."

"Jorgeson, Peter is inside that house with someone who is armed. Will you please go do something about it!"

"Lieutenant Rosen doesn't like me to interfere. Here come a couple of uniformed officers. Maybe you can persuade them to blunder inside and get their heads blown off."

Two officers scrambled out of their vehicle. "What's going on, Sergeant Jorgeson?" asked the older. "Gunshots reported from inside the house, we were told."

"That's most of it. Lieutenant Rosen went to find out

what's happening. Ms. Malloy and I were discussing lily ponds. I was thinking I could start with some cheap goldfish, and if they survive, maybe invest in some of those fancy Japanese ones."

I was ready to smack him when the front door opened and Peter emerged, his hand clamped on Chantilly's elbow. I noticed she'd washed her face and changed clothes.

Peter did not look as if he'd been dodging bullets for the last fifteen minutes. He stopped on the porch and said, "Miss Durmond expressed her frustration by shooting several panes in the conservatory. No person or plant was injured. She needs to be taken to my office and given a beverage. I'll be there shortly to take her statement."

Chantilly meekly allowed herself to be placed in the backseat of the patrol car. As the car turned around in the driveway, Jorgeson took Peter aside for a conversation. I perched on the hood of Peter's car and waited, my expression sublimely dispassionate despite the questions careening around my head.

Peter finally sent Jorgeson inside and joined me. "Adrienne's been found. According to what Jorgeson could patch together, she showed up at the Farberville Fitness Center about twenty minutes ago, stumbled inside, shot the guy at the desk, then drove away and wrapped her car around a tree. The tree survived."

"Oh," I murmured. "The guy at the desk being Randy Scarpo?"

"Is there anything you don't know?" he said, exasperated.

"Nothing very important, considering. Did she kill him?"

"He's being transported to the emergency room, but

he lost a lot of blood and the prognosis is poor. Could you please explain why she shot him? As far as we know, he's just some college kid who lives at Oakland Heights."

"With his wife and baby. Has anyone notified her?"

"Jorgeson sent an officer to take them to the hospital. I'm waiting for an explanation, Claire."

I told him what I suspected about the affair, then added, "If you question his wife, I think you'll find out that he didn't really have an alibi for the time of the shooting. He was probably planning to leave the fitness center at eleven-thirty, kill Armstrong, and be at home well before Adrienne and Chantilly arrived. However, his wife called and insisted that he come home early to help with their fussy baby. As soon as she went to bed and the baby quieted down, he must have come here and killed Anthony Armstrong. Adrienne must have been planning it for a long time, but she needed to wait until she could utilize Chantilly as her witness. Two sisters, exercising and then going out for drinks. So innocent."

"Then what about Daphne? Was her presence in the house a coincidence?"

"Not exactly," I said. "You have to take into consideration all this happened when Oakland Heights Phase Two erupted in the nightly news. Sheila started brooding about her lost legacy. She pulled out the family albums and remembered the old stories, including the ones about the fault line. The following day, Anthony responded to the media while his perfect wife simpered nearby, looking cool and coiffed. Sheila and Daphne must have decided the timing was perfect to retrieve the geological map and blackmail Armstrong Development."

"Did they?"

"It doesn't seem so," I said. "Sheila showed up early

this afternoon, probably hoping she could slip into the office. Finnigan Baybergen could have saved her the cab fare if he'd told her that he tried the same thing during the funeral."

Peter ran his hand through his hair. "But Chantilly—"

"Could we go inside? I'd like to wash my hands and have a glass of iced tea, or something more potent if you're going to have me hauled off to jail. I've had a very busy day, you know."

"That you have," he said as he offered me his hand. We went into the house and continued to the kitchen. He winced as he saw the bottles on the counter. "No wonder Adrienne was stumbling."

"I think the enormity of what she'd done caught up with her. She'd conspired to have her husband murdered, and although she couldn't bring herself to do the same to her sister, she must have known Chantilly wouldn't survive long in the barn. Textbook passive-aggressive behavior."

He handed me a glass of tea. "Until she shot Randy Scarpo."

"Okay, so that wasn't passive. Chantilly had threatened to blackmail her, and she must have realized that Randy could have done the same . . . except he couldn't. She'd be charged with premeditated murder, but so would he."

"Miss Marple doesn't have all the answers?"

"She might have thought he'd lost his nerve after she told him what she'd done to Chantilly." I watched a fly settle on a mushroom cap and begin to feast on the lobster filling. "I don't know why she would have, though, but she's not—she wasn't—the sharpest tine on the cocktail fork."

Jorgeson came into the kitchen. "Lieutenant, there's

a small problem, nothing we can't handle, but all the same, kind of perplexing."

Peter sighed. "You might as well tell Ms. Malloy and save her the trouble of launching a new investigation."

"Do you remember a guy named Arnie Riggles?"

"Arnie?" I squeaked.

"Yes, Ms. Malloy. He's passed out upstairs in one of the back bedrooms. He's wearing"—Jorgeson's face reddened—"a silk nightgown. There's a pile of wet clothes on the floor, presumably his. What do you want me to do, Lieutenant?"

"In a very obscure way, this is my fault," I said. "Do you want me to explain?"

"I don't think so," said Peter, then looked at Jorgeson. "Call for some uniforms and have them haul him to jail dressed as he is. It's liable to be a sobering experience."

"There's a cab parked somewhere nearby," I added. "It should be returned to a woman named Wanita, who can be found at the Tickled Pink Club, wherever that is. If there's any money in Arnie's wallet, give it to her."

"You know a woman named Wanita?"

"Not personally. What are you going to do about Daphne?"

"Yes, Daphne," said Peter. He opened the refrigerator and studied its contents. "Didn't these people ever eat real food?"

"Jacque would spit in your face if you so much as uttered the word *baloney*. Have a bite of caviar or a *coeur d'artichaut*. So what about Daphne?"

"If what you've said is true, then all charges will be dropped and she'll be free to go. It might not be so bad to let her stay in the psych ward for a few days, though. She became hysterical when I asked her about this baby you claim she had."

"I delivered him, Peter."

"What?"

"Let's go there later. I need to call Luanne." I moved to the desk and dialed the number of the Scarpos' condo.

"Hello?"

"Miss Parchester, this is Claire," I said. "Has a police officer been there?"

"I was so terribly alarmed when Jillian opened the door, thinking I was to be arrested after all those days and nights in the tree. But the officer, a sympathetic woman, told Jillian about her husband and offered to drive her to the hospital. I assured Jillian that it would be easier if I stayed and looked after her baby. He's a dear little thing, although somewhat pudgy. I shall stress the importance of monitoring his diet."

"Is Luanne there?" I asked.

"She left quite a long while ago, or so it seems. She made me promise not to return to the platform until she returns. I am sorry to admit that my resolve has been depleted, although I shall not give up the cause."

"Luanne didn't say where she was going?"

"No, not so much as a hint."

Luanne might have tried to call me while I was at the barn, I supposed, or not bothered if she had only a wild guess as to the whereabouts of Skyler, Inez, and Caron. I hoped she was right. "Miss Parchester, Jillian's really going to need your help and support. There's a strong possibility that her husband won't make it. She'll have to talk to his parents and her own, and make some decisions. She shouldn't be alone."

"But what about the tree?"

"Tomorrow's Sunday, so nothing will happen. What's more, Phase Two will be in limbo indefinitely. Howie come back?"

She giggled. "It seems Howie made a friend in the condo at the end of the building. A very good friend, if you know what I mean. After the rain stopped, they came out and went for a walk, holding hands so sweetly that I had to smile. He's much older than Howie, but I've always felt Howie lacked a strong paternal role model in his life."

Peter was glowering at me. I told Miss Parchester I would call later and hung up. I replenished my tea, then sat down on a stool and told him everything I knew about Skyler's first month, including the events of the last five days.

"So you believe Luanne's gone to find them?" he said.

"I don't know what else to do. Will you please give me a ride home?"

He had the decency to look embarrassed. "Yes, and I'll have an officer deliver your car to your house."

"That would be nice."

"I'm going to be floundering in paperwork for a few days, but after can we go out to dinner and talk?"

"I have a better idea," I said demurely.

Caron, Inez, and Luanne were in my living room when I got home. Skyler was back in his basket, snoozing peacefully. After ascertaining that all were unscathed (and giving Inez a decidedly dark look), I told them about Adrienne and Randy, as well as Daphne's exoneration.

"There's something wrong," said Luanne.

"I know."

Caron stared at me. "What? Adrienne arranged her alibi, Randy went up there and shot Anthony, and then everybody decided to blackmail everybody else."

"Miss Parchester told me she didn't hear Daphne go by, or Randy a few minutes later. What's more, she didn't hear either of them come back."

"Then she lied."

"No," I said, shaking my head. "Miss Parchester doesn't lie. She wasn't above misleading me, but she never told me anything that wasn't technically true. So why didn't she hear them?"

"She was asleep?" Inez suggested.

"Or she wasn't there," I said. "Daphne must have told Miss Parchester what she intended to do. Miss Parchester waited until Howie left and then went to the villa to protect Daphne. She saw the light in the office and assumed it was Daphne, searching the files. She was not expecting to find Anthony, who must have thought he could take a little old gun away from a little old lady."

"Miss Parchester had a gun?" said Caron.

"I'm afraid some well-meaning member of the Green Party gave it to her for protection. I suspect she found Anthony studying the geographic map, or even preparing to destroy it. He probably assumed she'd come to take it from him and tried to wrestle the gun away from her. The result was unfortunate for all concerned. Aghast at what had happened, Miss Parchester snatched up the map and headed for the back door, although it's likely she stopped in the kitchen to borrow a lemon. I know from personal experience that trying to find anything smaller than a watermelon in that refrigerator would be a challenge. When she heard a car drive up, she bolted out the back door, inadvertantly leaving it open. A few minutes later, she was able to slip around the house and return to her platform. Daphne had already driven away at that point, so Miss Parchester could not have heard her footsteps. Randy must have been telling the truth."

Luanne cleared her throat. "Adrienne shot him, though. Surely he told her he hadn't been the one."

"She didn't believe him, or perhaps he accused her of shooting Anthony. In any case, after she told him about Chantilly, they were both up to their respective necks in a conspiracy. And, well, she wasn't thinking too clearly—or driving too well."

"So what happened to the gun?" asked Caron. "Did Daphne keep it? I thought Miss Parchester told you this morning that Daphne did not have it in her possession."

I considered the question. "This I can't be sure about, but I have an idea. Let's say that Daphne was so frightened that she'd be apprehended with the gun that she tossed it onto the platform as she ran by. Miss Parchester would have figured out what happened and kept the gun until the police stopped searching the woods with metal detectors. Then, a couple of days ago, while Howie was either indisposed or running errands for her, she climbed down and concealed it where she could later retrieve it."

"Why not fling it off the bluff?" said Inez, blinking. "That's what I would have done."

"It didn't belong to her," I pointed out with a faint smile. "Miss Parchester would never fail to return something that had been lent to her. It simply wouldn't be polite. No, she probably wrapped it carefully in a waterproof bag and put it someplace not too far from the tree so she could be confident of finding it at a later time. Unfortunately, Howie found it during one of his patrols. Remember that I mentioned hearing a shot today shortly before noon? Howie must have been playing Davy Crockett. In fact, Miss Parchester told me he had a gun; she just didn't specify where he got it."

Caron nodded. "That kind of makes sense. What about the map?"

"She would never destroy it. It's likely to be tucked in the bottom of the sleeping bag. I'm sure Miss Parchester intended to return it to its rightful owner after things had been sorted out. She adheres to her moral convictions, no matter how misguided they might be."

"But she didn't come forward—or down, anyway—when Daphne was arrested," said Luanne. "She must have known Papa wouldn't have approved."

"I'm sure she intended to once the issue of the stand of trees was resolved. She could hardly think she could confess and then be allowed to stay on the platform. The court is scheduled to rule in two days."

"Are you going to tell Peter?" asked Caron.

"I don't see any compelling reason. Besides, this is all speculation. I will have a talk with Miss Parchester in a few days, however. She really needs to focus on her painting and stop meddling in murders."

Luanne, Caron, and Inez looked at me.

"So, Inez, you took Skyler to the high school?" I said at last.

Inez nodded. "I couldn't think of anyplace else. I was going to call you, but I didn't have any change for the pay phone and the office was locked. Skyler and I were real cozy in the teachers' lounge. I warmed his bottle on a hot plate and listened to the radio, hoping I'd hear about Daphne being taken back into custody. I couldn't let her run away with Skyler."

"She won't be running away," I said. "She stands to inherit a couple of million dollars."

Luanne went into the kitchen and returned with two beers. She handed one to me, then said, "But what about the condition in the will about righteous moral character or whatever?"

For Caron's sake, I tried not to sound overly cynical.

"Joey will see the story on the news, profess to be overwhelmed with remorse, and offer to marry her. Sheila will divulge that she's been a doting grandmother all along. A competent lawyer can then convince the court that Daphne has complied with her father's dictum."

"And they'll all live happily forever after?" said Caron.

"Who knows? In any case, we'll have Skyler for a few more days, but we won't have to keep him under cover. It will all come out once Jessica receives an anonymous tip."

"We may have another little problem," Inez said. "After Caron found me at the high school, we took turns pushing the stroller in the hallways, and . . ."

"And?" I said.

Caron attempted to appear contrite, but with marginal success. "Do you remember when Inez and I stole the frozen frogs destined for dissection? The biology teacher still keeps them in a freezer in the cafeteria. You'd think someone would have thought to put a padlock on the door by now."

I stared at her. "Rhonda Maguire's locker?"

"Phase Two."